ADVANCE PRAISE FOR *D*

"William Sterling Walker is a wonderful writer, fluent, warm, intelligent, and real. His stories about gay life in New Orleans are firmly rooted in place, and all his characters, gay and straight, are observed with a wise heart and a deep soul."
CHRISTOPHER BRAM, author of *Gods and Monsters* and *Eminent Outlaws: The Gay Writers Who Changed America*

"*Desire* is a sensuous, nostalgic, and evocative collection of stories set in sultry New Orleans before that dreamy dream got washed away."
VALERIE MARTIN, winner of the Orange Prize for *Property*

"These are stories that ask to be lived in—gorgeous, moody, sophisticated—not unlike the vividly conjured New Orleans that William Sterling Walker's haunted characters inhabit, flee from, inevitably return to. Walker is a brilliant guide through the labyrinth of this city and these seething lives, fluent in the mutually reinforcing tropes of desire and regret."
PAUL RUSSELL, author of *The Unreal Life of Sergey Nabokov*

"*Desire* is dreamy and affecting, stories of a New Orleans that was gone before Katrina ever got there. It's been a while since I've read a collection so well written, so intricately composed, with such beautiful and evocative descriptions of a time and a place."
CAROLINE FRASER, author of *God's Perfect Child* and *Rewilding the World: Dispatches from the Conservation Revolution*

"This beautiful collection is not so much a set of stories as an intricate song cycle, one that arranges and rearranges recurrent fragments of memory and sensation—light, fragrance, and music—like the tesserae of a mosaic, the shifting patterns converging into a haunting panorama of the life of our ecstatic, fated generation of gay men."
MARK MERLIS, author of *American Studies* and *An Arrow's Flight*

"William Sterling Walker's *Desire* feels to me like a welcome heir to Ethan Mordden's classic *Buddies*—picking up perhaps where he left off and setting us down amid the lives, loves, and sexual adventures of a community of gay men in New Orleans. These stories are alternately poignant and seductive, and the structure is elegant and deceptively casual—they build in force until you feel like they belong to you, or you to them."
ALEXANDER CHEE, author of *Edinburgh*

DESIRE

DESIRE

TALES OF NEW ORLEANS

William Sterling Walker

CHELSEA STATION EDITIONS

NEW YORK

Desire: Tales of New Orleans
Copyright © 2012 by William Sterling Walker
All rights reserved.

No part of this book may be reproduced in any form without written permission from the publisher, except by a reviewer, who may quote brief passages in a review where appropriate credit is given; nor may any part of this book be reproduced, stored in a retrieval system, or transmitted in any form or by any means—electronic, photocopying, recording, or other—without specific written permission from the publisher.

All of the names, characters, places, and incidents in this book are the product of the author's imagination or are used fictitiously, and any resemblance to actual persons, living or dead, events, or locales is entirely coincidental.

Cover and book design by Anne Richmond Boston
Cover collage by Laurin Hart
Author photo by Lenora Gim
Published by Chelsea Station Editions
362 West 36th Street, Suite 2R
New York, NY 10018
www.chelseastationeditions.com
info@chelseastationeditions.com

ISBN 13: 978-1-937627-02-7

Library of Congress Control Number: 2012943962

First U.S. edition, 2012

These stories appeared, in slightly different form, in the following publications:
Harrington Gay Men's Fiction Quarterly: "Aubade"
The James White Review: "Desire" and "Two Lives"
modern words: "Intricacies of Departure"
"Desire" was anthologized in *Fresh Men* and "Intricacies of Departure" in *Best American Gay Fiction 2*.

TO JEFFREY DREIBLATT,
VANCE PHILIP HEDDEREL,
AND PATRICK MERLA

"It's an odd sensation to recognize in oneself the need to be in a particular physical environment, when one longs for the home ground no matter how terrible the memories it holds, no matter how great the efforts made to leave it behind. So I have left this city again and again and thought myself lucky to escape its allure, for it's the attraction of decay, of vicious, florid, natural cycles that roll over the senses with their lushness. Where else could I find these hateful, humid, murderously hot afternoons, when I know that the past was a series of great mistakes, the greatest being the inability to live anywhere but in this swamp?"

from *A Recent Martyr* by Valerie Martin

CONTENTS

INTRICACIES OF DEPARTURE

I'M STANDING AT EIGHTY-FIRST STREET AND BROADWAY listening to this piece of music in my head when my eye catches a book going into a pocket of a peacoat behind the window in Shakespeare & Company. I look up at his face—it's a beautiful face, a vision—and suddenly I stop wondering where Sunday will take me.

Then he winks at me and disappears from the window, out of frame, off camera.

I'm wondering how he's going to get through the anti-theft device at the entrance. I wait at the doors of the shop. He's milling about the stacks and displays in front of the sales counter, buying time. His jacket is draped over his arm. The only way out is through that electronic turnstile; he'll never get away with it. Then I see the blue playing card in his hand, which means he must have something checked. I walk into the store and stand before the turnstile. I pick a name for him.

"Nathan," I call out. "Why don't you hand me your jacket while you get your bag?"

He doesn't look up immediately, but I know he's heard me. There's a crowd by the sales counter and constant traffic into and out of the store. No one is paying us any mind. His head tilts to the side like a parrot's. He glances up at me and grins. Then he moves toward me and hands me his jacket way over the turnstile. I stretch out for it. We must look conspicuous, but the alarm doesn't sound. I go outside, trying to be casual, and wait under the awning. It's colder now; the bite in the air cuts through me. The sun falls behind buildings as he joins me.

"Thanks," he says, looking both ways, up and down Broadway. "Good thing you're so damn tall."

I hand him his coat. "You didn't have it all figured out, did you?"

"Nope."

He pulls on the coat, wraps his scarf around his neck, and slings the book bag over his shoulder. My legs are rattling. We start walking.

"I'm not a klepto," he says. "I just need to come clean with that." He lights a cigarette and blows a long stream of smoke. "But once I started this, I couldn't stop. I had to go through with it." He has an accent.

"What book did you take?" I ask.

He pulls the book out of his pocket and hands it to me: André Gide's *The Counterfeiters*. He stops, drops his cigarette to the sidewalk, and grinds it out with his boot. Then he tells me he has never taken anything in his life, and I believe him, I don't know why. I look at him, and I think of a dozen questions, but all I ask is if he comes from the South.

"New Orleans isn't really the South."

"What's your name?"

"Nathan," he says.

Maybe it's a lucky guess. Probably not. I don't believe in lucky guesses. On second thought, the guy's a thief, maybe he's a liar. Now I'm a thief for helping him. Am I a liar? I think this as we continue down Broadway. We're both shivering. We have no idea where we're going. We've circled the block four or five times, I realize; we haven't gone through a crosswalk since we left Shakespeare & Company.

We wind up in this dive called Pier 72, though it's nowhere near the piers. Over coffee, cheesecake, and cigarettes, he tells me about what he left behind in New Orleans: the afternoon light, his favorite café in the French Quarter, coffee with chicory. He says he misses coffee and chicory the most. I tell him I've never had it, and he tries to describe its taste, muses on chicory's bitter delicacy. I listen to the lilt in his voice, the music of his accent. I glance at his reflection in the window, transparent over the rubble of ice and snow on the sidewalk. A cloud of smoke wraps around him. The snow falls through him.

"I took the train to get up here," he says. "I love trains. You have time on the train, time to think about where you've been instead of where you're going."

"That seems true enough to me. How long have you been here?" I ask.

"I've lost track," he says. "Not long, two weeks, maybe. I don't even know what day it is." He laughs and turns away to the window. He cannot look at me for very long. "Isn't it funny how when you like someone, you can hardly say a word to him?" he asks, watching the snowfall.

"I wouldn't call it funny."

"I guess not," he says. "I don't know. If I'm not into someone, I end up telling him my life story, for some reason. Or at least a version of it." He takes another cigarette from my pack on the table, rolling it between his thumb and forefinger before he lights it. This seems to be a way of absenting himself from me. "It's like you have this premonition of how the whole thing will end up. Maybe that's why you don't say anything," he says to the window.

"You? Or me?" I ask.

"Me. You. Yes, you. You don't say much either, do you?"

"I never know what to say."

"We could talk about movies or books," he says.

"Perhaps we shouldn't talk about books."

He laughs. We talk about movies. He loves silent movies, Buster Keaton movies, loves their rawness, the grainy quality of the picture, the wordlessness. He asks if I've ever noticed how riding the subway is like living in a silent movie. "No one talks to each other on the subway, do they?"

"Words sort of collect in your head when you ride the subway," I say.

"You see a face and you know," he says. "You just know there's something passing between you in the silence. But then he gets off before your stop, or gets lost in the crowd."

"People pop into your life all the time," I tell him. "Then they're gone. You try to accept it and move on. Or get waylaid." As soon as I say this, I wonder why I do. But then I tell him, "You can't connect with the world."

Until six months ago, Nathan Morrow—my other Nathan—kept his medications in wine glasses on the kitchen countertop. The assorted Crayola-colored pills and capsules had innocuous names, as if some chemist had culled them with kindergarten randomness from a bowl of alphabet soup. I suspect Nathan might have done better with something holistic. But I got tired of feeding him newspaper clippings, arguing with him about alternative treatments, and I left the glasses alone. Still, I can't stop thinking about them. Nathan had a glass for each day of the week. This is Monday, and the glass is empty. The seven glasses are all here, clean and in a row. All of them are empty.

My landlord sits with a half-full cup of coffee, rolling the rent check around his middle finger, lecturing me. "Those yuppies are all managers. No convictions. Bottom-line boys. No accountability. Just cut their losses."

"I know what you mean," I say.

"You do?"

"I'm not a yuppie."

"But you dress like one," he says.

"I don't dress like this all the time," I tell him. "Occasionally, I wear a smart little Donna Karan number and—"

"Ah. Don't tell me shit like that. You guys are all alike."

I've known this man almost a decade, but only today does he seem really old to me. As he slides his chair away from the table to leave, the glasses on the counter catch his eye again. They catch everyone's eye.

"I was just kidding," I tell him, laughing it off.

"Yeah, yeah," he says under his breath. "The wife had a nephew that was one of Those."

"One of what?"

"You know," he grunts. "The kind that like to dress in women's clothes. Came from good people, but he fell in with that Warhol crowd. Then once, when we were going to the clinic for her chemo, we saw him in Port Authority. He didn't even recognize us, family. Doris tried to talk to him, but he just started growling at her, and I had to pull her away."

He folds the rent check into a small square and sticks it in his shirt pocket. He clears his throat. "What the hell happened?" he asks, not expecting any answer.

In the city, you get the same what-is-the-world-coming-to-now that I got from the folks in the provinces, where I grew up. You still have to shut out, ignore what you see on the streets out of necessity. You become a New Yorker by a process of petrifaction. The inorganic subsumes the organic. It's gradual, though natives hardly notice how calcified they get. You wind up entombed by your own body, cracking under pressure, like sidewalks from the snow or heat.

After the old man leaves, I pass a boy sleeping on the sidewalk at ten in the morning. A cardboard sign tents over his head: AIDS BLOOD TRANSFUSION NEED 18 MORE DOLLARS TO GET HOME TO KENTUCKY. No cup, no change. A torn green army coat covers him. Is the sign fact or fiction? We want to believe people. We want people to believe us too. At least I do. Years ago, I used to give money to a panhandler who worked the block between two haunts of mine off the strip in Galveston. One Sunday I saw her waiting for the bus, done up with a veil on her head like some deaconess of a Baptist church, a pair of white pumps, and a bright dress the color of bird eggs. Now, what were the chances of me seeing her dressed that way instead of in the rags she wore on the corner by the Rawhide Tavern?

I guess it doesn't matter.

I like the thief. He stole a copy of *The Counterfeiters*. I like his sense of irony. He had absolute faith in me, if for only a flash. And he didn't get caught. The fearless of the world: someone will always look after them.

The wanting only seems to come over me now in waves. Nathan is sprawled across my bed, smoking a joint. I sit in a chair under the window. Steam wheezes through the pipes; the radiators are working overtime, so I have the window cracked open for air. Wind whistles through the opening. We are in darkness with the blinds drawn. Blue light from the street comes through the slats and stripes the wall.

"I'm in the middle of the only fucking city in the whole world," he says.

It amazes him. I can hear it in the way his voice catches. I don't have to see his face.

"Listen to it," he says.

I close my eyes and concentrate. Taxi horns blow short, blow long minor chords of flatulence. Sirens, major sirens, cacophony. Sirens, the sough of the city. Angry city. Six alarms, count them. Support units. Maybe seven. Maybe nine. Engines of the streets exhausting themselves. I open my eyes and the walls seem to waffle from the sound. I feel like I've been dropped through a well.

"Today, this man on the subway," Nathan says to the darkness, "was giving his spiel. He was preaching to us, saying shit like, 'Try and remember what it was like to be hungry.'" Nathan has the oratory part down pat. "Then he shoves a McDonald's cup in my face. I tell him I *know* what it's like to be hungry. He walks past me and yells in the subway, 'If I was a dog, would you give me a can of Alpo?' This woman sitting across from me—you could tell she had scads of money—she just wrinkled her nose. But this other woman—"

Nathan pauses to suck on the joint. It glows in his face, then subsides. "—this other woman was so convinced by the speech, she's shaking as she empties her pockets of loose change. It was like in those televangelist shows. I couldn't believe her. I thought she was going to hyperventilate."

"She must have been a tourist," I say.

He sucks on the joint and exhales. Then he tells me about the man he's been seeing every day playing the violin in the Columbus Circle station.

"Do you tip him?" I ask.

"Today I gave him the Gide book."

"Nathan, why did you come here?"

"Even a retreat is an advance."

"No. I mean now—tonight."

He ignores my question. I guess I shouldn't have asked. Now I don't want to know. Being stoned seems to amplify the stillness. Then he reaches on the floor for the ashtray, his arm's shadow arches over the wall behind my bed. It's meant to be a dramatic gesture and reminds me of how he reached to give me his coat Sunday. He rubs the roach out but smoke lingers.

"Someone told me to read the Gide, an older friend from high school. Said I would need it one day to live by. He told me on my eighteenth birthday. Said I should read *The City and the Pillar* too, but I couldn't fit both books in my pocket."

He laughs. I smile at the wisdom of his anonymous friend.

"I had gone to Shakespeare for a job Saturday. I swear it," he says. "I go up to the kid watching the book bags—you saw him, the gangly one—and I tell him I want a job. I say it just like that, 'I want a job.' It throws him off. He says I need to go to the information desk to see *Her*. So I walk with my bag over my shoulder and *She* says to me, 'Stop. You need to check the bag.' And I say I want a job. Again like that. And she says to wait right here and points to the floor.

"I stood there fifteen minutes. The woman forgot me. I could have filled up my bag with books and run out of the store. What could she have done? So I walk back to the counter and give the gangly kid my bag and he hands me the Ace of Fucking Spades. No use in going to see the woman now, because I'm doomed, but I do it. I go and see her and I wait. I don't want to wait, but of course I need a job. I give her my spiel, and she says that she wants to hire me but first I have to fill out this application. Then she thrusts a form in my hand and says in this really patronizing tone, 'Be sure you read the back portion first, before you fill the rest out on the front.'

"Fine? Not fine. Basically it says, 'Sure we'll hire you, but you have to get fucked for five dollars and five cents an hour.' How is someone supposed to live in goddamn Gotham City on that?"

"That's when you decided to take a book?" I ask.

"No. I didn't decide to do anything then," he says. "But Sunday, before I met you, I knew I would do something. I went back there. I didn't plan it, but I knew I'd do something. The Gide was Sunday. Today was this one."

He reaches for his coat lying on the rug. I watch the shadow of his arm arch on the wall. Then he flips a book at me. It seems to come out of nowhere, landing in my lap. I hold it to the light in the window. It's *The Selected Works of Rainer Maria Rilke*. I look up and strain to make him out in the darkness. I don't want to think how he smuggled the Rilke out of the store. But I wonder if he intends to bleed Shakespeare & Company dry, book by book.

"Rilke says we carry our desire and death around like a seed inside our bodies," he tells me.

I crack open the book in the middle and read the first thing I see.

I have my dead, and I would let them go, and be stunned to see them so comfortable, so soon at home in Death, so calm, so different from their reputation. You, you alone turn back; you brush against me, you linger, knock about, that the sound may give you away. . . .

"A gift," he explains. "For yesterday. Hope you haven't read it yet. Only thing handy."

Oh, don't take from me what I am slowly learning. I look at him long enough to see him, to have seen him. Then I close my eyes. *Don't take from me what I'm slowly learning.*

Thursday evening over dinner, Nathan tells me that a temporary agency sent him to work for a very old securities firm down on Broad Street, which needed someone to inventory their files for storage. He had to sort through files and ledgers in a cellar, some over a century old. Grunt work he calls it. The firm apparently didn't believe in throwing anything out and the cellar was very dusty and disorganized, but warm.

"Do you know what the irony of it is?" Nathan asks.

"What?"

"There's a lot of steady work as a temporary."

"Really now?"

"It's postmodern economics. 'Temporary' is a euphemism. What it means is that the company doesn't have to pay for your health insurance."

"And this is your own discovery?"

"I made it today." He reaches down into his book bag under the table. "I brought you another gift."

He hands me a large old ledger.

"Open it," he says.

It's from before World War I. The ink is brown and the entries are in a florid script that is almost illegible.

"You must return this," I tell him.

"They'll never miss it. Look how old it is. Do you think they'll go back and look for it in an IRS audit?"

He has a point.

"What will I do with it, Nathan?"

"I don't know. Look at it, put it on the coffee table."

"But you stole it."

"I prefer purloined. The Purloined Ledger."

I laugh. I can't help it. I'm beginning to amass a library. He tells me how he sneaked the book out of the cellar.

"They left you alone down there?" I ask.

"I have a sincere face," he says.

After we leave the Chinese restaurant, we trudge across Amsterdam Avenue again. I have the ledger and he has his book bag slung over his shoulder like a rabbit hunter. He also has his white takeout carton. The streets on the West Side are littered with slabs of ice and snow, like chunks of gypsum.

"I'm going to grow my hair long and get an earring. What do you think?" Nathan asks. He's wearing a baseball cap, ski parka, jeans, hiking boots.

"I'm not sure. I like you the way you are now, but if you want to, then go ahead. Who am I to say?"

"I feel like I need a change. But I'm afraid to spend the little money I have on clothes. I did buy this new Yankees hat."

He tells me how his roommate borrowed his favorite baseball cap and didn't return it.

"Says he lost it."

"I guess you're not really in a position to complain."

"Yeah, seeing's how I'm quite the urban nomad these days, and everything I left home with I carried in this book sack."

Nathan's been crashing at the apartment of old acquaintances from New Orleans, on a hide-a-bed sofa in the living room, and when the sliver of light goes out from under the bedroom door and their animal noises die out, Nathan lies there sinking in the middle of the tortured mattress, wondering what in the fuck he's gotten himself into. Then he beats off. He says there isn't anything remotely sexual about it, or that he gets any satisfaction from it. It's more medicinal, a sleep aid. He lies there with spunk on his chest thinking about New Orleans. Thinking about home is unavoidable.

"Thought you were pretty resigned to being here," I say.

"I thought it was what I wanted before I got here. I don't know. I spent a good portion of my adolescence believing nothing was ever going to happen to me," he says. "No. That's not true. I grew up never imagining anything significant happening to me. Now I'm here and I can't decide if I'm regretting it or thankful.

"Yesterday, I thought about going home," he says. "I mean I actually imagined myself on the southbound *Crescent*, staring at the countryside. But then it all started to dissolve into other thoughts and I decided I wasn't all that homesick.

"But the most significant thing I've done is leave," he says. "Guess I've mastered the intricacies of departure now. Trains make for great exits."

We cross Broadway and head for the subway station at Lincoln Center. There are old men in front of Tower Records with milk crates and planks set up to display coffee-table books, all unbelievably half-priced. We browse. They're beautiful, thick, expensive art books: Monet's water lilies, Mapplethorpe's women, treasures of the Hermitage. They're probably all hot, or have fallen off the truck, so to speak, and I think, This is why you can only get five dollars and five cents an hour for a job in a bookstore, Nathan. But I don't say anything.

We pass the frozen fountain at Lincoln Center as it begins to snow. It seems we have the whole plaza to ourselves. It's very cold, in the teens, and we walk to the station at a brisk pace. He grabs my hand and holds it, until a couple appears in the stairwell of the station. He's cautious about that sort of thing.

On the subway, a shriveled old man in cutoff shorts and tank top limps toward us. He has a genuine prosthesis. He pleads for something to eat. Nathan's face tightens. He looks at me, then hands the man his white container of leftovers. The old man snatches it and gets off the train at Times Square.

"I knew there was something about that shrimp and garlic sauce," Nathan says.

"I hope he eats it," I say.

The gentleman across the car from us, who has been watching stone-faced, asks Nathan if the takeout was tomorrow's lunch.

"It was."

"I could smell it," he says.

"I had this intimation when we left the restaurant about that carton," Nathan whispers to me.

"Yes, but you would have gotten to my house and stuck it in the fridge and left it there, and I'd have ended up throwing it out."

"Giving things to the homeless only encourages them to remain on the streets," the gentleman says.

"Fuck you," Nathan says to the man, who gets up and walks to the other end of the car.

"That was unnecessary," I whisper.

"I couldn't help it," Nathan says loudly. "I keep thinking of something my mother told me about my grandfather driving around town looking for an open grocery that would sell him a can of dog food on a Sunday, back in the Fifties when Louisiana still had blue laws. He wanted to feed this stray hound, you see. My mother said he hated to see animals neglected, but he'd only give it one can. He didn't have the heart to call the pound, because he knew they'd put the pitiful thing to sleep, and his daughters wouldn't understand. That's probably what happened anyway because it ended up disappearing. But when it came around that Sunday, Grandpa only fed it one can. My mother watched the dog lap up the food in an old hubcap, and she asked him why didn't he give it more, and he said to her, 'Now sugar, that dog wouldn't know when to stop eating. He'd eat and eat till he gorged himself to death.'"

I finger him until he writhes with whatever he's feeling. Before I enter him, this pinhole opens inside of me, and as through a camera obscura, I glimpse everything upside down and inverted. I think I've become him.

The expression on his face when I'm inside him, when he comes, is a kid's with something fragile in his hands, who suddenly, inexplicably lets it go.

"Why do you look crestfallen?" I whisper.

He closes his eyes, shakes his head. Then he climbs out of bed. He goes to the window, finds a pack of cigarettes, wrings one from the pack on the sill, and sits by the radiator.

He's told me he's never had a lover, but now I know: He's a widower. It comes to me in the simplest of gestures—the way he palms his cigarette, the way he furrows his hair behind his earlobe, the way he stares out the window. I see beneath his sedentary vigil anger, densifying on some focal point of concentration beyond the glass and whirling snow.

"You know what desire is?" he asks.

"What?"

"It's that throbbing numbness you feel after you've been truly reamed, after someone pulls out of you," he says over his shoulder.

I want to vomit.

He leaves me alone in the bedroom and stands in the hall. He sees the wine glasses on the kitchen counter, and I imagine him counting them; I imagine him knowing. I close my eyes. Steam courses through the pipes. The apartment is breathing in the silence. I hear him pad into the bathroom. Then he comes back to bed, wearing boxers.

"I thought I gave you what you wanted," I say.

He stands at the bed with his head bowed. I didn't want to fuck him, but I did. Now I want to blame him. I was giving him what he wanted. I didn't feel anything between my legs, just the rhythm, the motion of our bodies rocking.

He lies down next to me and I put my arm around his waist. "You're a fine piece of work," I whisper.

"You'll either hate me or not." He shudders against me.

"Which one should I feel?" I ask.

"I don't know."

After he has gone to wherever he goes, I sit on the sofa with the ledger on the coffee table and all the other books he's swiped the past week and I think about mailing them back to their respective owners. It would be the ethical thing to do. And I consider doing it, but these books are souvenirs and the owners, not missing them, now will never realize they've been taken away. Perhaps in some distant inventory, some far-off settling of accounts, they'll turn up missing, but what are the chances? I know I'm rationalizing. I know this, but I lie down in the dark thinking that every time he leaves, I never know if I will see him again. It's the nature of the city. It's that part of the city I hate. The snow whizzes by the window. The sky is leaden. I live in an insular, little world. I think I need these books as proof that he exists.

Grief isn't something that lessens with time passing. This is a lie so many old folks have sputtered out. They believe uttering these words makes grief dissipate. But they're dead wrong about it. Sometimes the coming of grief isn't as obvious as in a sad movie. Sometimes it can be the way two shadows follow, drift, merge over pavement; the unexpected sweetness of wood burning; the riff of an old song, long thought buried in the silt of everydayness.

I go to the bodega on the corner for cigarettes and the *Village Voice*. Snow sweeps across Bleecker Street in great swaths; street lamps disclose the gauze in motion. It still amazes me how snow muffles sound. The street has the silence of a museum. Nathan Morrow is gone. But in this silence I hear his music, or rather my own rendering of it, over and over in my head. I can't concentrate on anything else, but his music and the sound of my own breathing.

I asked him once to copy the music out for me so that I might learn it. He put me off, said he couldn't transcribe it. He had a wonderful ear but hardly any theory. But I think he liked the fact that no one else could play it. It was not meant for me. He did ask me what I thought of it but I couldn't tell him. I might've described what I heard as a series of moments drifted through, a succession of rooms, all suggesting some emotion, but what? Tell him I never knew how much desire could sound like despair?

Walking home in the snow, watching it fall, I think of the years we were together. We never said how we felt about anything. We played out desire on the body; it was never spoken of, never written out. I remember how frail he was, on the bench at the piano, a ghost in white pajamas, his feet hardly touching the floor, a wine glass filled with ice water on a plate next to him, slender fingers floating over the keys. It's what I picture when his longing to remember comes to me, the struggle to remember, as he slipped into dementia. It enclosed him. It encloses me. The rhapsody had become an interior for him, as it is for me now. I remember every note he played. But he left no score for me to find my way.

DESIRE

BUTLER AND I HUNG OUT AT ONE OF THE SIDEWALK TABLES where we could see up and down Magazine Street or into the café through the windows. Earlier that evening I had gone to meet Butler at the Restaurant Coliseum, off Coliseum Square, where he'd worked as a bartender since returning from an extended sojourn in the North. We'd left for the Abstract, but got bored and wandered up Magazine to the Zola. The Zola sat on the corner at Felicity Street, near Butler's apartment. Butler had made it his café. It was a fine café, though it didn't have air-conditioning. The bartender always played Satie or Debussy or Chopin on the phonograph behind the bar and kept the doors open so the music could spill outside. We liked the Zola because we could sit outdoors and not feel that we were missing anything. We also liked the fact that the Zola had a bartender with a record collection, a good toilet, an old phone booth, and strong coffee. But we weren't drinking coffee that humid May night. Butler had money, and we'd started on scotch at the Abstract and stayed with it.

"Hey, Duck, did I tell you? They were filming an independent movie in the neighborhood last week," Butler said.

"I don't think so," I said, lighting a cigarette and offering him my pack.

"I must've forgotten," Butler said, taking my Luckies. "They were doing a day-for-night scene outside the lobby of the old Happy Hour Theater, and I went on my balcony to watch."

Butler lived in the garret of a building on Magazine eyeball to eyeball with the abandoned cinema's marquee, which had announced LOST HORIZON LOST HORIZON LOST HORIZON for as long as anyone could remember, summing up, more or less, how we felt about living in New Orleans.

"Who was in it?" I asked.

"Some unknowns," he said. "I got curious about that and went downstairs to see them do this shot. One of the crewmen asked me if I wanted to be a walk-on—you know, for a few days—so I spent all weekend walking back and forth across the street."

"Did you get paid?"

"It wasn't union scale," Butler said, "but it wasn't too shabby either, considering we're drinking the walk-on money now."

"I wondered how come you were buying," I said, lifting my glass. "To walk-on money."

"Hear! Hear!" Butler said. "Are we cocktailed?"

I drained my glass. "Not too much."

"Then how about another walk-on scotch?"

"Maybe just one more," I said.

Butler signaled the waiter, who brought us another round.

"It was so funny," Butler continued. "I had this suit on Easter Sunday when I came home from working the brunch crowd."

Butler called his secondhand seersucker, yellow bow tie, old bucks, and Panama hat his Southern writer's drag, though he was a violinist. He wore it all summer, but never, as he would say, before Good Friday.

"And they asked me—get this—if I would mind changing into something less conspicuous."

"I can imagine how difficult that was for you," I said, feeling comfortable in my favorite pair of Madras shorts and an old Hawaiian shirt.

"It's strange being in the background," he said. "I'm so used to presiding over the action when I work behind the bar."

I wondered how conspicuous we looked sitting on the sidewalk of Magazine Street, getting crocked. I tried to focus on Butler. As always, he sat with the back of his chair facing him. He called it the "lotus position." Every time he sat that way, I thought of him telling me that was how he liked to screw. Butler had a knack for appropriating ordinary gestures and making them lewd or otherwise memorable.

"Where's Styborski tonight?" I asked.

"Probably reading tarot cards in Jackson Square," Butler said. "We don't fool around much any more, you know. He's been preoccupied."

"He has a crush on some Loyola person."

"You heard? He thinks I'm not jealous—"

"You?" I asked. "Never."

"But he is being led around on this kid's leash—I mean that figuratively, of course. Although one can't be too sure, given his proclivities."

"Styborski does have that beagle-like quality," I said.

"It's just as well."

"Why?"

"He's far too old for me," Butler said, grinning, then quickly adding, "I'm being facetious. You know?"

"I know."

"Really, he's too much a part of the fringe element."

"I was under the impression that we're all part of the fringe element, eccentricity being so highly prized here."

"The whole city is," Butler said. "But Styborski's way out on the periphery—like in another paradigm. He has some pretty outlandish fetishes, too. I can still feel bad for him, though."

"What's with this Loyola person?" I asked, wondering what exactly Butler considered outlandish.

"Cute kid from Natchez, with lips that could suck a golf ball through a straw. Blows glass in the fine arts department," Butler said. "Can you see it?" Butler arched an eyebrow. "Styborski gives the impression the kid hasn't really come out yet—Catholic guilt and whatnot. He and the kid got drunk together one night and the kid stayed over at Styborski's apartment. They slept together but didn't even touch. All they did was 'hint around it.' Now, how you 'hint around it,' I can't imagine. Styborski said the kid was too scared to try anything, but I don't believe it. I think Styborski was probably the one paralyzed, having to take charge. I'm glad I'm not that way. Another?"

Butler raised his glass, clinking the ice. I put my hand over my glass. Butler ordered another scotch for himself and we sat nursing our drinks.

"I was thinking how intertwined fear and desire can be," I said.

"And why do you suppose it's that way?" Butler asked.

"It's not always as simple as rejection," I said.

"True," he said. "Could be other extenuating circumstances." He rubbed his cigarette in the Cinzano ashtray and leaned on the chair, looking at me expectantly. "Cat got your tongue, Duck?"

We were beginning to lose our dignity in front of the Zola, so I suggested we take a walk. Butler downed his scotch, I lit a cigarette, and we started up Felicity toward St. Charles Avenue and the streetcar. We contemplated catching a cab to the Faubourg Marigny to hear a saxophonist we both knew. Then Butler said we should make an appearance at the Half Moon Bar and

Grill. I thought I should go home, but Butler insisted we have a nightcap to finish off his walk-on money.

When I had second thoughts about entering the Half Moon, Butler led me through the door by the elbow. Inside, he removed his hat and jacket and set them on a bar stool, stuck a ten-spot in my hand and went to the john. I sat at the bar with his things and our scotches.

Butler returned with a smirk on his face. "Jay's in the back room," he said, feigning surprise. "Playing pool."

"Of course," I said. "With Roscoe, no doubt. Don't suppose you said hello?"

"Had to," Butler said. "Roscoe is my boss."

"And you told him I was here with you."

"The only polite thing to do," Butler said.

I shook my head, and waited to see if he'd propose escaping to an alternate venue, but he didn't oblige me. I took out my wallet.

"What are you doing, Duck?"

"I'm sure I had some money," I said. "Here, bartender, two pitchers."

I extracted my pack of cigarettes from Butler's shirt pocket, lit one, and put another behind my ear. (Butler had a habit of appropriating cigarette packs.)

"We can't just leave now—no thanks to you—so I figure if we go back there, we might as well have an offering."

"You're smooth, Duck. Real smooth."

We gulped our scotches. Butler grabbed the pitchers and I grabbed his hat and coat. The room was dark except for the hanging yellow bulb inside a cracked Dixie Beer lampshade above the pool table. The Half Moon was a dive, but Butler liked it because it was close to Restaurant Coliseum and all the help from Roscoe's place hung out there. Roscoe had taken to bringing along Jay, his recent find. I stood in the archway, suspecting Butler had planned this little encounter all along.

We exchanged mildly enthusiastic greetings as we entered. Butler took our pitchers over to Roscoe's table in the corner.

"Rack 'em up, Duck," Jay called.

"Jay, I have to warn you," Butler said, feeding the pool table with quarters, "Duck feels inspired tonight."

The jukebox suddenly sprang to life with the Clash's "Should I Stay or Should I Go," reminding everyone it was there. Butler looked at me and chortled.

"So, Duck's the boy to beat tonight?" Roscoe asked.

"Afraid so," Butler snickered.

"Ten says Jay beats him," Roscoe said.

"Don't egg him on, Roscoe," I said.

"Twenty," Butler said. "Two more pitchers and I'll even spot you two balls."

"Deal," Roscoe said.

Midway through the game, I decided that both Jay and I were trying to throw it. Our respective cheering sections didn't seem to notice, getting more and more rambunctious as the game dragged on. Finally (out of exhaustion, I suppose), Jay scratched. It almost appeared accidental. I wished it had been an accident; I would have felt relieved of some of the responsibility. Roscoe groaned, but paid Butler graciously. Jay beamed. There was something clandestine about his smile.

Roscoe seemed reluctant to go for the pitcher refills and tried to get Jay to do it.

"He can't," Butler needled Roscoe. "It's like in pool, when the loser has to rack."

Roscoe went to the bar with a sour expression on his face.

"I've got to get home," I told Butler.

"Another game," he said. "Better yet, some cutthroat."

I looked across the table at Jay. "I'm not going to let the two of you fleece Roscoe tonight," I said, propping my cue stick against the wall.

When Roscoe returned with two pitchers of draft, Jay said to him, "Let's go to the French Quarter."

"Not me," Roscoe said.

I agreed with Roscoe, and he volunteered to drive me home.

Jay turned to Butler. "Then it's just the two of us."

"Guess so," Butler said, and went to get go-cups for the beer.

I plunked a couple of quarters into the jukebox, punched some numbers. Roscoe whined to Jay about barhopping in the Quarter. Jay pestered Roscoe to drop Butler and him off at Café Brasil, until Roscoe relented. Once Butler and Jay had filled as many plastic cups as they could carry, Roscoe decided he had better accompany them to the French Quarter after all.

We walked around the corner to Camp Street, where Roscoe had parked his convertible. Roscoe got into the car and put the top down. Butler insisted that he sit shotgun and jumped into the front seat, which pissed Roscoe off, I'm sure, though he didn't mutter a word. I climbed into the backseat with Jay. Roscoe asked if he should drive me home first, but Jay goaded me about wanting to turn in so early.

"Don't be such a killjoy, Duck," Butler joined in. "Just come with us."

We flew through the Irish Channel and downtown, into the French Quarter. I was grateful for the wind of the open car. Roscoe kept checking us out in the rearview mirror. I resisted looking at Jay myself.

We never made it to Café Brasil. Butler suggested a detour to the Louisiana Purchase, to watch the boys dance on the bar. By then I was on to Butler's game: Our barhopping wasn't as desultory as he would have liked it to appear. Roscoe groaned, but managed to find "celebrity parking" (as Butler called it) on the corner of Burgundy, across the street from the tavern. Butler, Roscoe, and Jay leaped from the car. I looked at my watch. It was one o'clock.

"This night," I called to Butler, "is fast becoming an abyss—the kind that stares back at you."

"Then prepare to return the stare," Butler barked as he sauntered into the tavern.

I knew I should go home then—the Louisiana Purchase wasn't a place I frequented—but I climbed out of the car and followed them. The tavern had a subterranean feel, with mirrored Mylar and chain-link grating over the windows and plenty of rowdy fringe element. The place reeked of cigarettes, beer, urine, commerce.

Jay maneuvered next to me in the mob by the pool table and gestured for me to scoot over a bit. I watched him survey the competition. I was uncomfortable standing, but I considered sitting on a pool table a sin, no matter how ratty it looked. When Jay hopped up, however, I followed suit. He called me a copycat.

"If you're looking for love around here," someone shouted, tapping Roscoe on the shoulder, "it goes by the hour."

"Thanks for the warning," Roscoe spat.

When Butler and Roscoe retreated to the bar, Jay and I started talking. I asked him if he'd wrestled in high school.

"Roscoe must have told you," Jay said.

"I can tell by the way you move," I said. "You remind me of someone I knew once, in my junior and senior years."

"Were you in love with this wrestler?" Jay asked.

"*Geez*," I said. "What a question. That was ten years ago. He's married now, with four kids."

"Did you two sleep together?"

"A couple of times," I admitted. "Mostly we'd get drunk on weekends and drive out to the West End boat launch, and I'd suck his cock. He told me he loved me, but he loved his girlfriend more. I see him from time to time—without the wife, of course. We never talk about what happened between us."

"I'll bet you've written a story about him."

I laughed. "See this?" I said, showing Jay the scar from the gash my wrestler gave me when I struggled to get free of a headlock and we both fell to the floor and my skull cracked on the armoire in my bedroom. Jay touched my forehead. I glanced at the bar and caught Roscoe staring.

Butler waved for us to come over and Jay and I dismounted the pool table reluctantly. A bald, bearded man perched on a stool at the end of the bar started plying Butler, and then Jay and me, with scotch, leaving Roscoe to pay for himself. Butler introduced him as Moe, the manager. Moe sat with a cute piece of trade in a white undershirt and go-go shorts. We watched as the hustler lit Moe's cigar with a blue Bic lighter. Moe sucked and puffed on the stogy, his stubby, bejeweled fingers twisting it back and forth in his mouth while Roscoe fanned the smoke away from himself.

Moe insisted he had seen Butler, Jay, and me in a porn film, and Butler kept throwing it in Roscoe's face. I stifled a laugh when Roscoe whispered in my ear, "Call off your dog, Duck, or he can find another place to sling cocktails."

"It's crowded for a weeknight," Jay said.

The hustler informed us it was Amateur Night.

"Why don't you get up and dance on the bar?" Butler coaxed Jay. "You know how to move. A body like yours? Damn, I bet you could make some pretty good tips."

"I don't think so," Roscoe said.

What did I care any more? I looked at Roscoe and blurted, "Don't you think Jay should put some of that Greco-Roman grace to good use?"

Butler laughed. Jay had that glint in his eyes, like he had at the Half Moon.

"Come on, Jay," Butler said. "Show these boys how a wrestler moves."

"Jay doesn't want to," Roscoe insisted.

"The hell I don't," Jay said.

"Do what you want," Butler urged.

Jay slowly took off his shirt, then his tennis shoes and socks, then his jeans, piling them on a stool next to me as Butler cheered him on. Roscoe fumed.

I sat watching the proceedings, remembering the frigid Sunday night before Mardi Gras when Jay and Butler stripped and dove into Lake Pontchartrain.

Roscoe didn't seem to mind Jay taking off his clothes then, even if it meant he had to ride around sopping wet in Roscoe's car afterward.

Jay jumped on the bar and began gyrating to the pounding beat emanating from the cassette deck behind it. (The Louisiana Purchase was not a high-tech operation.) Jay danced and the patrons stuffed bills in his jock. He worked the crowd. When he passed by me, I folded a five-dollar bill elaborately over the elastic belt of his jock. Roscoe was livid. He grabbed Jay by the ankle.

"Lighten up, Roscoe," Butler said. "We're only having fun."

"Go to hell," Roscoe said. "Come down off the bar, Jay. Now."

Moe told Roscoe in no uncertain terms that if he didn't leave the customers alone, he'd be expelled.

"I've never been thrown out of a goddamn bar," Roscoe groaned.

"There's a first time for everything," Moe said, winking at me.

"Jay, are you coming down off the bar or not?" Roscoe yelled.

Butler moved onto the bar, next to Jay, and shouted, "Hey, guys. Let's put it to a vote. All in favor of Jay dancing on the bar, please applaud." There was a fair amount of applause and some catcalls. Jay put two fingers in his mouth and whistled.

"All opposed," Butler declaimed.

Silence, except for the music.

Roscoe glared at me; I shrugged. He released Jay's ankle and stormed out of the bar. In all the years I'd known him, I had never seen Roscoe lose his cool. Jay slid off the bar to go after him. Butler intervened, catching him by the crook of his arm.

"You can't run out of here like that," Butler said. "Have fun, Jay. I'll talk to Roscoe."

Some boys came from the back room and took turns dancing on the bar. Jay propped himself next to me on a stool and bought me a scotch with tip money from his jock. He had collected about fifty dollars, which he counted out on the bar.

"I guess I was a hit," he said.

"Yes, but we really pissed off Roscoe," I said, reaching for the cigarette behind my ear and trying not to stare at Jay.

"He'll get over it," Jay said. He pointed to my ear. "Do you have another?"

"You don't smoke, Jay."

"I know. I feel like I want one."

"Have this," I said.

He took a few drags and stifled a cough, then flipped the cigarette back to me.

"I've never danced on a bar before, Duck."

"Remember what Moe said about firsts."

Jay chuckled. "That's my philosophy—try anything once."

"Did that bit of personal philosophy contribute to your hooking up with Roscoe?"

"Basically."

"Can I ask you a question, Jay?"

"Ask away."

"Never mind."

"Oh, no," Jay said. "You've got to ask me now." He draped a big arm around my shoulders and squeezed my neck.

"I'm not playing Truth or Dare with you anymore," I said. "You're too dangerous."

"I'll hold it against you if you don't."

"Okay! But you first."

"How'd you get your nickname," Jay asked.

"That's easy. Butler, of course. Do you recognize Ruthie the Duck Woman?" I asked. "She's a real character."

"I haven't been coming to the Quarter all that long," Jay said.

"Right," I said. "You'd know her if you'd seen her. She's eighty years older than God and four feet high. Petulant and bat-shit crazy. Carries her pet duck around in a Dixie Beer box. A few summers ago, Butler and I were wasted in the Bourbon Pub and she stumbled into the bar wearing a filthy, reeking prom dress, swaddled in a mangy mink stole. She plopped down next to me on a stool, hoisted her duck-in-a-box onto the bar, and snatched my Luckies from me, then had the nerve to complain to Butler and curse me because they weren't menthols. Apparently, Kool is her brand of choice. Butler turned to me after she left to harass the bartender, and said, 'You are *my* duck and one day I'll have to carry you around in a box.' He's since apologized for saddling me with that name over the years, but I guess not the sentiment."

"I see the name stuck," Jay said. "You shoot."

"Why do you go out with Roscoe—I mean, what do you see in him?"

"I don't know," Jay said, pulling away and contemplating my question. "I guess because Roscoe came on to me like a summer downpour. He just wouldn't let up."

"He was your first?"

Jay nodded.

"I figured."

"He's pretty smart—well, you know that. Smart and relentless."

Jay told me how Roscoe first followed him through the library's third floor maze of humanities stacks at the University of New Orleans, where he went to school. We drank for a while, but I could only bring myself to look at Jay in the mirror, sitting in the packed bar in nothing but his jockstrap. I was intrigued by how comfortable he seemed. We talked about wrestling. Jay said it was like dance: stylized.

"And erotic," I offered.

"Sure," Jay said. "For the spectator. But to experience it is something else entirely. It's brutal. You say good luck to your opponent, then you slam him to the mat and humiliate him. He gets what he deserves, because he's of the same mentality. He'd do it to you if you let him."

"Butler says pretty much the same thing about Roscoe," I said, watching Jay trace his fingers in the black cigarette scars on the wooden bar. "But I don't necessarily agree with him."

"Roscoe's only interested in what he can get from me," Jay said, his voice darkening. He was absolutely bug-eyed. "Sometimes I feel like a course in his restaurant."

"Look, Jay, I have to escape while Butler's gone. Otherwise he'll have me out all night, and I have work to do in the morning."

"Where are you going?"

"To Canal Street, to catch the streetcar."

"I'll walk with you."

Jay dressed and we left the Louisiana Purchase. We walked down to Bourbon Street and turned toward Canal, passing the Gunga Den, where a barker tried to lure us inside, and Galatoire's—dark and forlorn.

"I finally read one of your stories," Jay said. "Butler brought a copy of some literary magazine to the restaurant."

"Which story?"

"The one about the book thief in New York. Butler bragged it was about him."

"Possibly."

"I liked it," Jay said. "You're on the money about isolation shriveling people. I feel that sometimes—afraid of stopping, afraid of feeling, afraid of not feeling. It gives me the creeps."

"I don't wish it on anyone," I said.

Then Jay said he didn't cry at birth. His mother had cried—in her stupor, not from her C-section, when she heard the news of Robert Kennedy's assassination in Los Angeles. He said this with the clarity of a witness—how his mother listened to the nurses crying in the Miami hospital recovery room, how utter stillness seemed to loom before her, bringing tears to her eyes. How he carried this hungry, vacant feeling with him, and wrestling filled it. He wanted to know what it meant.

I didn't have any answers. I looked at Jay and wondered how this story had been passed down to him, what his mother was like.

"Your stories, how do you come up with them?" Jay asked.

"You should probably go back and look for Butler and Roscoe," I said.

"Roscoe won't leave the Quarter without me," Jay said. "Tell me what gets your stories going."

"They just happen."

"Write one about me," Jay said.

The streetcar wasn't there when we reached Canal. Two frat boys, propped along the wall of the drugstore like rag dolls, passed a green, screw-top wine jug between them. Jay hopped onto a newspaper box; I guess he'd decided to wait with me. I leaned against a street lamp. We didn't say anything for a long time. I kept thinking I would tell him about the story I had already started.

The Sunday night before Mardi Gras, I had gone to the Restaurant Coliseum in search of amusement, hoping to catch Butler before he left work. We—Roscoe, Butler, Styborski (sporting a new beard), and I—ended up sitting with a young black-haired student whom Roscoe referred to as Jacinto but did not introduce to us. Butler called him Jay. Roscoe held court at a corner of the bar near the makeshift stage where we'd gathered to hear his cousin, Fortunate Champagne, sing standards with her quartet. Roscoe fired a look at Jay and me. I bit my lip; no need to ask Butler to whom Jay belonged.

Jay and I ignored each other during Fortunate's first set—I wasn't forward enough to introduce myself—but I caught Jay stealing glances at me in the window's reflection as Fortunate began to croon "The Very Thought of You." Jay watched Butler lean over and whisper the lyrics in my ear. I punched Butler on the forearm. He snickered, then conveniently remembered it was my turn to buy, slipping my twenty from under my cocktail glass and pouring shots for the bar.

After Fortunate's set, Butler, Styborski, and Roscoe argued about Mardi Gras. I sat still, intent on the silhouette of a couple making love in a balcony window across the street. Butler asked Styborski if he'd been reading cards in Jackson Square. He flashed his de Medici tarot deck as if it were a police badge and said he'd done better the last hour of work, after the Bacchus parade passed up Canal Street, than he had the whole day, making four hundred bucks.

"So Mardi Gras has been good for you?" Roscoe asked Styborski.

"Actually, I hate Mardi Gras," Styborski said. "Don't like the parades, the tourists, or the snooty Carnival balls. Have you ever been to one?"

"Of course," Roscoe said. "My father's a captain in the Mystik Krewe of Shangri-La."

"I'm proud to say I've never been to one," Styborski said.

"They're boring—even the ones thrown by the gay krewes," Butler said. "And it's outrageous how much those queens spend on sequined gowns."

Roscoe snorted.

"Putting a crown on your aristocracy," Butler continued, "may have been quaint a hundred years ago, but now it's just stupid. Do we really give a flying freak who the King of Comus is?"

"Well, yes," Roscoe said. "When he's your uncle."

"Isn't that supposed to be a secret?" Butler asked.

"Those who count already know," Roscoe snapped.

"I'm sorry—" Styborski interrupted, waving his deck of cards at Jay. "Butler, who is this?"

Butler chided Roscoe for not introducing his new friend.

"Jacinto can take care of himself, thank you very much," Roscoe said.

"Jay doesn't say much of anything," Butler observed.

Styborski laughed. "That's okay. We like the strong, silent type."

Jay finally spoke: "I run out of things to say."

"Words, words, words!" Styborski bellowed. "Who needs words when you've got a good face?"

"Who are you quoting?" I asked, knowing how Styborski liked to make cinematic allusions.

"I'm paraphrasing Gloria Swanson in *Sunset Boulevard*," Styborski said.

"I bet Duck couldn't agree with you less," Butler said, turning to me.

"How so?" Roscoe asked.

"Ever read *Clothes for a Summer Hotel*, the play by Tennessee Williams?" Butler replied.

Roscoe shrugged. I couldn't imagine him ever reading a play.

"It's a later work," Butler said, "a memory play about the F. Scott Fitzgeralds. Zelda tells her lover, Edouard, that words are the love acts of writers." He grinned from ear to ear.

"What's all this about?" Roscoe asked.

"Never mind me," Butler said.

By now everyone was toasted. Jay kept looking at me with perfect animal stillness, though I doubted what I was seeing until he invited us for a drive in Roscoe's Mercedes after the Restaurant Coliseum closed. I found myself hovering between the surreal enormity of his furtive glances and the contentment I felt with a glass of scotch in my hand, poised at my lips—the chill, the heft, the shape of the glass. Scotch had a way of suspending everything.

When I emerged from my fog we were cruising Elysian Fields Avenue, then down Lakeshore Drive, listening to the B-52s, Butler, Styborski, and I in the backseat singing along to "Love Shack" at the top of our voices. Roscoe parked the car near a picnic pavilion at the Lakefront and we all scrambled out, whereupon Butler, Styborski, and Jay stripped to their skivvies and took a dip. Butler and Styborski called to us to join them, but Roscoe and I sat on the seawall steps and watched them in the tangerine light of a street lamp. Roscoe muttered something inane about the full moon. Jay emerged from the lake clasping his jock and shivering, water glazing his dark skin. He looked at me again, and I began to shiver.

Jay swiped Styborski's wide-brimmed fisherman's hat—the one that made Styborski look like Walt Whitman—from a pile of clothes. The hat had political buttons pinned on it like fishing lures. Jay took off running along the seawall, and Styborski gave chase until he was panting for breath. Jay slid onto the hood of Roscoe's car, waving the hat triumphantly. He read each pin aloud, savoring the words. He hadn't said much the whole evening, but now he recited each phrase—"Silence Equals Death"; "Greenpeace"; "No Blood for Oil"—like it was poetry. Jay claimed the hat for the rest of the night, and had it on when he got sick in the john of the picnic pavilion later, with Butler, Styborski, and Roscoe in the doorway watching him crouch at the urinal trough. Butler said, laughing, "It shouldn't be too hard to puke, what with the smell." Jay tried to say something and ended up heaving. Suddenly he seemed fragile, like somebody's kid brother.

I nudged Roscoe aside and stooped to Jay, kneeling on the floor. "It's best to get it out of your system," I whispered. "You'll feel better after you do."

Jay nodded, then grabbed hold of my leg and heaved into the trough again. I looked up at Roscoe and thought, How could you let the boy get this way?

In the background, Butler chattered about how easy it was to drink in New Orleans, what with go-cups and drive-through daiquiri shops and the bars staying open twenty-four hours. Jay heaved some more as Butler rattled on about three-martini Friday brunches at Galatoire's turning into happy hour at the Exile, then dinnerless dancing at the Parade Disco until the wee hours of the morning after many, many scotches; then recounted a tale about going home with a troll—a Tolkien troll. As the Saturday morning murk came through the windows, Butler had rolled over and moaned in the troll's face, "My mother'll be here early—you've got to leave." Then the troll had asked Butler, "Why would your mother be coming to my apartment?" Butler and Styborski cracked up as Roscoe sulked and I wiped Jay's forehead with balled-up tissue paper.

Later that week, on Ash Wednesday evening, as we sat at the Restaurant Coliseum bar and Butler poured us each a shot of fine nineteen-year-old single-malt scotch, Jay claimed not to remember a thing about that night at the Lakefront. Not a goddamn thing.

I had been watching Jay's reflection in the drugstore window, pondering my story as we waited for the streetcar. I wanted to tell Jay about it, tell him I had remembered everything for him (though I'd also remembered it for me). And I might have told him, but Jay abruptly decided to hunt for Roscoe in the Quarter.

Before he scampered off, he asked, "If we screwed, would Roscoe have to know?"

"Definitely not," I said, afraid that Jay would kiss me. "Roscoe wouldn't have to know anything."

Not five minutes after Jay disappeared, I heard the streetcar bell like the Good Humor ice cream truck that haunted my neighborhood as a kid. I watched the streetcar clank around the corner, then saw Butler running across Canal Street, holding his hat. The streetcar braked with a loud screech. I asked the driver to wait until Butler climbed aboard.

Butler sat down next to me, flushed and huffing.

"Why didn't you get Roscoe to drive you home?" I asked.

"Because he fired me," Butler said. "He called me a shit stirrer."

"Oh, no. I'm sorry."

"Don't be," Butler said, opening a window. "Where's Jay?"

"He left to look for you and Roscoe."

"I thought he might've gone home with you."

"I didn't ask him to."

"Are you nuts? The one opportunity in months you've had to be alone with that guy and you didn't ask him to go home with you? What kind of homosexual are you? How could you pass on that?"

"Why are you so hell-bent on hooking us up?" I said.

"Because I'm your best friend. Because he's beefy and smart and has the dick of death. Because I think you could use that guy in your life. Aren't you the least bit curious?"

"I'm more curious as to how you discovered he has the dick of death. But you didn't answer my question. If you think he's such a catch, why don't you go after Jay yourself? You certainly don't need me as a proxy."

"Low blow, Duck."

Butler sat seething while I regretted opening my big mouth. The streetcar creaked along desolate St. Charles Avenue, rounding Robert E. Lee Circle.

"Someone must have done a real number on you," Butler finally said.

"You know very well who did a number on me," I said. "But it really has less to do with him than you might think, and I don't see any need to drag his name into this discussion."

Butler sneered. As the streetcar crossed Erato Street, he asked me if I didn't invite Jay home because of Roscoe.

"Roscoe is one of my oldest friends."

"Oh, come on, Duck, give *me* a break. Roscoe's a freak and you owe him nothing."

"Look, Butler, I already know how the whole thing with Jay would end up," I said. "I have these ... hunches, and I can't just put them on the back burner."

"A lame excuse, if ever I heard one," Butler said. "I really don't get you, Duck. I don't understand why you're so intimidated, why you won't even call Jay on the goddamn phone."

"He lives in the dormitories, for Christ's sake."

"But it's so obvious he wants you."

"I really don't care to argue about it."

"Right. What do I know, anyway?"

"Will you give me a break? Please?"

Butler pulled the cord at Thalia Street and St. Charles Avenue and the streetcar ground to a halt. He stood and shook his head. "Live a little," he said, then stepped out the back of the streetcar and waved halfheartedly as it lurched forward. I used to worry about him walking alone late at night down to Magazine Street, but Butler isn't afraid of much. He once said that four years of living in New York on the edge of Crown Heights had taught him that trouble only happened if someone knew you were scared, that people made themselves victims.

My neighborhood isn't much safer; when I got to Lowerline Street, I hurried off the streetcar and trotted home. I went upstairs and opened the windows, and breathed easier. The heavy rumble of another streetcar passed like distant thunder as it moved far up St. Charles Avenue. I had gotten used to living within earshot of the streetcar, which was almost like forgetting it (until I needed to be someplace and had to wait for one). The sound was part of living along the line, like the river was part of the city, the one perpetual part.

I was sweating. I got naked and lit a cigarette, then padded to the bathroom and stood at the sink, setting my cigarette in the ashtray on the back of the old commode. Smoke ribboned into the mirror. I rubbed my sticky chin in the blue light, examined my face for blotches, felt my neck for swollen glands, finding nothing amiss. I remembered awaking this morning with the left side of my face in pain from grinding my teeth in my sleep. The bathroom was hot and close; when I sucked on my cigarette, I could actually hear it burning. The silence reminded me of hunting with my dad, huddling with him on a deer stand in the cold hollows of his land in rural Alabama, waiting, my breathing slowed, afraid to move, afraid of being reprimanded for scaring off our prey. I had to make an appointment to get tested.

I climbed into bed. A writer never finishes a story, Flaubert once wrote, he only abandons it. I remembered reading that somewhere. I closed my eyes and listened to the curtains flutter and the wild rush of wind through the trees—the dry, rustling sound it made—wondering if it would rain. And I lay there thinking of Jay until I fell asleep.

AUBADE

JACK FLIPPED SAM'S VEGGIE BURGER ON THE HIBACHI and doused the chicken with half a bottle of beer. The chicken seared. The grill steamed and smoked. Jack pointed the fork at Sam and me. "Don't get me wrong," he said. "I'd like to give you two the benefit of the doubt."

"Keep me out of it," Sam said.

"But anybody," Jack said, "that *chooses* to live in a goddamn climate like the Mekong Delta—and eats swamp bugs as a delicacy—has got to be plumb out of his gourd."

It was a hot Sunday afternoon, and it was only the middle of May. I turned to Sam. He shrugged. Sam had done a tour of duty over there as a photographer in the Army's public information bureau and knew what the Delta was like. He also worked picking beans on a Nicaraguan coffee plantation in the early Eighties to support the revolution and to make his art.

"The weather's only like this eight months out of the year," I said.

"But how can you stand this wretched humidity?" Jack asked.

"Better humidity than quakes," I retorted.

"Oh, I don't give a fig about quakes," Jack said. "What about hurricanes. It's a good thing I don't wear drawers in the summertime. I feel like I can tell you that, Miss Thing."

"Lovely," I said.

"You two really should consider moving to—" Jack said.

"Let me guess," I said. "The Promised Land."

"But San Francisco is the Promised Land," Jack said.

Sam and I live in a triangle of the Faubourg Marigny bounded by North Rampart Street, Esplanade Avenue, and Elysian Fields. It's a neighborhood of painted Creole houses reminiscent of Gauguin's Tahitian palette. The houses come to the edge of the sidewalk, or in local parlance, the banquette. In the evening denizens sit on their stoops drinking Dixie Beer, fanning themselves with the classifieds, and watching people walk home from work.

We have a new house in the Rue Chartres for which Sam paid an exorbitant amount by local standards. We have balconies and French doors and fireplaces. All the chimneys are sealed and the marble mantels are stained and pockmarked and have seen better days. Some of Sam's larger paintings lean on the mantels and along the walls of the room I use as a study. The other rooms are mostly empty and white except for a piano, an old iron bed frame left by the previous owner, a table and chairs, some linen curtains, an old Victrola I picked up in a French Market junk stand one Sunday for thirty-one dollars.

Time passes in such a way that it becomes a willful act to recollect what life was like before I came here to live. I might have discovered there's no more to love than other places, no more to remember. But there's much to remember. The ubiquitous smell from the riverfront coffee warehouses, the quiet bars, the grizzled men sucking stalks of sugar cane in the French Market stalls, the walled courtyards, the decrepit gardens glimpsed through verdigrised gates, the crepe myrtles and the sweet williams, the cathedral bells pealing, the café anarchists playing chess *al fresco*, the solitary walks along the levee, the dirty alleys, the new infatuations, the old regrets.

"Well, I suppose we should be grateful you've deigned to grace us with your presence here in the provinces," I said.

"In defense of New Orleans," Sam said, "I have to say there's only one other place in the world for the quality of light found here. County Kerry, Ireland."

"Interesting," Jack said, taking a swig off the bottle. "You find the quality of life there on par with New Orleans?"

"Sam said *light*," I said. "Get the cotton out of your ears, Jack."

"I expect I'm pretty baked," Jack said, turning the chicken. "Sam, what are you talking about? San Francisco has great light."

"Here, let me take over the grill," Sam offered. "San Francisco's light is rather lukewarm—fine for photography. But I prefer the ripe light in New Orleans for painting."

Jack surrendered the fork to Sam and slid into a chaise longue. He reclined shirtless under the ficus and the banana fronds, fanning himself with a pot holder. His long black hair held a sapphire sheen—quite the picture.

"You know, I'd like the two of you to sit for me," Sam said. "A family portrait. Do you think you both can take time out and stay still long enough?"

"He's the high-strung one," Jack said.

"I am not."

"Yes you are," he said. "It seems that whenever you walk into a room, the wheels are already spinning about what you'll do next. Or whom."

"Droll," I said, rising from my seat. "Very droll."

"If it ain't true, there ain't a cow in Texas," Jack called to me as I went into the house to fetch another glass of iced sugar tea. I stopped inside the French doors and glanced at him. Jack eyed Sam, then looked up toward me, squinting. I shook my finger at him and grimaced. He smirked. Then he put his thumb to his mouth and motioned for me to get him another beer. I shook my head no, but brought out another for him anyway and refills of tea for Sam and me.

"We really should pose for Sam," Jack said.

"Maybe Tuesday afternoon," Sam said. "I teach my life-drawing class tomorrow."

"Fine with me," I said. "How long are you here for, Jack?"

"It depends. I'm going to drive up to Natchez and try to talk my mother into liquidating some of her assets. I want her to sell a few parcels in the pecan grove near Section 42. I told her it would be a fool thing not to, with all the development going on, since she doesn't have the energy to deal with the upkeep any more. But she thinks I shouldn't concern myself with the family business, what with me being so far away."

"Does she know not to sell the mineral rights?" I asked. "Would you like me to talk to her?"

"She won't listen to anybody. She's so bull-headed since Pa died. I don't know why I bother."

"You do what you can," I said.

"I told her she ought to spend some of my inheritance, enjoy it, live a little. I'm here to tell you, Emmett, accumulating all that wealth did nothing for my Pa. Money is manure."

Jack took off his glasses and rubbed his eyes. I wanted to say to him, "Except when you don't have it," but I bit my lip. It still astounds me how often the ordinary lessons of someone born with very little money are major epiphanies to someone with scads of it.

"You know what she told me the day we graduated from Ole Miss?" Jack asked. "She said, 'Jack, you've got to run pretty far to forget where you come from. I don't expect such a place even exists.' I looked around the campus that day and I thought, You come from a farm, John Dunn. You come from a goddamn farm in Copiah County, Mississippi. But that's not what she meant. See, I warned her I was leaving home, and she whined, 'You don't know anyone in *San Francisco*.'

"She came once to visit when *Like Puns in Stein* was published," Jack said. "After the initial exhilaration wore off, I felt guilty for leaving home. Then it dawned on me that nothing would ever justify my exile into this *terra incognita* for her. I have to hand it to her though—she endured a cross-country train trip only to hear me say my piece. I asked, 'When did you know?' and she asked, 'When did I know *what*? That you would have some hard choices to make in life? I've always known that.' I told her I had to get out of the South, to reinvent myself for sanity's sake. So I went to San Francisco and became a professional queer. Our fathers were big bigots, you know. Did Emmett ever tell you that, Sam?"

"Not in so many words," Sam said. "Emmett said you've written another book. I'm sorry I haven't read your first one yet."

"Don't fret it. Does my little cousin even have a copy around? The new one's called *Khaki Is the Color for Sex Crimes*. I snagged the title off a stall in the library tearoom at Ole Miss. I love latrinalia. Some philosophy major must have scrawled it. It's about the summer I dedicated to giving up sport-fucking frats in public toilets. I doubt if anyone will publish it, after my first novel bombed. One obnoxious critic wrote that I was to narrative what Alban Berg was to melody, and he didn't mean it as a compliment. My agent says he can still get me a good advance since the book has a lot of sex in it. Not that I have a lot of sex these days. I imagine the two of you have a great deal of sex."

Jack and I looked at each other.

"I'm tired," Jack said. "Tired of the intense negotiations one has to go through these days just to get somebody's pants down. I'd been seeing this flighty Asian ergonomicist, but we broke up. I think I'll put my heart in a jar for a while."

I sat there not saying much. I wanted to talk to Jack but not around Sam. The evening had just begun to cool and the humidity wasn't unbearable. Yet the light was already so different. Sam was right about how the light thins as the afternoon wanes, how the light is pulled taut through the moisture in the air, refracted into blue and gold in the courtyard. Sam made several quick charcoal sketches of us sitting in the reflected light of the gurgling terra cotta fountain. Then we took our barbecue off the grill and went into the house to eat. I had fried some popcorn crayfish, cut some fresh avocados, steamed some asparagus, and made a hollandaise sauce and a shrimp Caesar salad. Sam had chosen a good, dry Bordeaux blanc.

Over dinner, his agitated mood passing, Jack gave us an account of his ride to the French Quarter on the airport bus and the gnomish man he'd watched having an animated conversation with himself. The gnome wore a baseball cap embroidered with the Confederate flag and a T-shirt with the slogan "Time Spent Fishing Is Not Deducted From A Man's Life."

"Strange little man," Jack said. "Everyone I saw today had a tic or a piercing stare or talked to himself. At first, because of a crease in his shirt, I thought 'fishing' read 'fucking,' and I laughed out loud. It was so fitting, so quintessentially Southern. He clutched a brown paper bag with another message written in green ink, holding it in his lap. I put on my glasses and pulled out my journal and jotted it down, 'And if you're real good, there's a bit more where this came from.' Am I babbling?"

"Not at all," Sam said, smiling.

"Jack was always such a reticent child," I said to Sam.

The next morning Jack and I got off to an early start with a workout at the New Orleans Athletic Club, where Jack made a nuisance of himself performing in the marble showers for a couple of older gents. As an out-of-towner, he was the star attraction. I retreated to the sauna and sat there for a while, eucalyptus opening every pore of memory.

We left the gym and walked over to my office in the Rue St. Louis. Jack relaxed on the settee facing my desk, reading the *Times-Picayune* and smoking Viceroys while I chalked up billable time on the phone.

I don't know why I had in mind Jack might want to do some touristy things. I suggested he join one of those Blue Line tours of the historic cemeteries or the antebellum homes in Destrehan, or take a trip on one of the river paddle wheelers, but he'd have none of it.

"I haven't seen you in four years, Emmett."

"Five," I said.

"Five. Do you think I want to go traipsing through the bayous? Besides, I don't hold for the love of ruins anyway, don't understand how someone could find a ruined cemetery quaint or charming."

"I'm just trying to make sure you're not bored," I said.

"I think I'll just hang out with you, see what goes on around the office. Your paralegal's pretty."

"He's straight," I warned.

"By your standards or mine? I'd like to get a piece of that."

"If you think you can, help yourself," I said.

"Not enough of a challenge there."

"I expect you need someone to tide you over, until you get back to the Promised Land?" I asked.

"Well, yes, as a matter of fact," he said.

Jack went to the Pair-a-Dice Lounge across the street and returned with two Coca-Colas in little green bottles, then sat sipping one from a straw and fanning himself with the Vivant section of the newspaper. His forehead crinkled as he shook his head yes or no, giving me incredulous looks or mouthing things to me, and I found myself watching for his reaction to whatever I said to a client.

Around three Jack reached into his leather backpack and pulled out a pack of cigarettes. "I have to take a breather," he said. "Back in a minute." He left the office and didn't return. Half an hour and two or three cigarettes later, I wondered if he might have found something to occupy him. Then I heard sirens on St. Louis. As I walked to the window, the telephone rang. Jack was calling from a pay phone on Royal Street.

"There's a fire at the Cabildo Museum. A hell of a commotion down here. Firemen all over the place. They've got Pirates Alley and half the square blocked off."

"I'll come down to meet you."

I grabbed my wallet and keys and trotted down St. Louis. Before I got to Bourbon Street, I could hear the wail of sirens, could smell the smoke, could see it churning into the air. The cupola of the museum was completely engulfed. Flames shot out of the dormer windows in the mansard roof.

I found Jack in front of the Court of Two Sisters restaurant. We made our way through the crowd to Chartres Street, then stood for an hour under the portico of the Upper Pontalba Apartments that flank Jackson Square. We watched firemen carry out damaged paintings of former governors and Jesuits and French aristocracy and prop them along the square's high, wrought-iron fence with the air and intensity of an elaborate ceremony. Thinking of the fire at Sam's warehouse studio last year, I pointed out Sam's old apartment. The fire claimed seventy-two of his paintings. The apartment's current resident began to hose down her hanging baskets of ferns. Water sluiced across the breadth of the balcony, then ran down the edge. Jack was, of course, more interested in the firemen and would comment on their merits at length.

"Why don't we get something to eat at Café Sbisa?" I suggested.

"Fine," Jack responded, pulling a red bandanna from the pocket of his jeans. "Man, it's hot." He took off his glasses, cleaned the lenses, wiped his forehead.

"Standing near a two-hundred-year-old blazing building doesn't help matters," I said.

"The humidity still has the heft it had when I first stepped off the bus," Jack said. "I thought I'd get used to it by now."

We walked to Decatur Street. Jack lagged behind, peering into souvenir shops.

"Ugh, I had forgotten them," Jack moaned.

"What?"

"Those," Jack said, pointing to the rows of Aunt Jemima dolls of various heights staring at us from behind the window of a shop. "Sad, ugly relics of Southern yore."

"I ignore them," I said.

"I'm sure you do," Jack said. "How, I don't know. You can feel the past here like the humidity. It's oppressive."

"Feel is the wrong sense," I said. "Smell."

"Like Paris and urine?" Jack asked. "I bet when it rains, the Quarter makes its own gumbo."

"Every time I return from a trip, I realize I had forgotten what it smelled like."

"I'll tell you what it smells like," Jack said, turning from the window. "Wood rot, mildew, and mud."

"It smells like Grandma Dunn's cedar armoire to me, with a dash of cassis. It's distinctive."

We crossed Monroe Street and walked by the bar at Tujague's. Someone called out my name and we stopped on the sidewalk. Out of Tujague's popped Claude d'Hemecourt.

"One of your cronies?" Jack asked.

"You could say that," I said. Claude was one of the Governor's environmental policy wonks at Wildlife and Fisheries. The three of us stepped into the bar. It was dark and cool inside. I introduced Claude to Jack and we ordered a round of neat bourbons. We stood under the painting of the former proprietor, a gentleman dressed in a white linen suit and Panama hat. Jack remarked how the old gent looked like Colonel Sanders.

"I didn't know you had a cousin, Emmett," Claude said. By the look on his face, I suspected he didn't believe Jack and I were kin.

"So, how do you know Emmett?" Jack asked Claude.

"It's a long story," I jumped in.

Jack arched his brow.

"Emmett and I have a history," Claude said. "At Tulane Law School."

"I see," said Jack.

"We were heading down to Sbisa for some oysters," I said. "Did you catch the fire?"

"God-awful," Claude answered. "Where did you go to school, Jack?"

"Ole Miss," Jack said.

"Fraternity?"

"Of course."

"You've got to be Delta Tau."

"Sigma Chi."

I looked at Jack, wondering why he lied. Claude grabbed Jack's hand to shake it, but Jack pulled a deft maneuver that caught Claude off guard.

"You *bastard*," Claude said, pulling Jack into a bear hug. "You are a Tau. He knows the secret shake, Emmett."

"I guess this calls for another round," I said, signaling the bartender.

"Damn. It's great to run into brothers," Claude said.

Jack lit up. "I tricked you, didn't I?"

Claude said he never ran across any gay brothers from Tulane. Jack said half his brothers at Ole Miss were gay.

"I didn't realize you had that much experience in college," I said to Jack.

"Hell. You should have seen what went on at Tau House," Jack said. "But I'm sworn to secrecy. Suffice it to say there was a lot of covert cornholing." He grabbed Claude's shoulder. "You should have dinner with us."

"I'm sorry," Claude said. "I really can't. Far too much work to do."

"That's too bad," I said.

Claude and Jack made a date for us to have lunch later during the week. Then Jack and I left Tujague's for Café Sbisa.

"Claude's kind of pretty," Jack said. "He favors the Reaganite brat on that sitcom, *Family Ties*."

"He's a good guy," I said. "Even if he is one of the Governor's slugs. Not that I concern myself with local politics too much."

"Does he have a big hooter?"

I looked at Jack. "He was sexier once," I said. "He's definitely a body in decline now. Too many late lunches at Galatoire's and not enough aerobic exercise."

"Oh, stop with the thinner-than-thou attitude, Emmett."

After dinner Jack didn't return to the office with me. I told him I had to work late and would hook up with him. I went back to the Rue St. Louis and drafted a letter to a new client who wanted to sue an oil company for spilling fuel on her property. I had bad news for her. The subject property abutted a gasoline station and convenience store in suburban Mandeville. Twenty years ago, an underground storage tank for the station had leaked high-octane fuel into the ground under my client's house. Cleanup crews managed to recover three thousand gallons. But she and her husband had remained in the house, living with the fumes, through the succeeding years. She had come to me a week ago, after she'd lost a son my age to cancer. My letter informed her that the environmental impact reports didn't look to favor making a case for wrongful death so long after the statute of limitations had run.

I worked until nine, then left the office and walked down Bourbon Street to the Exile, my favorite watering hole. Legend has it some local drag queens got kicked out of Lafitte's Blacksmith Shop by new proprietors who were surprised at the kind of folk frequenting the place. The undaunted queens moved down a block to open their own establishment. This was in the early Sixties when no self-respecting queer would be caught dead without a jacket and tie in a bar.

I stood in a corner near the fireplace and had a drink. Jack hadn't arrived yet. The wall of louvered doors across the bar—still thrown open from happy hour—gave onto Bourbon Street and I watched men parade up and down the sidewalk.

Jack came in and took a stool next to me. "What's up, Doc? You started without me. I'm so parched. Hey, Cap," Jack called to the bartender. "I'll have what he's having. What are you having, Emmett?"

"A Sazerac," I said.

"I thought only tourists drank that. Let's do a shot of something."

"Must we?"

"I've got some catching up to do," Jack said, glancing at the portrait above the fireplace, a pastel of a woman draped in a diaphanous sheet with one breast exposed.

"Sam did that," I offered.

"Did he now?"

"It was collateral," I said. "Against a tab one drunken night years ago. Then Sam got a bad bout of hepatitis, was jaundiced for months, and stopped drinking. One afternoon, Sam popped in here with me and we found it framed above the fireplace. Everyone calls her 'Mother.' Where have you been?"

"I ran into your slug and we had a drink at the Napoleon House. He convinced me I should move to New Orleans, said there was a whole colony of expatriated Mississippians here."

"But you already knew that," I said.

"We went to look at a couple of apartments."

"You can't be serious," I said. "You, giving up your glorious weather?"

"I found one in the Almonaster. Know it?"

"It's on Royal Street."

"Nice place. Big apartment."

"Are you going to take it?"

"I'm not sure," he said.

The waiter returned with our drinks and Jack asked for two shots of Chartreuse.

"I put a deposit on it," Jack continued. "This city does something to you, fries the brain."

"I'm not crazy," I said.

"That's debatable."

"Sam's certainly not crazy," I said. "What's crazy is a family poisoning themselves for twenty years and not doing a goddamn thing about it."

"What are you talking about?"

"Nothing."

"You see?" he told me. "Madness. You've been here too long and you don't even know it."

"Then why do you want to move here?"

"I don't know," Jack said. "Why did you move here?"

"I guess all those trips to Grandma Dunn's house had an effect on me." Then I suddenly remembered the summer picnic when our grandmother taught us to sprinkle salt on our cantaloupe to make it sweeter. As Jack and I took turns with the salt shaker, she swore us to secrecy, telling us she had been an orphan of the 1906 San Francisco earthquake and had come to New Orleans on the baby train to be adopted.

"Have you noticed there's not one black guy in this bar, except the bartender?" Jack asked.

"It didn't occur to me."

"Right. At least you're honest about your denial. Third-world poverty, mammy dolls and all."

"You're drunk, Jack, and I won't even dignify that remark with a response."

"I am feeling a little ill-conceived," he said. "Let's tell Sam I've decided to stay."

"If you say so."

"You think he'll be upset?"

"Of course not. He likes you. He wouldn't have asked you to pose for him if he didn't."

"Then what's the use?"

"What do you mean?"

"I just want to get him jealous."

"Sam's not the jealous type," I said.

"That's bullshit."

"Really, he's not."

"I bet you he has a green streak as wide as the river. Did you ever tell him about us at Rowan Oaks?"

"No way."

"Why? Are you ashamed of what happened?"

"That's not it."

"You're afraid of his jealousy," Jack said.

"I just don't think he'd get it."

"Then he has no idea we have a past?"

"What am I supposed to say? 'Sam, I fucked my first cousin on Faulkner's lawn'?"

"Sounds pretty succinct to me."

"He wouldn't understand. I'm not sure I do, either."

"If I remember correctly," Jack said quietly, leaning forward. "It was your idea." Jack grabbed hold of my hand. "I expect we were pretty fearless," he said. "Fucking on the lawn like that."

"We wanted to get caught," I said.

"You see, we were thinking of leaving even then," he said.

"I wasn't thinking of leaving the South," I said.

Jack frowned. "I get the impression you're still angry with me for skipping town after graduation," he said.

"I got over it."

"Did you? You let four years go by without calling me."

"Five. And you didn't call me either."

"I really didn't want to move to New Orleans and have a yuppie little life," Jack said. "And all you wanted was to go to law school and hang out your shingle. Look, yonder."

I turned and noticed a beautiful man standing transfixed under the street lamp on the corner. Jack had a photographic eye for moments like that, though sometimes I wondered if he realized it.

"He probably wandered too far up Bourbon," I said to Jack. Then it occurred to me the guy was drunk.

"Why are you here, Jack?" I asked him, pulling my hand away.

He took off his glasses, wiping them with the corner of a bar napkin. "I don't know what to do with myself any more," he said.

Jack wanted me to take him to the river. We left the Exile and walked down Chartres to St. Louis. As we passed the taxi stand in front of the Royal Orleans Hotel, three drag queens strolled by. "Looking good," a cabby called to them, gawking. "Want a ride in an air-conditioned cab?" They whistled and catcalled to him, then broke into a chorus of "*Voulez-vous coucher avec moi, ce soir?*" as they kept on walking.

Thunder and lightning started to the north, somewhere over Lake Pontchartrain. I pointed to a freighter with its spiderlike booms and cranes skimming along the crest of the levee, and remarked that we were about fifteen feet below sea level, which made for surreal vistas. We climbed the levee near the Governor Nicholls Street Wharf and watched a ferry pass across the river to the Algiers landing. The shoaling water darkened, dilated in its wake. We waited for the ferry to make the return trip.

"I like to go down to Fisherman's Wharf," Jack said. "Just to sit and look at the bay. Do you want to smoke some Mary Jane?"

"I'm not too keen on it these days. Thank you all the same."

"You know, anything inscrutable or mysterious—like love—can be explained with drugs," he said, pulling a joint out of his cigarette pack. He lit it and puffed a couple of times. "How did you wind up with Sam?"

"He courted me," I said. This was not exactly factual. Sam picked me up almost five years ago at Alice's Rare & Used Books Ltd. on Chartres Street. I was hunting for a secondhand copy of *Farnsworth on Contracts* one Sunday afternoon before I began my first week of law school. We cruised each other, lingering in the first editions aisle. I was quite taken with his salt-and-pepper hair and hazel eyes, his broad shoulders. He wore an old, olive poplin suit and red foulard tie, which seemed frumpy at first glance then grew on me. He looked unapologetically disheveled. I found it appealing. I overheard him tell the owner he had been to brunch at Antoine's with visiting friends. Ellen, a feisty and frilly woman, whose lover was the shop's namesake, asked Sam how the painting was going, then introduced him to me by way of a comment about his hair. "I used to have thick hair like you," Ellen said to Sam. "Before my chemotherapy." Grinning at me, Sam said that he didn't know Ellen was a cancer survivor. "Ten years," she said. "It's like I read it about someone else."

In our long conversation with Ellen that afternoon on the stoop of her shop, we plumbed the depths and breadth of each other's reading and it occurred to me that a sensibility, any sensibility, formed around an appreciation of how much knowledge and pleasure were linked. This realization seemed to mean more to me then than it does now as I write it. When Sam professed a profound aversion to books at the moment, Ellen and I didn't believe him.

That evening after dinner at the Mona Lisa restaurant with its two *hookahs* on display in the window, and drinks on the patio of the Napoleon House, Sam took me home to his apartment in the Upper Pontalba. What I most remember about our first encounter was my surprise at seeing him reach under the four-poster bed and pull out a can of Crisco, and the studious expression on his face when he looked at me in the bathroom mirror later that night.

"Was I too much, or what?" Sam asked me, concerned.

"I'm okay," I answered.

Without saying another word, Sam scalded a toothbrush under hot water for a good minute, collecting his thoughts over the running faucet. He handed the toothbrush to me. Was I to understand he didn't want me to leave? I brushed my teeth and rinsed off in the shower. Standing there, I thought how familiar and comfortable Sam felt to me. At that moment there were no coincidences. But how many times had sex with a stranger portended more than what turned out to be? I wanted to believe connections were made, meaning was made, in the press of bodies, that there was more to sex than random appetite. We had nothing to go on but this assumed intimacy—or was it a form of trust? My choice was to trivialize or glorify it, or I could just let it breathe.

Sam showered and climbed into a pair of paint-speckled surgical scrubs, tied the drawstring, and slid into bed. "You were leery about coming here, weren't you?" he asked.

"No," I answered, mustering as much indignation as I could.

"Then I'm disappointed," he said, smiling.

We listened to Bach's French Suites and awoke in the morning with our limbs intertwined. On the Uptown streetcar to the Tulane campus, I had the uncanny, breathless sensation of having made a decision.

"You seem perfect for each other," Jack said.

"That almost sounds insulting."

"I don't mean it to sound that way," Jack said, offering me the joint once more, and I relented. "Though Sam's not at all what I pictured him to be."

"Really?"

"I imagined him to be younger, wilder, more Bohemian."

"Bohemian for Sam is a five o'clock shadow."

"I can tell. He seems so straight."

"Trust me," I said. "Sam is a staunch homosexual. He fucked his first guy when he got Stateside—figured he'd served his country and deserved whatever pleased him—and he hasn't looked back."

"He's certainly domesticated you," Jack said.

"How so?"

"Just look at yourself, with your pretty white shirt, red bow tie, and galluses."

"Please," I said. "Like you were one to wear flowers in your hair. My costume has more to do with being an attorney, than anything."

"Are you happy, Emmett?"

"The older I get, the more I'm convinced anyone completely happy is a moron. Not that there aren't things that make me happy. But I try not to get too worked up or too low. It's exhausting just to stay settled. After all, love's only a temporary therapy for neurosis."

"But you always did like brief, intense relationships."

"That was you, Jack."

"We both have a bad habit of sabotaging relationships," Jack said. "If for no other reason than to keep anyone from getting too close."

I shrugged.

"You know it's true, Emmett. Ever loved anyone else?"

"Don't make me say things I'll regret later, Jack."

"I didn't think it possible," Jack whispered.

"You don't know what goes on in my head, any more than I know what goes on in yours, so we're even."

Jack's eyes twitched. I had to turn away. He grabbed my shoulder to search me out. I couldn't look at him. What did he want from me?

"I met this guy one Sunday evening on Green Street," Jack said. "I was hiking home from dinner. He wore motorcycle boots. He was this lithe man with a shaved head, before it was the fashion. We went back to the garret apartment he house-sat. Nothing but a futon on the floorboards and an old steamer trunk. No curtains on the windows. The light had that crepuscular quality I love. We smoked a joint and listened to music and then I ate his ass and licked his balls nestled in all that hair. His skin was the color of espresso and had a porcelain sublimity. I chewed on his nipples, his left one was pierced with a big barbell, and then I fucked him."

"You fucked him?" I asked, turning to face him.

"Impugn my masculinity, why don't you? Of course I fucked him. How could I not fuck him? How could I not hold him those mornings when we were in the clouds, until the fog burned off and the whole city stretched below us."

"Look, Jack, I'm sorry," I said. "I'm not so numbed out that I don't have a sense of what it must be like to lose someone, appearances to the contrary."

"I still think about the love we made in that apartment," Jack said. "His name was Pablo. Pablo from Laredo. He was a nurse. Said he lived in Key West but left because his lover was crazy, though he still carried around this nostalgia for him. That's what he called it, his nostalgia. It only goes to show you how all love is unrequited. The crazy lover had turned him on to Mozart, and Pablo had an old boxed set of Clara Haskil and Arthur Grumiaux recordings he absconded with in his flight from Key West. He called them his desert island records and played them over and over. The *andante* of one particular sonata for violin and piano in E minor. Apart from its associations with him, the music seems weary with so many questions. That piece makes me inconsolable, to hear it. I discovered Mozart wrote it when he was just a kid, after his mother's death left him alone in Paris."

Jack took off his glasses and wiped his eyes. "Pablo died early on," he said. "From a sudden, mercifully quick attack of pneumonia. He left this world a far cry braver than I would have with no hope of treatment. We can thank our Great Communicator for that. FDA's process for approving new drug therapies resembles the Vatican's for making saints. You've got to present three verifiable miracles. A year later, Pablo came back to me in a dream. I remember him clearly, seated in an overstuffed chair at a party. He was beaming, Emmett. He wore the strangest blue silk turban on his bald head and a black kimono and a double strand of floor-length pearls and I shocked myself awake by thinking how many pearl fishers offered up their lives for so much beauty. After that I let go of him. Somewhat."

I held Jack. I watched over his shoulder as the ferry made its slow advance toward us. A bracing wind whipped off the river. We heard a clack like plate glass shattering, and I felt Jack flinch. Then came a tinseled streak and guttural thunder, sputtering into a hum. Any minute it would rain.

"We'd better go," I whispered.

Jack stared at the water for what seemed like hours until I led him by the arm down the levee.

We came into Decatur Street disoriented and anxious. We paused and looked around. The electrical charge in the air had sucked sound and movement out of the street, but the stillness had its own tremor. We happened upon an old man standing between two vehicles, urinating on the grill of the parked truck. Then the sky opened and it began to pour.

We ran for cover under the balcony of Jules, a leather biker bar on Decatur. Neon lights popped and buzzed in the bar's window. A slew of men spilled out of the saloon, onto the sidewalk. Several gleaming, parked behemoth hogs listed in a line, as if moored to parking meters. A bearish man with "Tough Guy" tattooed on his arm jumped off his Harley and grabbed his sidekick around the waist, a nude male mannequin with a blue fright wig and chipped lips. The two joined us under the balcony. A cab honked at a carriage loaded with snickering tourists as it slowed in front of the bar. The poor horse pulling the carriage wore a wreath of purple plastic roses and wet, funereal tulle around its neck. The coachman flipped the cabby the bird. Then, in a fit of irony, Peggy Lee's sultry voice, remixed over a cloying, techno-tango rhythm, began to float out of the bar like a squall of smoke, telling us to keep dancing, to break out the booze, to have a ball.

I pulled Jack around the corner. We made our way up Barracks Street and huddled in a doorway. We were drenched. The rain came down harder. Jack ran along the sidewalk, rattling and jiggling gates to alleyways until he found one unlocked. I followed him. He slipped into a dank, vaulted corridor and I stumbled after him through the darkness. It was close and cool as a cavern. A dim light framed an arch that opened onto a private courtyard,

next to a staircase that spiraled upward. Rain sizzled on flagstone. My back
was pressed against the wall.

I pulled Jack to me, biting the nape of his neck, fumbling with the buttons
on his jeans, smelling his hair and the places he had been that day. We got our
pants down around our ankles and I sank into him. He shuddered against
me. We were both sweating. I took him from behind as we groped in the
darkness for footing underneath the staircase. Above us, laughter and shrill
voices floated over raucous music. We fucked as quietly as possible, wordlessly.

Someone ran down the stairs into the carriage way and out the gate. We
froze. I stopped breathing and closed my eyes. I covered his mouth with my
hand. Nothing like a downpour to lend what we were doing an urgency I
hadn't felt with Sam in a long time, maybe never. It no longer mattered if
we came or not. We didn't. We succeeded in exhausting ourselves. We pulled
up our pants and slinked out of the corridor undetected and hurried back
to the house in silence as the rain tapered off.

A drizzle still hung in the air. Our clothes were soaked and we shed them in
the courtyard. I showered downstairs, then nearly tripped over the dog as I
climbed into bed with Sam.

"What time is it?" Sam whispered.

"Three. Did I wake you?"

"Yes."

"Sorry."

"It's okay. You boys have a good time?"

"We went to the Exile," I said, sitting up in bed.

"Where are you going now?" Sam asked.

"To get some water."

"Wait. Come back to bed."

"Let me get a drink first."

"Would you find me a cigarette?" he asked.

I found a pack of cigarettes in the bathroom. I lit one and we passed it
back and forth. He told me how he'd watched two boys on the roof of the
adjoining building earlier that night.

"They had one long, excruciatingly slow fuck," he said. "I sat listening to
Mendelssohn and jacked off."

"You jacked off?" I asked.

"I couldn't help it."

Then I climbed into bed. Sam held me. He whispered in my ear he wanted to be inside me. I like to think he wanted to be inside my head, to see what I see. I wasn't much of a bottom before I met Sam. The dog took little interest in what we were doing.

Later I listened as he slept with his arm draped across my midriff. The soft pulse of his breathing fell through the stillness, like a squeeze box. It soothed me. I lay there, squinting to read the digital alarm clock across the room, blinking 88:88. The rain drummed a rollicking paradiddle on the banana leaves outside our window, imparting density to those hours. It dawned on me, surveying the dirty towel on the floor, the jar of petroleum jelly, the ashtray on the nightstand brimming with butts, I had better own up to the fact that there were only so many fucks left in this world for me. I watched as daybreak bloomed in the bedroom, burned brighter through the slats of the louver doors. After a while, I gave in to the light and at some point drifted off to sleep.

I dreamt I had been swallowed by the brackish water of a flooded cemetery. Thinking I had drowned, I wandered a maze of tombs slowly morphing into frescoed rooms like a submerged palazzo and I asked, Is there a lesson to be learned from this? What a rip-off, I thought. Then Sam woke me and asked if something was wrong. I told him what I remembered of my dream. My body felt tentative and uninhabited. My eyes burned as if I had been crying in my sleep.

I left Sam in bed, showered, shaved, and dressed. I packed my briefcase and passed the guest room on the way out to the Morning Call for coffee and beignets before work. I heard Jack snoring in the guest room. Opening the door cautiously, I beheld him in a swirl of white sheets, the room now blazing with light through the French doors. I couldn't take my mind off him all day.

That evening Jack came into the courtyard *garçonnière* Sam had made his studio, the "slave quarters," as Jack called it. Jack prowled about with his shirt off. He wore faded khakis, starched to a crust with frayed cuffs, which hung just shy of the tips of his scuffed loafers, swallowing his skinny ankles. He wore no socks—and no underwear, as evidenced by the outline of his thick cock.

"Must be murder on your feet?" I asked.

"What's that?" said Jack.

"Wearing no socks."

"You get used to it."

He sat down next to me on the old church pew and crossed his legs. We watched as Sam hung a canvas with roofing tacks on an empty wall. Working with a stepladder, he moved a gesso and medium mixture around on the canvas with a trowel. His technique was to plaster the canvas, creating a textured layer that would lend a sense of movement under the painted surface.

On the paint-splattered cement floor Sam arranged coffee cans filled with turpentine and linseed oil and brushes and water. The box fan churned in a high window and made a low, steady hum. I rose and stood in the doorway to smoke, wondering if Jack would make good on his threat to move to New Orleans. Jack studied several canvases that leaned against the wall.

"Now, this is painting," Jack said. "Great composition." He bent over to examine the texture of the canvas surface. "Who's the boy?" he asked.

"A student," Sam said.

"Keeping things from me now?" I said. "What's his name?"

"Karl."

"Has he had all his shots?" I asked.

"He's a good kid."

"I'm sure."

Sam had painted him kneeling on one knee in nothing but a pair of slippers; it was the slippers that made the painting so intensely erotic.

"How old is he?" I asked.

"Twenty-something," Sam answered.

Jack praised a certain juxtaposition of line and brushstroke as a revelation. By Sam's modest or guilty blush, I suspected that the gesture had been total happenstance and Sam wanted to steer clear of any discussion of it.

"You do have an appreciative eye," I said to Jack. "It's a crying shame your optic nerve is connected to your dick. Just kidding."

"The painting's yours," Sam said to Jack.

"I couldn't possibly," Jack whispered, resting his hand on his neck, his mouth agape.

"Jack's decided to move to New Orleans," I announced. "Permanently."

"That so?" Sam asked. "That's quite a change since Sunday."

"I haven't made up my mind yet," Jack said. He lit a cigarette. "How will you pose us, Sam?" he asked, changing the subject.

Sam shot me a glance. "Back to back," he said. "I'll paint you both in profile." He turned to a steel rack of shelves where he kept the phonograph and some tubes of paint and brushes standing on end in rows of mayonnaise jars.

"If you stay long enough, I won't have to finish the painting from memory," he said to Jack.

Sam placed a record on the phonograph. He wasn't quite willing to surrender his raspy vinyl albums yet for CDs. I slouched in the doorway, watching the old album spin on the turntable, the stylus coaxing lovely music from it. A windowpane in the skylight pinged from the crack of thunder. The evening light in the studio had shifted, become elongated. The mustard plaster walls seethed with incandescence. The light declined, giving everything a patina of yellowed ivory. A Mendelssohn string quartet seemed to do the same to the air in the room. I began to feel queasy. The turpentine and paint fumes were getting to me.

Jack found a half-empty bottle of Early Times and two clean Mason jars in the kitchenette and poured a snort for himself and me.

"You seem to be weathering this visit well," Sam said to me under his breath as Jack wandered to the back of the studio.

"I'm sorry it's on such short notice," I said, watching Jack through the corner of my eye.

"Don't be," Sam said. "He's family."

"It's fine. Really," I said, watching Jack flip through a series of watercolor illustrations for a children's book that never happened, blue and orange pastel studies of noon light and shadow along the stucco garden wall. I couldn't take my eyes off his back, his tapered haunches. Jack had the bottle of bourbon by the neck and rocked it absently as he turned to a folio of chiaroscuro studies in charcoal of coffee pickers Sam had done before he left Nicaragua. Sam told Jack they were all committed *Yanqui* leftists with a sense of humor.

"Do you know the Grateful Dead song 'Uncle John's Band'?" Sam called to Jack. "We were teaching our Sandinista friends an alternate lyric—'Uncle Sam's Band.'"

Jack forced a laugh, then moved to some canvases on rolling frames in the wall unit. He found Sam's largest pieces rescued from the studio fire last year, an enormous study of fallen, mulching leaves and skeletal birch trees advancing from behind a membrane of fog and violet sky. I secretly didn't want him to, but Jack yanked the heavy frame and the painting slid into the open. I watched Jack back away from it. The painting had caught his interest.

"Everyone makes much of Monet's drift toward abstraction," Jack called from across the studio, staring at the canvas. "But it's because the old man was going blind. He was only painting what he saw. Painting is about process. Process and interpretation."

Sam squeezed globs of paint onto a thick piece of glass he used as a palette. "It's about the vagaries of light," he countered. "It's light's movement on surface incident, on the topography of something. Light is never the same, always relative to time and place. In an instant, it will all change. That's why it seems so necessary to me to lock the memory of light in paint with a brushstroke, a gesture. Painting is different than photography because it doesn't leave the moment to the whims of chance. I'm ready for you to take a seat now."

I sat in one of the bentwood café chairs under the skylight. Jack turned away from Sam's painting, slowly rolling his head and removing his glasses in one gesture. He rubbed the bridge of his nose and closed his eyes for a moment. Then he hung his glasses by the seam of his front pants pocket.

So this is how he wants to be remembered, I thought: without his glasses.

We were seniors in high school the first time Jack and I fucked. My parents and I had driven down from Vicksburg for my uncle's funeral, late in October. Uncle Clay had died when his truck battery exploded as he tried to jump-start my Aunt Aileen's Volvo. Jack was in their house on the telephone with Triple-A to see about getting a tow truck to take the car to the Montgomery Ward's. The battery had destroyed my uncle's face, but the heart attack he suffered on the way to Jefferson Davis Memorial Hospital actually killed him.

After the funeral, Jack and I had gone into the house to change out of our Sunday clothes. We put on some jeans and jackets and walked along the gravel road that cut through my uncle's thousand-acre pecan grove. As kids we often walked this road to railroad tracks that formed the western boundary, looking for Choctaw arrowheads or glass bells that birds sometimes knocked off telephone poles. It was evening. The road crunched beneath our boots. The woods were cool and still. We left the road and hiked down into the hollows, cutting across the crest of a ridge where the pecan and hickory trees sloped into the bottom country, near the creek. The farther we made our way through tangled underbrush, the closer we heard the rush of water, like a monotonous ribbon of sound. When we got to the creek, about two hundred yards from the road, Jack turned to me and said, "The world is darkening."

I shivered. I didn't know what to say. He hadn't cried at the funeral, not in front of his mother, which didn't surprise me. But I thought he would cry in front of me.

"I've got to piss," he said, and unzipped his fly.

I stood next to him and did the same. I glanced down and saw he had an erection. My prick shot up. I stood awkwardly, straining to urinate. The trees rustled; a light mist settled in the briars around us with its smoky smell. And again a sudden chill, like a stern glance. Cold air passed over our dicks. Then Jack's warm hand grabbed hold of me, pulling me to him.

We went slowly. I don't want to diminish how I felt by saying it was because he had lost his dad and I was sorry for him. What happened between us had been in the works for a long time. We were each solitary children in our respective families. We spent whole summers with each other. We had been pissing together in the woods for a long time before.

After we finished, he unbuttoned his flannel shirt, pulled off his T-shirt, and stood there shivering in the cold with his small chest and nipples and ruddy, freckled shoulders.

"Here," he said, handing me the T-shirt.

We wiped ourselves with it and then Jack forced the shirt under a fallen log, saying he'd return for it tomorrow.

"Do you think we smell gamy?" he asked.

"No. You smell like Old Spice."

"It was Pa's," he said.

I remember it got colder as light passed out of the woods. We heard the pop and crackle of pecans dropping into the thicket. Then we heard Aunt Aileen's voice in the distance. Jack fought through the brambles and up the slope. He reached the road before me and called back to her. When we got near the house, Jack cursed himself for losing his glasses somewhere in the woods. I told him I didn't remember him having them on when we left his room, but he insisted.

What is it about memory that demands the first time to be played out in an endless stream? Memory wants only to become sensation, to reenact the past. Sam had no idea how much that last painting reminded me of the woods behind my uncle's house.

I remember this all like it was yesterday.

TWO LIVES

1.

CHASE DECIDED TO COMMIT HIS MOTHER the Saturday she admitted to eating cat food. He had gone to her place in Gentilly to mow the lawn before dusk, and when afterward he went into the kitchen to wash his hands, shirtless and sweating from the heat, he found an empty can of Kozy Kitten tuna in the sink.

"Momma," he called out to her in the next room. "What is this? You don't have a cat."

She did not answer him.

It occurred to Chase she might be feeding a stray. He rooted through the pantry, behind boxes of cornflakes and grits and a bottle of whiskey, and discovered four more cans and a bag of Cat Chow. Opening the dishwasher, he found dried cat food on plates and a putrid fish smell.

He stormed into the living room, where his mother sat in the recliner watching a Lawrence Welk rerun. She wore a calico robe over her flannel pajamas and had her white hair tucked into a hunter's orange ski cap. Mr. Welk waved his baton and "Lush Life" bubbled out of the old Philco. Chase turned off the television set and dragged his mother into the kitchen.

"Explain this!" he shouted. "Why are you eating this crap, Momma?"

"Because," she cried, "I'm hungry."

He raised his hand to slap her, then recoiled as she cowered. He dashed through the screen door into the backyard, laughing uncontrollably at the clarity of her lunacy.

For the next six months, Chase spent Saturdays visiting his mother at Bolingbroke Nursing Home, across the Lake Pontchartrain Causeway Bridge to Mandeville. It was the only time he drove. The rest of the week his Volvo stayed garaged at the Monteleone Hotel, a few blocks from his apartment on Royal Street. He hated driving.

Every weekend, Chase brought along family photographs, hoping to jar his mother's memory. Blithely she would invent stories to fill the gaping holes. There was something childlike about it. She lived utterly in the present. Rationality was in full-throttle retreat. She hoarded useless objects. She wandered the halls, searching for nothing. The doctors told Chase his mother's condition would only get worse.

Chase listened to the hollow wind through the pines as she sat in her wheelchair on the terrace, babbling about movie stars. It was a clear morning for December; dew glazed what was left of the thick summer lawn. The lake lay flat and slate-gray beyond them, the light here so . . . lucid, away from the city.

"What's that?" she asked, pointing to the white wicker table.

"I brought you a present," Chase said. "Some chocolates."

His mother fumbled with the yellow package. Chase helped her remove the cellophane wrapping and set the open box on her lap. She peered at the candy inside, fingering the chocolate pillows in their brown tissue cups. Chase stared at her gnarled and swollen arthritic knuckles. Gingerly she picked up a chocolate and bit into it, then looked at Chase and frowned.

"Nougat," she said. "Sticks to my dentures."

"I thought you liked them." He retrieved the box, putting it back on the table. "You used to like them."

She examined the back of her hands, pulled tentatively on the loose skin at her wrists.

"The nurse told me you've been wetting the bed," Chase said.

"Rubbish," she bellowed.

"Okay," he whispered. "I believe you. Do you want to try a different chocolate?"

"I want to go home!"

"We've been through this before, Momma."

"I need to take care of your sister."

"No, Momma. I don't have a sister."

His mother started to scream.

"Don't cry, Momma, please. I'm sorry. Have a chocolate. Look. Here's one with cream in it."

"I don't want a goddamn chocolate. I want to go home."

To settle her down, he took her for a ride in his car, as he had done the last few times he visited. The nurses were glad to be rid of her when she got like this. In her excited state she caused a chain reaction among the other patients. Chase once overheard a nurse assistant compare his mother to the one dog in the neighborhood that incited all the others to yelp. He resented the comparison, resented overhearing it, but didn't say anything.

Whenever his mother got this disturbed, he promised to take her home. They would go for a long drive in the back roads of the Florida Parishes. She had a short attention span and forgot things from minute to minute. Riding in the car tired her and she would fall asleep. On the way back to Bolingbroke, he'd listen to her snore, and think of how she used to drive him around the neighborhood streets to put him to sleep when he was a baby.

2.

Most weekdays Chase observed a rule of silence. He hadn't noticed the song that Friday until around lunch, when he heard it seeping into his cubicle. He'd spent the morning at the computer, drafting orders to show cause and poring over case law. It wasn't that he minded the radio. Kamlesh had the thing on all the time and was considerate enough to play it low, and Chase tuned it out. But now it had broken Chase's concentration. The singer's velvet warble washed into the foreground of his mind: "You'll be doin' all right with your Christmas of white."

Chase choked up a little. He felt a welling in his chest, tears coming. He couldn't stop them and he didn't know why. He sat at his desk, aware of the whine of copy machines, the *tisk-tisk* of keyboards, the incessant ringing of phones, the glum, muffled voices of one side of telephone conversations. How absurd, to be crying over an Elvis tune.

"Chase?" Kamlesh called from the other side of the partition separating their cubicles.

"What's up, Kamlesh?" Chase hoped his colleague wouldn't stand and see him crying. The radio had been flipped off, but the song still lingered in Chase's head.

"I'm walking over to Eat No Evil for lunch. Care to have a salad or something?"

"I'll have to take a rain check."

"Do you want me to bring you back a pita and sprouts?"

"No, thanks."

Chase put his head down on his desk. "Blue Christmas" kept playing, the voice of Elvis smooth and menacing. He tried to finish reading a deposition but gave up. He packed his leather satchel with work and the newspaper, dug his gym bag from the bottom drawer of his file cabinet, and left the office before Kamlesh got back from lunch.

Chase walked over to the New Orleans Athletic Club on Rampart Street and worked out, Elvis still moaning. A younger man cruised him in the steam room; Chase ignored him. He closed his eyes and tried to think of other songs, other voices. Elvis kept winning the battle; whatever song Chase recalled inevitably segued into "Blue Christmas."

He showered and left the gym, and walked down Bienville to the Gramophone on Royal Street, where he bought a few CDs. Then he walked the six blocks to home and sat on the floor in the living room sorting through his purchases. He took two ibuprofen and loaded the carousel of his disc player with Mozart divertimenti, Patsy Cline, Gregorian chant, Kate Bush, The Cure. He lay on the rug with his headphones in place. It worked until a disc ended and the carousel rotated; in the brief interval, Elvis floated back to torment him. He grabbed the phone and called Walt at Charity.

"You've got to be joking, Chase. 'Blue Christmas'?"

"What's wrong with me?"

"Perhaps you're channeling. I'd lay off the Shirley MacLaine books for a while."

"Be real, Walt. I'm serious."

"I'm an anesthesiologist, not a shrink," Walt said, "and I'd rather not offer you anything pharmaceutical—"

"That's fine."

"You take life too seriously," Walt said. "I would imagine this problem is something like my occasional fits of insomnia. The more you dwell on it, the worse it's going to get. Tell you what, let's go out tonight."

"I don't think so."

"You don't get out nearly enough, Chase."

"You go out too much."

"Hey, you called me for help."

"Sorry."

"A little Dixieland will take your mind off Elvis. God, I can't believe what I'm saying."

"I know. Look, maybe we'll hook up later. I'll call you."

"Sure."

"I will. But now I think I'll plug myself into a Walkman and go running."

"Don't brood. Beep me later."

Chase hung up the phone. He'd have to remind Walt that he was driving across the lake in the morning and couldn't be out all night. Chase would try and convince him to order in pizza and rent movies instead.

Chase changed into sweatpants. He hunted for his running shoes, then grabbed his Walkman off the kitchen counter and popped in an Art Tatum tape. He ran in the neutral ground of Elysian Fields Avenue, up the five miles to Lakeshore Drive. It was late in the afternoon and getting colder. To the north, storm clouds gathered.

Gentilly is a neighborhood of bungalows and shotgun houses, with statues of the Virgin Mary or a patron saint enshrined in cement clamshell grottoes on many of the thick lawns. Most houses were decorated with plastic Santa Clauses and reindeer and colored lights, which winked on as Chase ran. Some residents had strung Christmas tree lights to the bare oak trees along the avenue. He passed a donut shop on a corner, then a kid on a red Schwinn bicycle too big for him throwing the late edition of the *States-Item* from a basket. Chase shuddered slightly when he passed Brother Martin High School, his alma mater, remembering how football players in his freshman gym class had showed him their dicks in the locker room, how his presence had seemed to incite them. He caught an erection, and lost it as the temperature fell with dusk.

He crossed the avenue and rested at the bus stop in front of his childhood home, recently sold. The new owners had installed a big "Merry Xmas" sign in lights on the roof. He stared at the house for a while, shaking his head, until a NOPSI bus came and he climbed aboard, exhausted, for the trip back to his apartment.

It turned out to be one of those December evenings when, between bouts of warm and cold weather, fog shrouds the French Quarter. Chase watched from his balcony as Royal Street disappeared in the murk. He had just finished off a lukewarm beer, a piece of cold pizza, and, for the first time since law school, a Lucky Strike. He'd bummed it from a downstairs neighbor he'd run into in the stairwell, checking her mailbox. As Chase leaned against the banister, waiting for Walt to return his call, "Blue Christmas" popped on his mental phonograph again.

He drank another beer. At eleven, he put on his jacket and walked up Royal Street to Dumaine and over to the Exile. Walt stood by the door chatting with Rick, the beefy bouncer. They looked funny together—Walt well-built but short, gesturing wildly with his hands, still dressed in his hospital scrubs and lab coat, stethoscope around his neck; Rick in standard-issue T-shirt, jeans, and leather jacket, fingering Walt's stethoscope and laughing.

"What's so funny?" Chase asked, joining them.

"Walt playing doctor," Rick said.

"You forgot about me?" Chase said to Walt.

"Sorry. I've had a little too much to drink."

"Have you been out since happy hour?"

"More or less. I left the hospital late and rushed to finish my Christmas shopping before Maison Blanche closed. I needed to celebrate. I can't wait until you see what I got you. You're not angry, are you?"

"I guess I can't be."

"Crowd's good tonight," Walt said, surveying the bar.

"Pretty good," said Chase.

"What's eating you?"

"Nothing."

"You need a cocktail, Miss Thing."

"No, thanks."

"One shot of Jägermeister, then."

"You must be joking."

"I'll be right back."

"Wait."

"Don't tell me you're not drinking, Chase. I can smell the beer on your breath. You can be stubborn all you want, but I know better. You really want one, so you might as well have one. I promise not to tell."

"Who are you going to tell? My mother?"

Walt looked at Chase like he understood him. "Wait here," he said. Then, to Rick, "Don't let him go."

Walt evaporated into the crowd. Chase felt stupid. He thought of leaving, but drunk as Walt was, Chase knew he would follow him home anyway.

Walt returned, brandishing drinks and smiling triumphantly. "Here," he said, thrusting a plastic cup into Chase's hand.

"This is a double, Walt."

"So. Suck up. Like a good boy."

Chase took a sip of the liqueur. "I hate this crap."

"Drink it. That's it. Drain the baby. See. It's not so bad, is it now?"

"Are you satisfied?"

"I should be asking you that."

"Hardly," Chase said.

"I'm not the least bit surprised. When's the last time you had a stiff one?"

"That's none of your business."

"Or a good lay?"

"I don't remember."

"Liar-liar-pants-aflame," Walt said, laughing.

"I'm going home."

"You know what your problem is, besides having 'Blue Christmas' stuck in your head? You've got blue balls. And you're emotionally constipated, to boot."

"Good night."

"Hey, just one minute."

"Let go of my arm, Walt. You're crocked."

"I'm still stronger than you, Chase."

"What? What the fuck do you want?"

"Aren't you going to ask me what I would prescribe for your condition?"

"I know what your cure-all is already. Feel 'em, fuck 'em, fool 'em, and forget 'em. I've had enough tonight. And I'm not the one who's emotionally constipated."

"I'm not so sure you do know, unless you've been scoping out the bar like I have. See? Standing by the fireplace over there? That's your cure."

"Don't point. The guy in the USMC sweatshirt?"

"You can read that without your glasses? He's been cruising you since you walked in."

"That's his misfortune."

"But I thought you liked chocolate."

Chase looked at Walt. The needle scratched across his mental record and dug into a groove. Elvis crooned, crooned. Chase wanted to bolt from the bar.

"He's definitely that," Walt continued. "Real Godiva, bald—and a soldier."

"Don't you dare say it."

"I'm not belittling your sexual tastes, Chase. I'm only pointing out someone who might be worthy of your lofty standards."

"Why are you so crass?"

"Your stoicism brings out the worst in me. Why don't you go over there and smooth on the boy? He's awfully cute and he looks interested."

"Where are you going?"

"Down to the Louisiana Purchase. You don't need me to hold your hand."

Walt waved to the marine as he left. The bouncer laughed. Chase mumbled something to himself and went to the restroom, where he urinated, then washed his hands at the sink. As he gazed at his reflection in the mirror, he saw the line formed to use the urinals behind him. Half on instinct, he felt the glands in his neck through his turtleneck sweater. He stared at the wolf eyes of his black Irish father until they no longer seemed his own, then focused on the face standing in the background: the marine, who knew how to wield a smile.

Chase left the john and stood by the bar. The music in the Exile pounded, with Bronski Beat hitting that perfect *beat, Boy, beat, Boy.*

When the marine returned to the fireplace, he sent Chase a longneck. Chase nodded and walked over. They exchanged names, stood a minute watching music videos on the monitors above the bar. Then Chase motioned for the marine to follow him upstairs, onto the balcony.

It was foggy outside, but at least there they could hear each other. The marine said he was shipping out to the West Coast in a couple of days for a tour of duty in Saudi Arabia. Images from the recent war flashed in Chase's mind like a CNN special report, oil wells billowing black smoke, highways in surreal desert expanses littered with debris and death.

Chase began speaking of past Christmases, when he and Walt couldn't wait to get home from Ole Miss, how they would spend winter break floating from party to party, café to half-remembered flat to garret and back to a bar or another café, night after night, in endless search of diversion.

"We had these delusions of sophistication back then," he told the marine, "but now I think it was all the acid we dropped in college. We'd observe things with an eye to the irony of the situation, with this extreme detachment. Or we didn't think about it. We tended to fuck the same way."

The marine looked bored. Chase went on anyway.

"We were doing it for the experience, or so we thought, like it was a renewable resource. We never thought that the law of diminishing returns might apply. My friend, Walt, tells me that, knowing everything, he'd still leverage it all—looks, youth, health, everything—to the hilt."

The marine checked his watch. Chase knew it had to be after midnight. The marine was expecting something, was on some sort of timetable. But aren't we all? Chase thought. He regretted his Saturday morning drive across the lake. If he took this guy home with him, he might finally get to sleep by three or four. He had a presentiment of dozing off at the wheel, of slamming the Volvo into the guardrail on the Causeway, getting pinned, crushed. He knew what want of rest can do to a driver, how hypnotic the mile markers can be, zipping past the windshield.

Then the new dread seized him. Walt wouldn't leave a bar alone at night's end, seeing it as a public admission of defeat. Much as he hated to admit it, Chase had come to feel the same. Either way, it was useless.

"I hate the holidays," he said to the marine.

"Man—man," came the response.

They left the bar together, walked down Dumaine toward Royal Street. Did Chase really want to take the marine home with him? He was definitely to Chase's liking. But in the morning, he would awaken with the taste of this stranger in his mouth, on his skin, and everything would have an edge to it, as if what had transpired might be significant, portentous. Yet Chase would know it had been a waste.

3.

Saturday morning came in cold after a night of rain. Chase got up, showered, shaved, and dressed, then walked the six blocks up Royal to the Monteleone Hotel garage. He climbed into his Volvo and idled the engine. Bing Crosby came onto the stereo, dreaming of Christmases he used to know.

Chase drove up Elysian Fields to Lakeshore Drive, past the deserted parking lot of the old Pontchartrain Beach Amusement Park. Weeds grew through cracks in the asphalt. Behind the iron gate he could see the abandoned ticket booths and turnstiles, the graffiti, half-dismantled trellises of roller coasters, the dilapidated arcade and bandstand on the littered beach. He remembered the night of his eleventh birthday and imagined he could still smell the burnt popcorn, the hot and smoky arcade. He had pressed his palm to the colored mirror of Madame Zatarain's Fortune Telling Machine while his mother fed it quarters and he waited for the garish gypsy mannequin in the glass box to spit out his fate.

"My palm says I'll be unlucky in love," Chase said, reading the small scroll. "Boring."

"There're two breaks in my life line," his mother said, puzzled, about hers. "I'm supposed to go crazy. I think they got ours mixed up." She punched his arm.

They had stayed at the park all evening. He took her on the Ferris wheel, and the Wild Maus roller coaster, and the Haunted House ride. She sat in his lap, shrieking with delight. Her hair smelled like mint and strawberries.

Later, they walked out to the beach and watched heat lightning fork over the lake.

Chase thought of his mother lurking the halls of Bolingbroke, somewhere on the North Shore. In the evening, after their long drive, the orderlies would help Chase put her in a chair, wheel her down the maze of corridors to her small blue room, and help her to bed. "Mrs. McInnis?" Chase would ask her, dropping his voice an octave or assuming an accent. "Are you sleeping?" When she didn't answer, he would kiss her on the forehead and quietly leave. Then he'd drive back to New Orleans, wondering who would take care of him when he got that way.

ODD FELLOWS REST

WHEN I WAS A SOPHOMORE IN HIGH SCHOOL, I took a job as a cashier at the tiny A&P on Royal Street in the French Quarter and I've worked there ever since. I've been putting myself through college this way and it's what I know. It may take me a dozen years to finish school but who's rushing to a fire? My fate is that I listen well to people. On the streetcar or at the K&B lunch counter or standing behind the register—everywhere I go, people tell me their stories. I have a regular clientele.

Like the one-armed Café du Monde waiter who buys three bags of sugar-free hard candy a day. Or the big woman with the frizzy hair and black sunglasses who owns the junk shop on Frenchmen Street—she buys Bunny Bread, Campbell's chicken and rice soup, and Charmin toilet paper. She opens her tattered coin purse daintily with elaborate hand gestures. Most of my customers shop every day. One customer who'd lived in Dublin told me that's how the Europeans do it. I'm not surprised at how much personal history I glean five minutes at a time, when I see someone every day.

I've noticed types of people are loyal to certain brands, like the junk shop owner. It makes sense when you think about it: advertising becomes personality becomes identity. I wrote this down one day in my journal, sitting in the Croissant d'Or. Call it niche marketing in reverse; ask a Marlboro or a Camel smoker what he feels about his image. I can spot a Lucky Strike smoker a mile away, partly because that's my brand. I'll see him in the checkout line or here in the mornings at the café during breakfast and I'll say to myself, "I bet he smokes Luckies." He's one of the post-Camelot generation, generally wears glasses, sits in cafés, incessantly reads as a form of recreation, worships Sidney Bechet and Shostakovich, shops at thrift stores for clothes because he thinks he wants to. But more than that, it's the expression when he inhales, the tilt of his head as he exhales, pretentious in a way that might irritate, say, a Winston smoker. No doubt he would tell you without a shred of self-irony that he gets great satisfaction from the tar and the taste and the rush from that first cigarette of the morning. You know he's an existentialist because he smokes cigarettes without a filter. He's resigned to his addiction.

I stand back and form mental snapshots of people, paste together pieces of their biographies, puzzling over their purchase patterns like a Rorschach blot, looking for clues to what's in their lives beyond the evidence of their frugality or extravagance, how much gin they drink in a week, or if they eat tofu instead of beef.

The store manager once caught me scribbling my impressions of a customer on the back of a receipt tape—his attributes, his purchase profile.

"What the hell are you doing?" the manager asked.

"Documenting examples of conspicuous consumption is my other life," I told him.

He didn't get it. I don't think any of my customers would get it either—and I'm aware that my impressions of customers probably say something about me. But they wouldn't be shocked at how much about them I've picked up over the years. Some might feel vulnerable but most would be indifferent. They might believe they want to connect with someone as they volunteer spoonfuls of personal history and I'm the guy they see every day, but really they only want the illusion of intimacy and I have a sincere face.

For a few, however, the yearning for connection is blinding and they don't even realize how sad it is unless their routines are broken and they're forced to examine their actions. And being a cashier is not like working behind a bar where you can shut up someone with a cocktail on the house. When a Lucky Strike guy stares at me and I recognize his neediness, I turn away. I can't look his desperation in the eye. Then I feel guilty. I may wonder what he feels but I can't give everything away. I have to save something for myself, numb myself enough to keep from going bonkers. No?

My curiosity about people—my sleuthing, if you will—comes from learning at an early age that I didn't fit in, couldn't pass for normal. When I was in middle school, the neighborhood kids would wait for the bus on the corner of Canal Street and City Park Avenue in front of the gates of Odd Fellows Rest, where the tombs are all aboveground and the vaults are stacked along the stucco wall one on top of the other like bread ovens. One boy, Billy Reubens, would point to the gate and sneer at me, "You'll be buried in there someday, because you're an odd fellow." Then he'd prance around me, flipping his wrist in my face and letting his hand dangle, crooked and affected. Everyone would laugh, not at him but with him, which was absurd considering how ridiculous he appeared.

Why did he single me out to pick on? I always minded my own business. Was it because I was slight? Because I made better grades, took piano lessons, was fastidious about personal hygiene? Or was it because Billy Reubens was a shark and something I was or did made him smell blood in the water? At the time I had no idea; it took years of sleuthing to figure out why he reacted toward me the way he did. Did Billy Reubens make me a connoisseur of human nature? An aesthetic snob and ardent socialist, however contradictory the two may be? He did force me into a kind of invisibility.

I learned to hide my humiliation. I daydreamed about vanishing, working out fantastic if not illogical scenarios, turning and twisting them in my mind and admiring the flecks of color like some marble I might hold up to the sun. Most of these fantasies involved the theft of huge, liberating sums of cash or negotiable instruments, absconding with sufficient resources to enable a dramatic Houdini-esque escape from one life to the next: stealthy, clean, miraculous. I would steal away to Buenos Aires (I'd have to learn Spanish) or cross the border into Quebec and become a painter. I admired painters. But this line of reasoning, although appealing, had limited practicality. Sometimes I felt a cold, distant stare behind me, sure someone was following me, two steps back. Turning quickly, I realized it was only a trick of light in my peripheral vision or the shadow I cast as I walked from bowl to bowl of lamplight on a desolate stretch of Ursulines Avenue.

I came to believe these experiences made me a better observer. It might have helped if I'd discovered sooner that the Odd Fellows were a secret benevolent society like the Masons. But at a certain point my life altered: I invented a facade to hide behind, this idea of sleuthing, a way to assert my difference without anyone noticing. I imagined it to be a calling, not realizing that it had become a necessity.

Most of what I remember I absorb without even trying, like a reflex. My head is filled with checking account numbers, addresses, phone numbers, dates of birth, UPC codes, drivers' license numbers—all parts of the stories

I hear. Weekday mornings before work, I sit in the Croissant d'Or and jot everything down in my Big Chief notebook—the kind my mother bought me for school—to make some sense of it. I come here after a run in City Park. I'm used to getting up early, though I don't have to be at the grocery until noon. When I was in middle school at St. Dominic's and served as an altar boy at Mass every Friday, my mother would wake me, have me dressed and out of the house at the crack of dawn, and I never complained about it.

Once I asked Father Declan, a thin, devout little Irishman, why we had to say Mass to the almost empty church. He told me it didn't matter if the church was empty, the life of the Church was important and the Mass was the life of the Church. I was a little young to fully appreciate this, he said, slipping the chasuble over his head, but I had not entirely missed the point and hopefully someday I would understand. Of course, now I know very well what he meant. I couldn't function without my morning rituals.

I like it in my café. It reminds me of a certain Brassai photograph of a Parisian café interior. At the beginning of the last century, it used to be an Italian ice cream parlor. The Croissant d'Or has a white tile floor and a high, pressed-tin ceiling. Blue-lettered tiles embedded in concrete declare one threshold to be the LADIES ENTRANCE. The café is tucked out of the way in a far corner of the Quarter, which is probably why I like it. In the tarnished, mottled reflection of the old, gilt-framed mirrors, I feel submerged in another world.

I grew up in Mid-City, near the Cemeteries, and live Uptown where rents are more exorbitant, not far from the house where I was raised and my mother still lives. She works part-time as a secretary to the priests of St. Dominic's Parish. My father was a boilermaker in the trade union who died before I was two. The doctors at Charity Hospital told my mother the cause was tuberculosis, but the family knew that meant asbestosis. The neighborhood is quiet and dilapidated and a bit dangerous.

Sometimes when I stroll to the bus stop after my run, I pass the high wall of Odd Fellows Rest and think how mornings like this are what I live for, especially now at the beginning of March when the light is so pure and the cemetery is a blazing white, windowless city. Today is Ash Wednesday. The blooms are saturated with color and the crepe myrtles are just catching the wind. Every time someone opens the café door I get a whiff of what we call the "Municipal Aroma"—the charged pepperiness of a storm brewing. The proprietor has the radio set on the local classical station and it's playing Bach now; I recognize the prelude in C-sharp minor from Book II of *The Well-Tempered Clavier*. I'm having my daily brioche and a cup of coffee with chicory. And my Lucky Strike. I allow myself one, usually while I write in my notebook. I used to think I could quit smoking but I can't. I need that one cigarette; it helps me to focus when I'm jotting things in my notebook. I like to hold the smoke in my lungs, let it sit there; somehow it makes the coffee taste better. Psychologists call it an addiction chain: a certain activity triggers the desire to smoke.

I learned this from a customer who comes into the store twice a week at three o'clock looking like a Weatherman on the lam—skittish, caffeinated, always dressed in the same tie-dyed T-shirt, blue jeans, and sneakers. (Funny, I can remember his brand but not his name. It will come to me.) For him it was driving; he couldn't get into a Volkswagen without lighting a Benson & Hedges. He told me this one afternoon as I rang up his usual groceries (two cans of generic albacore tuna, a half-dozen eggs, Ex-Lax chocolates, French Market dark roast coffee, and a carton of extra-light menthol longs) and watched him snap a thick white rubber band around his wrist. I asked him why he did it. He said it was "Negative Smoking Technique": whenever he craved a cigarette he popped the rubber band. He'd learned it from a New Age guru who looked like the late Karen Carpenter, at a seminar in the airport Hilton ballroom that cost him a thousand dollars. He had tried the patch and it gave him seizures at night, shudderings in the brain he knew must be nicotine withdrawal. Hypnosis hadn't worked either.

After he left with his two bags of groceries, I couldn't stop thinking about those exhausted moments before sleep when I balance the day's emotional debits and receipts and ponder the infinitesimal choices I made during the day, wondering why I did something, what the hell was I thinking? One way or another there isn't any explanation save intuition or luck of the draw. You collect and collect and collect, and then what do you do with it?

The other afternoon, an elderly couple came into the store and the wife asked me out of the blue if I had a girlfriend. We had been familiar before, but not that familiar. I told her no, then felt obligated to offer a reason— senior citizens have that effect on me. I sputtered out the facts: that there had been one girl in my life, a fiancée who married someone else. Sensing a good story, the couple asked how long ago this had been. A decade, I told them. I could feel the tops of my ears burning red as I continued to tally up their groceries in silence.

I guess they decided not to press me further, to leave me some dignity. I wondered if they assumed I had been pining after Morgan ever since. The irony was rich. I had unintentionally created an aura of loneliness about myself; at least that was how they seemed to interpret what I'd said. They gazed at me with knowing regret. Maybe I read them wrong but suddenly they seemed happier than I ever remembered.

The truth is that Morgan and I are still close friends, even after me telling her I'm gay two months before our wedding—water under the proverbial bridge. Marrying Morgan was the one choice I reversed at the last minute, but I had been confused. In the end, I offered us both a reprieve.

Vernon Daglio, a guy I know from the old neighborhood, the man who sold my mother her funeral insurance, says that we all have to have at least one unreasonable fear to keep us human. But aren't all fears inherently unreasonable? Not long ago I spied a young man in jeans, a pullover, and hiking boots at a table near the ladies' entrance. He was bowed over, elbows on knees, shaking, his forehead and cheeks red. He stood up, distractedly dragging his ketchup-colored backpack, knocked his way through empty tables and chairs, and left. Why was he sobbing? Suddenly I flashed on my mother, imagining she was dead. "Nothing assuages the fear," I wrote in my notebook, inconsolable.

Vernon makes a living on fear: he hawks funeral packages called "Assurance Plans" from his father's mortuary chain. He's been trying to sell one to me for over a year. This morning he comes into the Croissant d'Or, stands next to me at the counter, orders a cup of decaf—he's the only New Orleanian I know who drinks decaffeinated coffee—and shoves another brochure in my face: "Today's Decision Gives You Tomorrow's Peace of Mind."

"I don't need a prepaid funeral and a plot in Greenwood," I tell him. "I want my ashes spread over the Grand Canal in Venice." (I've only ever been to Venice, Louisiana, at the mouth of the Mississippi River.) But even of this I'm not so sure, though I'd never tell Vernon.

Seeing Vernon reminds me of my bus ride down Esplanade Avenue this morning. I gazed at my reflection in the glass blurring into the cityscape—an intimation of a double life. Or have I been wrenched into this life during a dream, living under an assumed name? I have been mulling over how I might be able to leave New Orleans. Thoughts creep up on me but I keep putting them in the back of my mind with all the other trivia I've collected.

I do wonder what it would be like to give in. Vernon says the everyday life we live isn't really life, that life is only a string of vivid moments. Vernon is also a frustrated comic book artist.

I'm working on another cup of coffee, writing this down in my notebook, sitting and watching two young students standing at the counter holding each other's hand, their faces so close together they seem about to kiss, talking intently in French, completely unaware of the din in the café, the clatter of china, the Quarter denizens and tourists murmuring all around them. How beautiful they are. I can feel electricity pass between them.

Vernon asks me what I see. I tell him that I imagine them about to embrace, and that they don't makes it even more sublime. He says that he can understand my fascination; he's attracted in the same way to the innocence of young women. I think we must be the only ones who've noticed them.

What a contrast to yesterday's brouhaha. It was a gloomy morning like this one. An old man dressed in army fatigues crept into the Croissant d'Or—not in itself out of the ordinary, it being Mardi Gras. Mobs of people loitered outside, mostly in costume. Fatigue Man cornered a porter mopping a spill near the counter and told him that no one mopped floors in Paris. I stood at the counter with my cup of coffee, surveying the crowded café. Fatigue Man lumbered to the back and swung open the door to the courtyard, allowing a cool draft to course through the room, then slipped outside. Finding my usual window seat empty, I sat down to write in my notebook.

Fatigue Man appeared before me and announced in a thick accent, "You are sitting at my table."

I looked at him, then at my notebook, brioche, coffee, cigarettes. I distinctly remembered the table being clear of anything that might have staked a claim, and I had no intention of abandoning it.

"*Parlez-vous français?*" he snapped.

"*Oui! Je parle français très bien,*" I answered.

Fatigue Man sat down in the chair opposite me and stared. I returned to my notebook. The old man watched me read. I felt his eyes peering into me. Words seemed to ferment inside him; he mumbled to himself as he fidgeted in his chair. I looked at him over my glasses. Was he starved for attention? Angry to vent words? Or just hungry? He took one of my cigarettes, lit it, and gestured at the parade of sopping-wet costumed people on the sidewalk.

"Am I disturbing you?" he asked in French. He had withdrawn from our duel over the table.

"Not at all," I said.

"Are you a stockbroker?"

He blotted his high, wrinkled forehead with a paper napkin. I wondered how I must appear to him. I didn't believe he thought I was a broker but it was an opening to conversation.

"I work in a grocery store," I said. "What do you do?"

"I am a satyr," he said, taking a short sip from his cigarette. "I was born in France. I have always wanted to write. I have stories. Here"—he stabbed a finger into his temple—"in my head. They are real as my bleeding asshole.

"Here is something for you to write about," he said, suddenly switching to English. "Write about all the women in the men's room. It is full of desperate women squatting over the urinal. You do not mind me talking about urine? Everyone has to urinate. Your Abraham Lincoln did it, even Christ. We are human. The French, they do not mind talking about urine. Sometimes when you have to hold your piss and you are desperate like these drunk women, it is better than sex when you do go. It is true, no?"

"Sometimes," I said, laughing.

"But it is not a funny thing, pissing," he continued. "Really, I saw a man in my youth, a peasant where I was born who spent half of his estate to fix himself. He had a bad bladder and he had"—the man snapped his fingers—"one, two, three, five operations. I saw this, no? They had to put a pipe in him to urinate. He could not use anymore *son membre.*"

He turned away as if to peer into his memory. I imagined that he had forgotten how he got here and what went haywire in his brain. We watched the garish parade outside and every now and then he shook his head. The smell of coffee brewing in the copper samovars was almost more than I could bear in the stillness. I took off my glasses, rubbed the bridge of my nose, lit another cigarette.

Then two policemen entered the café and stood by the door. The blond policeman walked over to our table. "Get up, Al," he said. "Time to leave these good people alone."

As Al meekly scraped his chair away from the table and stood, clicking his teeth nervously, the older policeman, joining his partner, explained to me that Al usually haunted the Bywater neighborhood. The police would drop him off at the St. Bernard Parish line but Al always returned the next day.

"He's a French national," I told the policeman.

"What are you talking about? Al's from the Ninth Ward, been here all his life. He's whacked, a certified basket case. You've never seen him in his motorcycle helmet, to protect himself from the gamma rays."

"Then why don't you take him to Charity Hospital," I demanded, "instead of just depositing him in another jurisdiction?"

"We do," he said. "But lunatics have civil rights too."

"Yeah, the right to remain silent," the blond deadpanned.

They escorted Al away without any cuffs, the older policeman gruffly gripping Al's elbow. Al stopped at the door and bowed toward me in one last courtly gesture, then seethed, "*Vous devriez quitter tant que la chose est possible.*" Leave while you're able.

After they'd gone, I wondered what New Orleans had done to Al, what ordeal had changed him. I imagined whole incunabula lost inside the man. Then I remembered Proust saying that books are like cemeteries where all the names have been obliterated from the headstones. I'd been of the mind that a certain type of man becomes a cop, that as a class they lack any sense of irony. But I was wrong. They become inured to it.

Later the porter told me a customer had complained about a scene Al made in the restroom and pressured the manager to call the police. I'd left the café depressed.

I always said one day I would write a story about what it's like to live in a cultural backwater. This is my third or fourth cigarette. I'm late for work and the boss won't like it. But I can't leave my notebook yet, or my café. I'm going to have one more cup of coffee and another smoke before I go.

Sometimes I come here and I get this notion that I live in another country. I start thinking that I'm not alone, that out in the city there's someone for me. I have him in mind, no more than a mental snapshot really, and it takes some effort to hold on to—I've seen his face yet I can't place him. This feeling is irresistible and it colors my impression of everything around me.

I picture him sitting in the window of a café or standing outside on the sidewalk and I can't tell if he's a ghost, an echo, or a premonition, or if he's looking at me or through me. In a way, it doesn't matter; the whole story hinges on how shadows from the tree branches fall across his eyes. He's a guy with a cigarette and a cup of coffee sitting in an old bentwood chair in some strange café that could be anywhere but here. There are days when I even sense him following me when I leave for the A&P. And when that happens, I let him.

FAREWELL TO WISE'S

THE TELEPHONE RANG AND I FUMBLED WITH THE RECEIVER, my eyes barely open.

"Hey, it's me," Remy said.

"You have *some* nerve," I said. "Calling me this early on a Saturday."

"What are you talking about? It's noon, for heaven's sake, Chip."

"You shanghaied me last night. That's what."

"Do you have company? Am I interrupting?"

"Goodbye—"

"*Wait.* I called to see if you would drive me out to River Road to look at a car I saw in the classifieds. The ad said it's twenty years old and only has eleven thousand miles on it."

"I don't want to do anything but stay in bed. I have a splitting headache. Besides, the listing is probably a misprint."

"There's only one way to find out. Were you sick this morning?"

"I was out cold. But give me time."

"I drank a Bloody Mary."

"We drink too much."

"I know. So how about it?" Remy asked.

"I'm going back to bed."

"Be a sport. When can you pick me up?"

"No."

"Think about it."

"Goodbye."

I hung up the phone and closed my eyes. But I was wide awake now.

The refrigerator light blinded me when I opened it for something to kill the sour taste of last night in my mouth. I looked through the boxes and packing crates for a glass, then went out onto the balcony in my robe, thinking of last night. I sniffed under my arm—the smell of a worn cotton T-shirt, sweat, a hint of cologne, stale smoke.

I showered and shaved and dressed, packed my satchel with letters I needed to mail, then walked to Napoleon Avenue for my car and drove into a scattered afternoon downpour on Magazine Street.

I parked the car opposite Remy's building, dashed across the street, and rang his doorbell. The streets had emptied of people. Heavy swags of rain blew from light pole to light pole. Remy lived above an antique shop. I climbed the two flights of stairs to his apartment. He greeted me at the door with a tattered beach towel to dry my head.

"Where did you wind up last night, after you ditched me?" he asked. "I looked all over for you."

"Here and there."

"Is that a new bar?"

"I had a date."

"You mean a trick."

"No, I don't mean that."

"With whom? Not that person I saw you with at the Exile?"

Remy sat down on the futon in his living room and pulled a Godiva chocolates tin from under the stack of *New Yorkers* on the old ebony piano bench that served as a coffee table. He opened it and began rolling a joint with the weed and the wrappers inside the tin.

"Which one?" I asked.

"The brunette."

"No. I was on my best behavior with him. Do you have any ibuprofen?"

"Check the john," he said.

I went through Remy's bedroom to the bathroom. Opening the medicine cabinet, I was stunned to see so many prescription bottles.

"Hurry up," he called from the living room. "I've almost got this bad daddy rolled."

"What's the Silly String for?" I shouted, opening the cap of the aerosol can and sniffing the nozzle. It smelled like poppers. "Do you use this for something lewd?" I set it back on the toilet tank.

"I torment Nico with it."

"How could you name your dog after a dissolute cult figure? Don't roll a cigar. I can't hang out with you all day," I said. "I have to work at least thirteen hours tomorrow."

"Why?" he called.

I pretended not to hear him. I popped two ibuprofen in my mouth, swallowed, and returned to the living room.

"How is your pet, anyway?" I asked.

"Petulant, as usual, but she's not here." Remy had already taken a hit on the joint, and was flinging his head back and staring at the ceiling medallion, blowing smoke rings.

"We should go soon," I said, peering out the window. "It looks like the rain has slacked off."

"Okay. Have a hit."

I took the joint from him.

"Should I put on some music?" Remy asked. "I get sick of music though. Believe it or not, I don't run home from rehearsal and throw on a record. I have to have some silence. Otherwise I wake up at night with something playing loudly in my head. Last week it was the second Shostakovich *Jazz Suite*—so loud, I jumped out of bed."

I understood. I recently had awakened to the ringing of my vintage telephone.

Remy selected an album from a stack on his desk and placed the vinyl disc gingerly on the turntable. The needle popped and hissed until it found its groove. Remy watched it spin on the turntable a second, then slouched in an armchair. Remy was an old-school audiophile who refused to give up his LPs. I thought of my Aunt Vivian, who would play my grandfather's jazz albums on the Philco console stereo in the living room when I was a child. We listened to the snap, pop, and crackle of the worn vinyl. The music stopped when Remy abruptly lifted the needle. "Let's listen to something else," he said, pulling another record from its sleeve and placing it on the turntable. "I love these Bach cello suites."

I smiled, no longer sharing our odd synchronicity from last night. The music unfurled in a continuous ribbon of sound.

"Are you stoned, Remy?"

"My head feels like Styrofoam," he said. "You?"

"The walls are waffling and I have this dismal ringing in my ears. This is good stuff," I said.

Remy stood and floated from the living room. I heard cellophane crackling in the tiny kitchen. He returned brandishing a Whitman's Sampler box. He turned to me and let out an exasperated sigh.

"Don't you just hate cheap chocolates, Miss Thing?"

"Where did you get these?" I asked, laughing.

"The neighbor lady gave them to me for helping her go to the grocery the other day."

I popped one in my mouth. "That's sweet. But take them away quickly, before I retch. Don't you keep any real food in this apartment?"

"I'm never here. I eat out."

"So do I, but that's no excuse. Don't you even have chips?"

"No."

"We're going to get as big as houses, eating out all the time."

"I don't care."

"You'll care tomorrow, sweating your balls off on the recumbent bike."

Remy threw himself again into the stuffed chair and flopped his hairy legs on the coffee table. We were really stoned, I realized, stretching out on my large pink satin pillow in the middle of the room and gazing blankly at the window, listening to a *Sarabande* unspool. I loved the way the music took me on an excursion, wending its way, careening then receding. I could see Remy watching me, from the corner of my eye.

"Does this bozo you had a date with have a name?" he asked. "Your recent tricks don't usually have names, just attributes."

"What the devil are you talking about?"

"I'm talking about last month's 'Latino with the rocket cock' or 'the red-headed writer bottom who was a sour beauty.' Or was it 'tart asshole'?"

"I said 'dour beauty.' The only asshole in this conversation is you."

"I'll ignore that. Whatever happened to the boy you met last summer? The one with the little potbelly who was still in high school at Brother Martin."

"I liked his little potbelly. He was cute. But I got tired of his little sidekick tagging along everywhere we went. Her I didn't like. They were up each other's butt all the time."

"Where, of course, you wanted to be," Remy said, laughing.

"They reminded me of Shaggy and Velma on *Scooby-Doo*—each other's constant shadow."

"He smelled," Remy said.

"I never noticed."

"Liar. How could you not?"

"He might have been a tad musky."

"It was those black turtlenecks he wore all summer."

"He complained of poor circulation."

"I thought it was to hide the hickies he was getting from the Brothers. Just kidding."

"I wish you would have helped me find his sidekick a girlfriend—to get her off my hands."

"What happened to him?"

"I don't know. He disappeared."

"Remember Thaddeus?" asked Remy.

"Thaddeus? From St. Aloysius?"

"Yes. Pigpen. Another stinker."

"He always had cool comic books though. And *Mad* magazine."

"Boy, have your tastes come full circle since middle school," Remy said. "You remember my cousin Emile from Chalmette, who lived with his dad's mother in the Bywater so he could go to Jesuit?"

"Of course."

"He used to say you were so 'autistic.'"

"Oh, yes. I liked him. He wasn't too bookish, but then intelligence would have taken the bloom off his carnality, to paraphrase Nabokov."

"I thought he made good grades at Jesuit."

"I suppose. I never had a class with him."

"Didn't you do him?" Remy asked. "At that birthday party Rene and I had in college, when we lived in the Quarter with those crazy lesbians who made Alice B. Toklas brownies?"

Remy had a fraternal twin, Rene, who was also gay. Their father, Dr. Peychaud, had been an assistant superintendent of archdiocesan schools in Orleans Parish in the Eighties. Remy and Rene had their mother's rounded face and amber eyes and thick brows, but they had their father's darker coloring. Remy did everything with *brio*—even in high school. But it was Rene, not Emile, who had initiated me into "the joys of cocksuckery."

"I never had the brownies," I said.

"Really? They were in a pan on top of the old Frigidaire."

"This was in that apartment by the Mona Lisa?"

Remy nodded. "You must remember that. We were all downing Chartreuse shots when Heather came into the living room in a black bodice and a slip—she was doing underwear as outerwear long before Madonna—and said her one immortal line, 'Don't you just hate cheap chocolates, Miss Thing?'"

"Now I remember," I said. "Heather was practically bursting out of that bodice. Those heinous queens were taking bets on whether or not it would happen before the cake was cut."

"That was the very same cake they give the Queen of Comus on Mardi Gras day," Remy said.

"You don't say. Did you know that the *Mona Lisa* was a self-portrait?"

"Vaguely," Remy said. "Did I read that somewhere?"

"You and Rene were such fixtures at the Mona Lisa," I said. "Like the two *hookahs* in the window. I always knew where I could find you two—drinking 'Mona's Brew.'"

An hour passed. Remy and I drove out to River Road in Harahan to see the car from the ad. The owner had bought it for his wife on their thirty-fifth wedding anniversary, he said as the three of us walked up the driveway to the garage behind the house. Remy helped the old man yank up the door and we went inside. The garage smelled of turpentine and sawdust. The car was a red Karmann Ghia convertible. Remy ran his hand along the polished hood.

"Then the husband next door had to go and buy his wife a Lincoln." The old guy took off his fishing cap and palmed back his thick gray hair. "When Edith saw it in their driveway, she copped an attitude with me, said hell'd freeze over before she drove this thing again. So I said, 'Fine Edith, you can walk.' And here it's sat ever since. I've had it up on cinder blocks for twenty damn years. You think she was *stubborn*? You like the car?"

"What's not to like?" Remy said. "It's a beauty."

The old man and I stepped out of the garage into the hot sunlight while Remy lingered, peering into the car's interior. Then he followed us onto the drive. The old man squinted when he took off his glasses to rub the bridge of his nose. Remy went back and circled the car in the cramped garage. He kicked one of the tires, not swift or deliberate, more like he needed something to do while he mulled over his decision. Then the three of us stood at the foot of the driveway. The old man offered Remy and me a cigarette. Remy accepted and they smoked and talked about the price quoted in the classified advertisement.

"Edith died last year, you know. Emphysema."

"Sorry to hear that," I said. I felt like I had to say something.

"I held on to the car, I don't know why. I don't have any children to give it to and I hate the damn thing."

"Mister . . . ," Remy said.

"Falatti."

"Mr. Falatti, the car is immaculate and the price is good and I like it."

"Fine, then. Sooner you clear her out of the garage the better. Understood?" They shook hands.

"Might need a battery though."

"We can run out and get one," Remy said, looking at me. "To be on the safe side."

I walked to the road and sat listening to the stereo in the air-conditioning of my beat-up Honda Civic. I rolled down the window when Remy tapped on the glass.

"How's it look, Remy?"

"I'm buying it. We need to go for the battery. Then we'll transfer the title."

I drove us to an automotive parts store on Jefferson Highway where Remy picked up a new battery, then back to the old man's house. Remy and I lugged the battery up the driveway, into the garage, and the old man helped us install it in the car. Remy slid in behind the wheel and cranked the engine, revved it a little. It purred.

I climbed in on the passenger side. "Don't you think it's a bit impractical, Remy?"

"What do you mean?"

"It's a two-seater, for one thing."

Remy shrugged his shoulders and shook his head. "I want it. Picture this car on a stretch of open road as far as the eye can see—nothing but desert on either side and this red beauty flying like there's no tomorrow."

"I see it, but I don't necessarily see you in it."

"All I'm asking is, if you can't help then don't be a hindrance, Chip. I feel ready to hit the road again. I'm ashamed that I settled back down here so soon. Returning to New Orleans was only intended as an interim measure, a place between where I was going and where I had been. I believe we should move every five or so years for personal growth. But New Orleans sucks you in. Things don't change here. You could go away for a decade and it would be like it was yesterday when you come back. My first thought when I returned was that I'd buy a big Uptown mansion and turn it into a frat house. But now I just want to take a long vacation to California. New Orleans is too small to contain my curiosity."

The old man came out of the house and said he would drive the Karmann Ghia to the notary public on Jefferson Highway to have the title changed.

"I've got the pink slip—you meet me at the notary with a cashier's check." He folded the pink slip three times and stuck it in his bifold wallet.

In the parking lot of the notary public later that afternoon, Remy asked Mr. Falatti if he needed a ride home.

"It's only a mile down Colonial Boulevard. I think I'll walk. Thanks all the same."

The two men shook hands again. When Mr. Falatti was gone, I told Remy that the old man didn't look forlorn enough about the transaction for my tastes.

"Doesn't that worry you?" I asked.

"Not in the least. I think he's glad to have his garage back. I know what you're thinking. It wasn't his woman's church car."

"The thought did cross my mind."

I've known Remy since high school, and at the risk of sounding loony, I have to say he has an uncanny talent for knowing things. It's like we're plugged into each other on some paranormal wavelength. Remy often answers the phone on the first ring, saying, "What's up, Chip?" or "I've been waiting for your call, Chip," in a breathless, almost relieved voice—and this is without caller I.D. Now here he was, speaking my thoughts again. I wondered if he knew that I had decided to follow his example and slip from the city's gravitational pull myself. When I considered it (I tried not to think about it at all), I saw myself as an underachiever. As my tenth high school reunion approached, I was still a teaching assistant at the University of New Orleans, a commuter school. I had come up in the world from being a weekend clerk in D. H. Holmes department store in Gretna. Going bald, I had embraced baldness by shaving what was left of the red hair on my head. But I did not feel free so much as unmoored, and it bothered me. I wanted to run away and find my way back, as Remy had. But to what?

Remy and I had a friend—an acquaintance, really, someone we saw at gatherings five or six times a year—who refused to fly. He never traveled too far from where he grew up in Lafayette. Presented with the opportunity to trek in the Himalayas free, this acquaintance politely but firmly declined. He preferred to stay at home in his apartment in the French Quarter, have friends drive him to Pensacola every summer, take the train occasionally to New York. He would not get into one of those goddamn planes. Of course, there are plenty of people who, for one reason or another, are afraid to travel. Remy says that travel is ultimately fictitious anyway, that you only go places you want to, see places you want to see. He once remarked about this acquaintance, "If he can walk down Pirates Alley and imagine seeing the Rialto Bridge instead of the crepe myrtles and live oak trees of Jackson Square, far be it from me—far be it from anyone—to judge him for choosing not to get on a plane."

On Sunday afternoon, Remy picked me up in his new convertible.

Remy hated going to the movies alone. His friends were his family, the family he chose. He admitted to me that he often wondered what it would be like not to have a history, like Sarah Jane in the movie *Imitation of Life*, which had also been revived at the Prytania Theatre, but we had a history with *Vertigo*. Remy arrived at my apartment an hour late, ringing the bell. I met him downstairs—I hadn't told him about moving yet, and I didn't want him to see my apartment in disarray. He wore sunglasses, paint-splattered, ripped-in-the-knees dungarees, and a T-shirt printed with the words "Violent Femmes."

"The shirt isn't really mine," he said. "It materialized in my laundry bag. It's just a shirt."

I was wearing an ancient T-shirt emblazoned with the handsome face of Vance DeGeneres of The Cold. "Don't worry, Remy," I said. "I didn't take you for a sudden VF buff."

"Isn't it macabre to think how Eighties bands like Depeche Mode and the Dead Kennedys are considered hip these days because they're so retro?" he said.

"I know. The *Repo Man* soundtrack is a main cultural reference for some of my students."

As we drove around town in the Karmann Ghia, I imagined that we looked cool in our sunglasses. Remy suggested we drive past the Café Brasil. We parked around the corner on Elysian Fields, in front of the derelict Elysium Theater. A guy bundled in an army fatigue jacket with "Ryker" across the pocket stood in front of the building. Remy stared at him as we passed on the sidewalk. The guy wore a red cap, pulled down over his ears so that he could not look at anything without turning his head. Consequently he revealed his interest to everyone he cruised, including Remy. But why was he dressed for polar climes in the middle of May?

"Isn't that the porn theater where you used to sell tokens after school?" I asked Remy.

"Did you know me when I worked at the Elysium? I was sixteen. Men cruised by in faded blue Impala sedans and Dodge Darts, and the neighbors complained until the city had it condemned and shut it down, and I was out of a job."

We walked over to the Café Brasil but found it empty of patrons. We sat at a table outside and ordered coffee.

"So, do you still want to go to the Prytania to see *Vertigo*?" I asked.

"Yes. Do you know what Hitchcock once said? 'I don't film slices of life. I film slices of cake.' But let's do the Fruit Loop in my new car first."

We circled the block in the convertible. I was going to miss cruising past the queer bars on a Sunday afternoon, I thought, when all the boys hang out at the Parade Disco's tea dance, practically dripping off the balconies.

"Speaking of food," I said, "I'm starving. Let's have lunch."

"Where?"

"You decide. I feel uninspired today."

An idea sparked in Remy. "*Vee* must go to *Vice's*."

"Wise's? Isn't that a little out of the way for cafeteria food?"

"Let's go," Remy reiterated in his best *fräulein* German accent. "*Vee* haven't been *zere* in years."

Apparently his idea was fixed. We walked back to the car and sped up Elysian Fields to Mid-City where Remy grew up.

At Jesuit High School, when Remy and I were seniors, we would sometimes skip Father Patout's first-period biology class and hitch a ride with our friend Styborski to Wise's, across the street from the Barq's bottling plant, near the Cemeteries. That's when we'd see the owner, a real codger, who seemed perpetually agitated, as if he were on a bad caffeine jones. Mr. Wise would shout at the staff and customers alike, his big voice booming for someone his size. Remy called him the "Anti-Host." But he was theatrical and lent the place some atmosphere, which was one of the reasons we went there. He was also one of the first restaurateurs in the city to have a nonsmoking section, before any city ordinance. He'd have to tell smokers to move to the correct section, because they were not labeled *per se*, merely set off by blue and red lines of tape across the white terrazzo floor. Remy, Styborski, and I smoked Marlboros, and we learned the hard way where to sit when we sat in the wrong section, away from the entrance, the first time we went to Wise's for the Belgian waffles. The old man bit our heads off. This doesn't really have much to do with anything, but I used to stare at those blue and red tape borders on the white floor and think of the veins and arteries in the *Gray's Anatomy* poster that hung in Father Patout's lab class that we were cutting.

The food at Wise's tasted good, for cafeteria food. At least Remy and I thought so. Styborski hated it. He only came with us because we tended to skip class together and Remy and I always outvoted him on where to go. Sometimes we would venture to the Double Happiness, but Styborski wasn't too keen on Chinese food either, though he ate whatever was put in front of him. He complained that the food at Wise's tasted as blandly Middle American and conservative as a Betty Crocker bundt cake, but to Remy and me, natives weaned on Tabasco and cayenne, it was a relief to eat something a little farther north of Spiceville. Styborski was originally from suburban Baltimore (his grandfather was Maryland's Kielbasa King), and he would tease us by drawling "The Gret Stet of Luzianna" instead of "The Great State of Louisiana." In return, we called him a "Baltimoron." His family had moved to New Orleans in our junior year at Jesuit, and Styborski tended to want everything blackened or in a roux. Then again, you always want what you didn't have growing up.

I used to get the turkey and stuffing, because my family had shrimp and oyster dressing and turtle sauce piquant for Thanksgiving. Or I'd get the macaroni and cheese with big rotini shells and gooey Velveeta, and of course a Barq's Red Creme Soda or a Dr. Pepper. We would sit in our olive green Naugahyde booth in the corner, past the red veins in the floor, and if we were stoned—which, in those late years of our high school careers, was frequently the case—we would stuff ourselves like pigs and stare at the galaxies on the linoleum table top and giggle about all we had eaten.

It was about four in the afternoon when Remy and I stepped into the twisted maze of chrome railings at Wise's entrance. We walked down the long corridor of art deco sconces and old, silver-framed newspaper clippings of the cafeteria in its heyday. It was a little too quiet. Most of the Uptown maids and cooks had Sundays off and it was a ritual for their abandoned employers to take their families out to eat. But when we got to the serving line there was no one else there. We scoped out the long row of empty stainless steel serving pans.

I stared at Remy.

"What's wrong with this picture?" he asked.

"Where's the turkey?" I said.

He shrugged his shoulders and asked the counter waitress.

"We don't have none," she said.

"What do you mean, you don't have turkey?" I exclaimed in horror. "You always have it."

The counter woman had us pegged. "*Get a grip, girlfriend.* We don't be having no turkey because the kitchen bitches don't be making none." She snorted. "Now what do you need, Louise?"

"She just *read* you," Remy said, snapping his fingers at me. "*Gimme* the roast beef, Miss Thing," he told the counter woman.

We pushed our trays down the burnished rack, past the windows of the serving line, and looked at the plastic blue titles above empty pans. Remy pronounced the invisible selections "very low-cal." We mimed picking our imaginary feast. For the first time, we were unimpressed by the menu at Wise's. I told Remy it made me think of grimmer days at Jesuit, before we were seniors and could leave campus for lunch on Fridays and go to Liuzza's for po-boy sandwiches. When we reached the dessert section, Remy exploded.

"What kind of cafeteria is this?" he demanded in high dudgeon. "No apple pie? I want my apple pie!"

We must have hit a sensitive nerve. All of the counter women gathered in a huddle to confer, arguing among themselves. A woman stuck her head out of the serving window from the kitchen, her copper-colored forehead crinkled with a quizzical expression under one of the warming lamps. "What's all the commotion?" she hollered.

We had succeeded in creating a scene, one of Remy's favorite pastimes. We slouched farther down the line, forced to make do with what little they had, scrounging together two trays of third choices and retreating to our *good-ole* booth, where we distracted ourselves with gossip about our clique and who we had seen lately while eating most everything on our plates and drinking something red. And smoking.

"Have you seen Styborski lately?" Remy asked, changing the subject. "He seems to have dropped off the face of the earth."

"Last time I saw him, he was a bouncer at the Parade Disco," I said.

"Last time I saw him, he was reading tarot cards in front of the cathedral. That was last year. I told him, 'If you go on like this, you won't be able to enjoy what's left of your life.'"

"You told him that?"

"If not me, then who? He said he wanted to be a poet, but spent more time in the Half Moon than he did writing."

"I regret," I said, "ever telling that boy an artist shouldn't give up his vices."

"When did you tell him that?"

"Years ago. In this very booth, in fact. Look how he's lived up to that silly advice." I thought of how Remy and I had kept a bottle of bourbon in the bow of my father's pirogue in the backyard. We would walk around the corner of the house to retrieve the bottle, then drive off to the Lakefront in Remy's old car and take turns passing the bottle all night.

"And where was I?" he asked.

"I don't remember," I said. "I don't necessarily disavow anything. I just shouldn't have said it to him. He didn't need that particular kind of encouragement from me."

"That's bullshit," Remy said. "It's not your fault Styborski drinks the way he does." He took a long pull on his cigarette. "Actually, I worry about you."

"Here we go again."

"I've been watching you sniff along that boy's trail for months," Remy said. "Taking your sweet time in your inimitable way."

"What boy?"

"Allen. And I was good. I didn't try to run interference or cockblock you. I kept my mouth shut—"

"Till last night."

"Well, like it or not, Chip, you don't have time to be housebreaking these pups every six months." Remy raised a hand to my objections. "Wait until I've said my piece. I don't mean to be judgmental, but someone has to tell it like it is and I've known you longer than anyone else. Your other buddies are incapable of telling you anything or don't know any better. I'm the only one to tell you this. You've had quite the sex-sodden years since college, but I don't understand your attraction to these *youths*. You need to change your life. There's nothing for you in this city anymore. No opportunity. *No more turkey, girlfriend.* The buffet is closed. You need to move on to something else. Save yourself. Get out while you can. You've been too complacent. You need to see the world. You've been on the party jag too long."

Remy's words stung me. He had never said anything like this to me before, not so harshly. For a long time, I couldn't look at him. I sat there pushing my food around on my plate.

"I know my job's a shitty one," I finally said. "I know I need to do something else. And when I find out what that is you'll be the first to know, Remy. As always. In the meantime, I've applied to graduate school out of state."

"I don't know what to say."

"You could be excited for me."

"Of course I'm excited for you. When were you planning to tell me? You let me run my mouth and now you're pissed. You're so angry you could spit. But you won't show it. You just sit there, shredding that napkin."

"I'm tired. I want to go home."

"Let's skip *Vertigo*," Remy said. "We'll go to my place and smoke a joint."

I could name all the arguments we've ever had by the restaurants in which they occurred. They usually started while we waited to be served, when my blood sugar plummeted or Remy had a nicotine fit. He seemed never to have made the connection that if he would go outside and have a cigarette and wait, everything would blow over.

We gulped down our red drinks and snubbed out our cigarettes and left Wise's. Halfway to Remy's apartment, I remembered I had left my Ray-Bans on the table. I asked Remy if he thought they'd still be there later, and he said we probably should go back now if I wanted them. So we sped back to Wise's. One of the waitresses had saved them for me.

Leaving the cafeteria, I stumbled off the curb and twisted my ankle. It swelled instantly, throbbing painfully. I sat down on the pavement and grabbed it. The ankle didn't feel broken. I hopped and limped across the street, then another ten feet in Remy's direction. He offered his hand and pulled me to standing, slung his arm over my shoulder, and held me by the waist as we moved toward the car.

"Do you think we should go to the hospital?" he asked.

"No hospitals," I said. "It doesn't feel broken. I'll call my doctor tomorrow. But I've got to have a cigarette before I go on."

I dug into my pocket, pulled out a pack, and placed one in Remy's mouth. He lit it with a Zippo lighter and took a few drags.

"I'm having a flashback," he said. "I'm remembering how my grandmother used to complain how uncouth it was for a lady to smoke when she was out on a walk."

"Give me a drag, will you?"

He handed it to me, then helped me into my seat. At his apartment, Remy filled a blue plaid ice pack with ice from the freezer and brought it back with two lagers. He sat down next to me, eased my foot up onto the piano bench, and set the ice pack over my ankle. Then he put an Art Tatum album on the turntable.

"It looks really swollen," he said.

"It's only twisted. It looks worse than it feels."

"You're sure you don't want to go down to Baptist?"

"I'm sure. You know what summer in an emergency room is like."

"Right. Hey, did I tell you my Betty Carter dream?" Remy asked.

"No."

"The other night I dreamed I sneaked out to a recital and was standing in a gigantic dark lobby with sheer curtains for walls. I'm standing there, waiting for Styborski to pick up Nico, and this homely woman slips a postcard under the glass door. She was tall and gangly, with long arms and stubby fingers and nails. She wore a small strand of black pearls—aubergine, really—matching in hue if not in sheen the radiance of her eyes, and her silver hair was in a chignon. She loved violets, the essence of violets. The note read, 'To Betty Carter from Isabel. I arrive tonight.'"

"Who was Isabel?"

"Hell if I know. So I show Styborski the note when he arrives. Next we are in a restaurant and I ask him if he knows who Betty Carter is and he says, 'Of course, a jazz singer.' There's no way Styborski would ever admit not knowing who someone is. When I woke up, Nico had her snout on the futon, next to my face, and was staring at me like she knew what I was dreaming about. It was really weird."

"Where *is* Nico?"

"My brother's dog-sitting her for me until tomorrow. She's so pokey these days. But she knows when it's me on the phone. Rene says she patters across his apartment and lies down at his feet. When it's not me, she gets up and goes under the sofa."

"So you can't figure out this Isabel, and of course, why Betty Carter?"

"No earthly idea."

"You must've been channeling something," I said.

"I will not be miffed if you move away from New Orleans without me," Remy said. "Okay?"

"I know that, Remy. All I'm asking is, if you can't help then don't be a hindrance."

"*Touché*, bitch."

Remy removed the ice pack and went to the kitchen to refill it. He returned with a cigarette dangling from his lips, which he handed to me.

"You have no idea of the herd mentality you inspired when you cruised City Park after school. You could have led the whole group of us off a cliff," Remy said.

"What in hell are you talking about?" I asked.

"I was one of those who followed you. I was your biggest fan."

"You're joking."

"I held on to this lopsided lust for you for so long. But to you I was purely ornamental."

"You were not. I fell in love with you at first sight. You *and* Rene. It was hard to tell you two apart back then."

Remy picked up the album's ratty cover sleeve and stared at it, as if trying to decipher its meaning. "I will miss you all over again," he finally said. "I moved back to New Orleans because of you."

"And I'm moving away because you inspired me to. Don't go maudlin on me. You get weepy when you're stoned."

Remy drove me home, but after his red Karmann Ghia pulled away, I decided to risk a detour for a snack. I hobbled the few blocks up St. Charles Avenue to the K&B Drug Store on Broadway, and waited in line to buy a pack of Twinkies and a quart of milk. I watched a youngish man walk to the dairy case. He was dressed in black bicycle shorts, a sweatshirt, and cyclist shoes slightly longer than a regular cleat, curled on the ends—he walked funny in them. I loitered by the counter, looking at tabloids until the cyclist approached. He jumped ahead of me, then turned to apologize.

"Were you in line?"

"No, go ahead," I said.

The cyclist looked at my Twinkies. "Wow," he said. "My fave."

"They're buy-one-get-one-free," I said (not too smooth, I thought).

The cyclist paid for his juice and waddled out of the store. Why didn't I offer him one to help me home, I groused. I paid for my Twinkies and milk and hobbled out of the store. The cyclist had unlocked his bicycle and unhitched it from the parking meter. I watched him straddle the bicycle and ride away.

Tuesday morning early, Remy called at work, his voice harried, breathless.

"Did you see the paper yet, Chip?"

"I haven't even had my first cup of coffee."

"We had the last supper at Wise's."

"You're kidding."

"Check out the front page of the Living section. Got to go," he said.

On my coffee break I walked to the Student Center to buy the *Times-Picayune*. When Remy left New Orleans the first time for the Manhattan School of Music, years ago, I felt queasy for weeks. That queasiness returned as I flipped through the paper to the front page of the Living section and found "FAREWELL TO WISE'S" in big, bold, sans-serif type befitting the passing of a local institution, with nostalgic photographs and a sidebar giving a brief history of the place.

It seems old man Wise had had enough of running the business and wanted to retire. But he didn't tell anyone, not his family and definitely not his employees. He simply fired everyone at closing time on Sunday. There were signs, to be sure. The head cook (the one who popped her head out at us through the serving window), who called the paper, told the staff reporter that she had suspected something was amiss when the old man let the inventory of food stuffs fall the past few weeks from fifteen thousand dollars to about three thousand dollars. She said Wise walked into the kitchen at around six p.m. and told everyone not to bother coming to work the next morning. Mr. Wise declined to be interviewed.

Reading the story, I shuddered, realizing something had indeed passed between Remy and me. Remy didn't believe in coincidences and there was no way he could have known beforehand this was going to happen. I would not ordinarily consider myself superstitious either, except when it comes to Remy. Though I admit that I took guidance from the son of the proprietor of the witchcraft shop next door to the Mississippi River Bottom tavern a few months ago, when I was hoping for a telephone call from Allen. The shop is a tourist trap, I know, selling snake oil. You'd get better advice from a tattoo parlor by the airport, if anywhere. But the young Goth said he had a spell for every occasion and necessity and he was cute despite the long, blue-black hair, nose piercings, and grommets in his ears. He told me to singe a single strand of my beloved's hair with a white candle, sprinkle cinnamon over the flame, and place his picture upside down behind a clock, if I wanted contact with Allen.

I lacked any of Allen's hair but I did place a photograph of him upside down behind my digital alarm clock. Of course, Allen never called, although with his picture hidden my mind dwelt less on him. When I later quizzed the Goth about my poor results, he asked if the clock had a face—the hex didn't work without a clock face. Then he warned me against wishing for anything too much or for something I didn't want—the first practical advice I had had in months.

Later that night Remy called to tell me about his own little detour on Monday. When he left orchestra rehearsal that evening, he drove to Wise's, and in the car wondered why we hadn't gone there more often in later years. He parked in front of the deserted building and got out of his car, and felt like he had stepped onto the back lot of a movie studio. It reminded him of the silent film *Sherlock Jr.* where Buster Keaton plays a projectionist who falls asleep and awakes to find himself inhabiting the film he is screening. Remy had made the same crossover and, like Caliban in *The Tempest*, wanted to forget it was a dream. But illusions are as treacherous to navigate as reality, he told me. He peered into the cafeteria window, cupping his face against the glass, then walked to the glass doors and shook them to see if they were locked, he didn't know why, feeling tentative and disturbed. "It was one of those moments you wish was on film," he said, "but know that it wouldn't necessarily mean as much unless you had been there."

"Our Sunday *was* rather cosmic," I said, using Remy's euphemism for the *Twilight Zone* occurrences we had come to expect between us. I told him I was glad we had gone back for my glasses.

"That'll teach you to be more careful about where you lay them, Chip," he said.

MENUETTO

1.

WHO COULD BE HERE SO SOON INTO VISITING HOURS, Bernard Percy wondered, his face buried in his pillow, his mouth drooling, only half awake. Maynard wouldn't come this early.

Bernard felt drained. Every muscle ached. His arm twitched. He scratched his cheek, lolled his head to one side, listening. Had he imagined the knock on the door, the trill of knuckles on glass?

Thunder rended the velvet swath of evening; a streetcar clanged.

Another bad dream. If only he could remember. He traced the rhumb line of associations backward, hating the fuzzy sense of self, the blurred spatial relationships, the quicksand of forgetfulness.

He'd discovered a lost Mozart manuscript. The page was visible as he fingered the violin strings to see how it felt. Then he awoke, desolate, unable to recall a single note, a voice ringing in his ears.

A radio voice drenched in cigarettes and booze, wanton pleasure, and regret. "I will hate him for this," Bernard remembered saying. But to whom? Maynard? Stan? Michael? Rudy? Was he at Stan's old apartment on Royal Street, clicking off his most recent conquests as Stan did a two-step, hiking up his pink silk dress, thinking he really did have great legs for a forty-five-year-old and handing him an invitation then morphing into a woman in a Givenchy coat on the ledge of a building preparing to jump?

He remembered blood, its ferrous scent like rusty water, remembered the boy in a flimsy hospital gown laid out on a gurney, his sinewy gossamer body packed in ice with tubes for breathing and pints of hemoglobin, the paramedic priest giving him electroshock and extreme unction. And everyone grieving except Maynard, who shouted, "Now I'll have to pay for the ambulance."

Bernard fixated on the boy's oval face, his high cheekbones like a Byzantine Madonna, his short black hair, his furrowed forehead, his onyx eyes beneath thick brows, his caramel skin glowing under the street lamp, shivering with anger.

Suddenly he's on the road with his father, suffering his poisonous silence, driving back and forth from Las Vegas to Palm Springs on the stretch of Route 66 that runs through San Bernardino County. His father berates him for being a momma's boy, for growing milk breasts, for reading tabloids and sissy magazines instead of Zane Grey novels. It's night, the summer that belonged to his father, and he's standing in the desert with an Indian chief in headdress amid gnarled bristlecone pines and tortured rock formations. "Stay still while I take this goddamn picture for your mother," his father says, then puts him on the auction block in blazing sunlight. As the Polaroid reveals itself, Bernard sees that he has become his father. "In the canyon you can hear your soul breathing," the elderly Navajo says.

If this keeps up, I'll go berserk, Bernard thought. He heard chatter and canned applause from the television on a swiveling platform suspended from the ceiling, the low, garbled voice of some game show host crooning.

And then the knock again.

Bernard blinked. He rubbed his eyes, glimpsed movement behind the door's frosted pane, a silhouette peering into the room as the door eased open. He shifted his torso in bed.

"Ahoy," someone called coyly from the threshold.

Well, now, Bernard thought, Miss Mary Congeniality. Finally.

The door swung open. The hall light was like a punishment.

"Ahoy, my ass," Bernard said, squinting. "It's about time you showed your face." He tried to rouse himself.

"Don't get up on my account," Stan said, arm outstretched. "*Goodness!* When did you get your nipple pierced? Why did you do that?"

Bernard adjusted his hospital gown, pulled the sheet over his waning erection. "To feel it, silly boy."

"That's extreme," Stan said, tentatively stepping into the room, past the comatose old man in the adjacent bed. He appeared as relaxed as Bernard had seen him in months, his red hair cropped short, wearing a new pink polo shirt and blue jeans. "I'm sorry I couldn't come sooner. I arrived back from Venice a week ago. I got here as quickly as I could."

Stan took a seat between the side of the bed and the dirty window overlooking a dreary patch of Uptown and peered over the tops of his glasses, scanning the hospital room like a conductor in the pit to see if everything and everyone was in place. The drab room was as Spartan as the set of *The Honeymooners*, enough to make one sick, Bernard thought, though he had tried to leave his imprint. A stack of books sat on the aluminum nightstand and cracked open on the floor as if snacked upon and discarded and the *Times-Picayune* lay strewn around the bed beneath a glossy photograph of the new Calvin Klein model, ripped from *Vanity Fair* and taped to the wall. A profusion of flowers from well-wishers—violets and a white crocus in cobalt and tangerine ceramic pots, green iris shoots and dahlias sent by the women from the Herstory Project—and cards from the volunteers at NOAIDS Task Force where Bernard freelanced, writing grants between gigs, lined the windowsill.

"My, you really are mellow yellow, aren't you?" Stan finally said. "How are you feeling?"

"It's japonica yellow, I believe," Bernard said. "And I feel ghastly. I ache all over, I itch all over, all the time—the result of the jaundice. I've hardly slept in days. My bowels are in a tizzy and I've lost twenty-five pounds in the past week—I know you can't tell—and I experience sudden dilations of memory. Last weekend I coughed and had a weird synesthesia of taste and breath and smell, like an electrical charge. I felt as if a chasm had opened inside me. I had this intimation—I don't know if it was hypochondria—that something was gravely wrong. Maybe when I coughed my heart skipped a beat. Then there's the nausea. I can't keep anything fatty down for more than ten minutes. I alternate cold and hot flashes, chills and fever. And the dreams! My jaw hurts from gnashing my teeth in my sleep. Even my semen is yellow."

Stan's eyebrow arched. "Way too much information, girlfriend. I bet you couldn't wait to tell me that. Do you feel like company, or should I leave?"

"Stay," Bernard said. "Maynard won't be here for a while."

"Where is he?"

"Cureton's—where else? I think he's smitten with his trainer. Ask me if I care."

"Do you?"

"I don't have time for those hooligans at the gym and I don't feel the least bit threatened by them. Besides, Maynard doesn't have the stomach for an affair."

"How long are the doctors keeping you here?" Stan asked.

"That's just it," Bernard said. "My immune system has gone a little haywire. The intern, his name is Dr. Payne—appropriate, don't you think?—says I may be able to leave in a few days but I'll be housebound for at least a couple of months, maybe longer, and I'll have to see my regular doctor every week for a liver panel. I didn't have the courage to hear my T-cell count. I told him to tell me tomorrow, for—"

"—tomorrow is another day. I know, Scarlett. Your count's that bad?"

"He said he's going to talk to Dr. Bell about putting me on another cocktail. What I really need is some sympathy."

"You'll have no pity from me," Stan warned.

"Then I guess two fingers of bourbon is too much to expect? I'd love to get pickled."

"Please, Louise. How long do you have to stay off the sauce?"

"At least a year and a half."

"What about smoking?"

"You know I take the view that the eggs I eat will probably choke my arteries with cholesterol before the tar clogs my lungs," Bernard said.

"Medically, that's not necessarily the case."

"What you're really asking is, do I fear death?"

"Dr. Bell says you'll outlive us all."

"Anyway, Dr. Payne said the withdrawal would wreak more havoc on my immune system, so I shouldn't worry about kicking the habit right now. Talk about something else. You're supposed to cheer me up."

"I did bring you a care package," Stan said, opening his backpack and producing a decorated silver foil bag brimming with blue tissue paper. "And I stopped by your apartment to fetch the mail—lots of bills and this box."

"*Hmm*, an unmarked package. I know what that means. My DVD-of-the-month club." Bernard pulled open the cardboard box. "*Ass Wide Open*? Shoot, I've seen this already. Have you?"

"The porn version of *Eyes Wide Shut*? No."

"Without Kubrick's misanthropy or pretentiousness. Want to take it with you?"

"The last one you gave me—"

"I have to admit that *Homeboy Homeopaths* was a little *outré* even by my standards. The thing with the acupuncture needles?"

"Indeed."

"This one has more nudity in it—a relentless parade of pectorals and pricks. And it's quite elaborate and trashy."

"Sure, I'll take it. I hope the leads have more chemistry than Cruise and Kidman."

"They do. And it's the same plot: dark-haired, buff doctor; wispy-blond art historian bottom. They go to a holiday party where the doctor hooks up with that delicious Czech porn star with a huge cock named Lucky while the art historian flirts with two Abercrombie & Fitch models. The doctor chases the porn star all over Greenwich Village and then out to the Hamptons to the beach house of a record mogul, a 'Friend of Bill's' played by Bang-Bang LaDesh out of drag, who hosts a weird dungeon party. And at each point in the doctor's odyssey, he's cockblocked while the rest of the cast sucks and fucks with abandon. Later, during a bizarre fisting ritual—these boys give each other enemas like we give each other Altoids—the host humiliates the doctor by saying, 'The Black Party's not for dilettantes but for hardcore sybarites!' That is an actual line. I almost busted a gut."

"But did you bust a nut?" Stan said.

"You are such a potty mouth, Stanley Bond."

"I thought you didn't like porn versions of mainstream films."

"You're right, I usually don't go for highbrow porn. But I gave it a shot—so to speak. Parts of it are too funny to be erotic. But it totally skewers the Kubrick style, literalizing the satire, showing the extremes gay men will go to for sex."

"I didn't think the original worked precisely because it was about straight couples."

"What gay man hasn't done stupid things for sex?" Bernard agreed. "Except maybe you. You do stupid things not to have sex."

"Very droll."

"Anyway, the doctor ends up back in the Village with his lover at the Pleasure Chest, reaffirming their love among the dildos."

"Don't give away the end," Stan said. "Speaking of parties, how was yours?"

"So you did remember." Bernard fidgeted in bed with his hands around the cardboard box. "It was as horrible as a forty-fifth birthday party could be. But you were missed. And there were lots and lots of gifts. Maynard gave me the new Uchida recording of the complete Mozart piano sonatas. Of course, he got shit-faced and had the nerve to say—in front of everyone, mind you—that he was dating someone below his station. Wait, it gets better. He called me no-account coon-ass trash from the bayous. You have no idea what it's like to be mortified in front of fifty of your closest friends at your own goddamn birthday party by—I can hardly bring myself to say it—your own *boyfriend*. My *jaw* dropped. He made such a scene. I was about to throw the cake at him when Rudy came over to us in the dining room and said in that stern, quiet little drawl of his, 'May-*nerd*, you need to leave my home immediately or I'll have Bubbles throw you out on the sidewalk.' Last month, he ran up a thirteen-hundred-dollar phone bill using the wank lines."

"You need someone who makes you feel important," Stan said.

Bernard exhaled loudly and closed his eyes, thinking he wished he did not find Maynard so sexy. "Forgive my exaggeration," he said. "Maynard's okay when he's on his Wellbutrin. I'm on it myself now. I've felt so haggard lately and a hundred-fifty milligrams is just enough to round off the edges. But my libido suffers. I bet you never thought you'd hear me say that. Maynard's terrible sex, anyway. Dull as dishwater and paranoid about semen—even his own. He's so afraid of catching, he can't enjoy the intimacy. He has a laundry list of safe things he won't do. He hates messiness. Won't even let me read the Sunday *Times* in bed for fear of getting newsprint on the sheets."

"I thought that was you," Stan said, smiling.

"But that cock of his is thick and wicked. And I've managed to draw him out somewhat," Bernard said, ignoring him. Then, abruptly: "Why do I do this? Why do I go out with these nut jobs and unattainable men? Michael made me feel I was the center of the world."

Stan nodded in his annoying, empathetic manner, the jerky gesture of one who liked sincerity in small doses and cut with broad silences, Bernard thought. "There's something else in the bag," he said.

Bernard dug through the tissue and extracted a magnifying glass with a mother-of-pearl handle and a filigreed silver ring holding the lens.

"A belated birthday gift," Stan said. "I found it in a shop in Venice. I suspect it's odd, but it was the most beautiful object I saw when I was browsing the antique shops."

Bernard wondered if Stan intended it as metaphorical. He held the glass moon up to his eye and peered, turning it in his hand, opening his other palm, examining it through the lens, turning to the dirty window. The silver corona caught a glint of light from the table lamp.

"It's beautiful, Stan. It'll come in handy—I stepped on my glasses last night going to the toilet. Thank you. It reminds me of the one Michael had on his desk. He inherited it from his father who bought it from a woman in Hiroshima. It went through the bombing." Bernard shook his head. "Enough about me. I didn't ask you about Venice. Did I tell you I want my ashes spread in the Grand Canal? You'll forget to visit my grave here, but you adore Venice and you'll always return to the Grand Canal."

"Don't be so melodramatic."

"Melodramatic nothing. I no longer buy green bananas. I buy thinner books. Tell me about your trip. Did you go to the Guggenheim?"

"I did go to the Guggenheim," Stan said, "but I didn't do much writing. Mostly I worried about money. I've been thinking I shouldn't have quit my day job, even though the lawyers at the firm were positively icy when I went to pick up my last paycheck before I left for Italy."

"What did you expect? You foreclosed on any opportunity they had for making you an offer to stay, said it was non-negotiable. Now you resent it when they don't try to keep you? Don't be ridiculous. You wanted to work less and write more, so do it. Don't give in to that kid inside you saying you can't succeed. Your memoir was published in an anthology. Eventually you'll write the novel."

Stan bit his lip. "Who reads novels anymore? What was the last novel you read?"

"Write a biography, then. You know I like those."

"I know. They're hot, hot, hot."

"Write a biography of Michael. He's a worthwhile subject and there's lots of interest in him."

"That would require me writing about you also," Stan said. "It would be too weird. And I have been working, just not in Venice. I got dicked by the editor of *Chelsea Style*. He deserves a special circle in hell."

"I have dish about him. Years ago I overheard Martin telling friends that he had just blown some cute usher in the loo at City Center during a matinee of *Promises, Promises*. An unimpeachable witness who happened to be in the adjacent stall told me what really happened: Martin groped the kid at the urinal, who told him, 'Get your hands off me, you fucking faggot.' You're not amused. What did he do to you, dear?"

"As you know, I don't have a lot of free time to write on spec. Martin asked me to review the latest Generation Why novel—that's the reason I didn't come to see you before now. I turned it in on time and I panned it. Aside from calling the book aimless, joyless, and lurid and its emotional palette— as you would say—entirely in primary colors, I had the temerity to suggest that its subtext is straight out of Leni Riefenstahl and this fascistic emphasis on perfect young bodies as an indicator of worth is not only disgusting but plague-denial at its most reprehensible. If you're not healthy, you're bad, bad, bad; sex belongs only to the young and hung and everyone else can go to the Devil; sex is meaningless if you're not healthy and beautiful. And somehow it's your own fault. I pointed out how dangerous it is being an apologist for the gym subculture, how this fantasy of perfection and sexual utopia feeds on the fear of death. Martin was not pleased. He killed it."

"No surprise there; he's a gym bunny himself. But I wonder if we were any more egalitarian about sex when we were in our twenties," Bernard said.

"What on earth do you mean?"

"Do you think we were more inclusive?"

"Certainly you were pretty democratic," Stan said.

"You mean I was a tart. Did Martin give you a reason?"

"He sent me an e-mail saying he 'disagreed with my analysis.' I fired off a response, told him he wouldn't know shit from Shinola if his nose were rubbed in it. Then he rang me up and said I'm a self-hating asshole."

"Consider the source, Stan."

"I know. But it still rattled me. And he's not paying a kill fee, like I can afford wasting time working on something that won't see print. But it's not worth suing over. I should be thankful he won't publish it. I don't need the flak. I blame it on these odd times we're living through. On one hand there's panic about any sort of sexual expression and on the other there's a breakdown in pragmatism about the crisis, an attitude that you can be only so dead. One queen actually said that to me in Pensacola last summer. I saw these two guys going at it on Navarre Beach, in front of God and everybody—"

"Sounds hot," Bernard said, flashing on his first foray to Fire Island in the off-season some fifteen years before: the throngs gone; the island stripped to its bare essentials, scrub cedar, mulberry, and pine; the shock of the cold, pounding surf along the golden beach stretching into infinity. He'd stopped to watch the spectacle of two boys in the throes of passion, their moans carrying down the beach amid the salty crash and lull of waves while a shirtless artist with white hair painted their lovemaking *en plein air* from a discreet distance, hopefully capturing the chromatic light on the sand, the roaring wind, the expansive leap of blue from sky to horizon. He'd seen the trio again later in the sunburned silence of the ferry ride to Sayville.

Stan frowned. "They were fucking bareback, Bernard," he said.

"And how could you tell that?" Bernard asked. "Were you hovering?"

"I was close enough to see but I was not hovering. 'What are you people doing?' I hollered. 'Just because you *will* the crisis to be over doesn't mean it is. Do some good for the gay community and use a goddamn condom.'"

"I can't imagine you saying that. You're not that confrontational."

"Tell me, Bernard, how can people let passion overtake their common sense?"

Like I'm the expert, Bernard thought; how could passion *not* overtake all sense? "It was probably the Ecstasy," he said.

"I hadn't thought of that," Stan said.

"That's because while most kids in school were exploring drugs, we were otherwise occupied," Bernard said. "In any case, that was a long time ago. I find it amusing that you should be a defender of sexual expression now."

"Whatever made you think I was a moral scold?" Stan asked.

Bernard laughed. "I seem to remember you registering your disdain for my City Park revels. What was it you called them? 'Grubby ruttings'?"

"I found them nutty, those nocturnal couplings and circle jerks in the thickets of City Park that you described in lush detail. *Dangerous*. You worried me. I couldn't have cared less about your slatternly barroom behavior and sloppy steam room sex. At least you conducted them indoors, in safe places."

"What about when you came to visit Michael and me in New York and we marched in the freezing cold in that ACT UP protest against excessive drug prices? When I eyed the policemen lining Maiden Lane and whispered in your ear, 'Cute boys in uniform'? What did you say to me? 'Don't eroticize the *oppressor*.'"

"That's different," Stan said.

Bernard wrinkled his nose and gazed out the window. He sighed, yawned, closed his eyes. He was so over this illness-as-metaphor thing, that health was a measure of worth. One day scientists would discover there was no such thing as death from natural causes—that death itself was a virus—he was certain of it. He thought longingly of the boy with a blue guitar case leaning against the wall across from him in the emergency room, who wore his cock to one side of his jeans, Bernard could not help noticing. He resembled someone, Bernard couldn't remember who.

Stan interrupted his reverie. "Have you been working?"

So they both wanted to change the subject.

Bernard's eyes twitched. He stared at the globe of the lamp above the bed. "It's not that work feels pointless," he said. "It just seems absurd and unnecessary when you have a finite amount of time left in the world."

"You're being maudlin. What about the quartet?"

"I don't give a flying Ford about the quartet. I wish I could sit propped up in bed and read all day and not see anyone."

"Shall I go?"

"Stay. The truth is I hardly read anymore," Bernard said. "Reading reminds me of things I used to feel, and I don't want to be reminded. I'm too exhausted, too disconnected from that part of me. When I read it's impossible to keep from falling asleep. But I can't stay asleep. And you know how I hate to read anything piecemeal. There, I just revealed a secret. The voracious reader reads no longer. I've even soured on biographies."

"You can't stay idle forever," Stan said.

"I'm not. I've been staring for days at the same page of a commission from the Equinox Quintet. I have gigs with them in the fall. It's a set of variations I originally started for one of Rudy's salons, based on the last motive of Scott Joplin's rag 'Solace.' And you knew I was set to conduct graduate composition recitals at UNO? I was working with the department head's *wunderkind*. (I don't get her fascination with him—they're such a conservative bunch in that program and the kid's unregenerately atonal. But you never know what way the aesthetic winds will blow.) The first rehearsal was needlessly strenuous and I came away thinking his thesis project was tripe—a suite from his opera based on *Breakfast at Tiffany's*."

"The movie or the novel?"

"You have to ask? The movie, of course. The piece was pointlessly difficult," Bernard said. "We'd been going through it for over a week and it still sounded like crows cawing. Cardboard has more depth. The little snot came to the last rehearsal with more revisions, rhythms scrawled out in blue ballpoint—on a yellow legal pad, mind you—no key signatures, accidentals all over the place, four time signature changes in as many bars. 'No, *no*, Nanette,' I told him, 'this is totally unacceptable. Sit your butt down and write it out *in finale*, with the codas.' Just because I fucked him a couple of years ago doesn't mean he can take liberties with my time now."

"You screwed him?"

"He wanted it! Anyway, that was long before I knew I'd be conducting his graduate recital. Fast forward: he complains about the rehearsal to his faculty advisor, who slaps me on the wrist and says, 'Indulge him. *Please*. He's the chairman's darling.'" Bernard grimaced, scratched his balding pate. "Instead I called him up at the last minute to say I couldn't do the recital. There wasn't any time to find someone to fill in for me, so he had to postpone. He certainly couldn't conduct it himself—that would have been too accidental even for him. But there wasn't a snowball's chance in hell I'd participate in that crap. I didn't want to conduct a twelve-tone mathematical proof, a jigsaw puzzle where you have to fasten your seatbelt and mount the piece like a hell-bent rodeo horse hurtling toward some nerve-racking, earsplitting finish. I pity the poor undergraduate slave turning pages for the rehearsal pianist, stuck in sight-reading hell counting like a madman under her breath, having to cue the singers with broad gestures and head nods. I *had* to cancel. I probably sullied my reputation with the department, just when I was hitting my stride working with students, too. But you know what? It was worth it. I'm happy I did it. Am I a snob, Stan?"

"Indubitably," Stan said.

"Don't get me wrong. You know I love challenging music. *Harmonielehre*? The rhythm of those opening chords like depth charges? I love that."

Bernard remembered playing John Adams's *The Chairman Dances* with the Brooklyn Philharmonic years ago, the rush that settled into a kind of floating contentment.

When Bernard read notes on the page, he heard the music in his head like people hear an inner voice while reading a book. When Bernard picked up the violin, anxiousness swelled his chest, his adrenaline pumped. From idea to execution, from impassive notation to the warmth in his curled knuckles, from listening to, anticipating how the honeyed voice of the wood at his cheek sounded from gliding the bow across the strings until that nanosecond before decisions had to be made—reactions of his bow-hand to the musicians around him, to the instrument, to the pressure—these were the places where technique, learning to choreograph the movements so that the body remembered them during performance, ameliorated the cold little terrors. The conception of how it should sound abided in him, a voice unique as a fingerprint—astounding, thrilling—the memory of the first time he'd heard the piece sublimely played. Each performance attempted to return to that cadence in his head; each performance summoned that voice of memory.

Bernard shaped his playing to this conception, intuited what colors to scumble, claimed it for his own. But sometimes the emotions evaporated before the core of him that felt could express it, as if he didn't have the wherewithal to move through them. But he was learning from Rudy.

"It's a shame," Bernard said. "Under the right tutelage the kid might have created something worthwhile.

"I was fortunate, Stan. The violin chose me. My earliest memory is with a violin in my hand. Then Professor Bateman came into my life and made me memorize Bach partitas. Bach commandeered my adolescence. But Professor Bateman doted on me and I didn't work one hundred and ten percent. I didn't have enough discipline to become a virtuoso. I skated through college on my gifts. I wrote a couple of preludes, a sonata, some bagatelles, but I'll never be a great soloist."

"I don't know, Bernard. The first time I heard you play the Mozart E-minor with Rutherford Minyard, I got goose pimples all over and cried. You really put your heart into it."

"I work hard now and I know I play with expressiveness," Bernard said. "But I'm not satisfied that I work hard enough, except maybe when Rudy and I play together. I love our dynamic. Those sonatas are so elegant and sad, even in the major, and they require such concentration—their ebullience masks their difficulty. They beg for reciprocity between the piano and violin, a lightness of touch, a graceful lilt, a restraint—all of which Rudy has. He could have had a concert career. But he wanted to be a poet. Life is so funny that way."

Bernard sighed. "Did I ever tell you about when I auditioned for Benjamin Kielmanowicz to get into Juilliard, Stan?"

"You went to UNO."

"I did. But it wasn't my first choice. My mother begged Professor Bateman to arrange a private audition with Maestro Kielmanowicz. We took the train to New York and stayed with her sister; my aunt put us up for a week at her house in Prospect Heights.

"At Maestro's apartment in the Ansonia, my mother sat on a settee in a far corner of his studio while I played. I thought I presented well. 'What do you want to be?' he asked me, clearing his throat. 'A violinist,' I answered solemnly. 'Your interpretation was deficient,' he said, without taking a beat. 'You're not good enough even to be a page turner.'

"I couldn't speak, I couldn't move. I glared at him, too shocked to sob while Mother defiantly asked him to explain himself. He told her that if I didn't know what he meant then I had spent a needless hour of my time, and matter-of-factly showed us to the door.

"When Mother asked what I would do, I said I didn't know. The train ride back was endless. But as soon as we reached New Orleans I went to D. H. Holmes and bought the best stationery I could find, then locked myself in my room and wrote Maestro a long letter thanking him. He telephoned me a week later, telling me how impressed he was by my graciousness and that he had decided to recommend me to Juilliard's admissions committee.

"And then I politely declined, astonishing him and my mother. That's how I went to study with Madame Musson at UNO."

"Well, it seems the story had a happy ending."

"Mother was furious. She never forgave me. To add insult to injury, those four years at UNO were a total washout. I went on a binge. I was quite the library glory hole fiend. But fucking was my major occupation. I collected eager frat boys by the dozen, one right after the other—I was a big top then, can you believe it?—fished them out of Fat Harry's on the weekends. I never let any of them get close to me. Most of them couldn't have cared less; they didn't want intimacy, or to be known by anything as insignificant as a name. But that didn't stop me from hiding my violin when they were there—don't ask me why. Or when I found time to practice; maybe I picked up the violin once a month. Mother was not pleased."

"She knew about this?"

"Apparently someone clued her in, hopefully not to the details. She'd known I was gay since I told her I wanted to kiss Remy Peychaud, on the way to a lesson with Professor Bateman. 'Nothing you can tell me will change how I feel about you,' she said, then added, 'There are things you might do that would disappoint me.' Like smoking, and later mucking up Juilliard. When I moved out of her house to go to school, she qualified it further: 'No matter what you do,' she said, 'I will always love you.' By that time I resented her condescension. Of course I'd just found out the truth about my father.

"After I'd confided to her about Remy Peychaud she'd suggested that we wait until I was older to tell my father—he wouldn't understand. I was afraid of him, so I went along. After that she'd threaten to tell him, to keep me in line. Then all those years later she admitted that he knew. She'd told him everything at the start. She said that I was my own worst critic and that I refused to accept that she had always been proud of me, but I felt betrayed.

"The point of all this is that Maestro Kielmanowicz was right. I wasn't good enough."

"On this one I have to agree with your mother: you are your own worst critic, if only on the subject of your playing."

"Don't misunderstand me, Stan. I love to play. It's a great consolation. I love growing a piece, putting feeling into it. So much depends on what you bring to the music. I learned that from Professor Bateman. He had an unmistakable sound. He's always in my inner ear. I emulate his coloration constantly, his musical personality, his awareness. But the fact is I'm not a great soloist and never will be. Don't argue. I've thought long and hard about this.

"But now that you have me wandering down Lookback Lane, this morning I was listening to NPR and heard an interview with a young cellist in New York for music camp. He came from a farm in Nebraska and it was his first time away from home; his youth orchestra was scheduled to play Gustav Holst's *The Planets* at Carnegie Hall. He sounded so glum, my heart sank. It reminded me of Lenny Stein."

"Who?" Stan asked.

"The lead singer of that garage band, Edith Head. He was from Oklahoma. I used to call him the Tulsa Slut. We tricked almost daily in the practice rooms my first year at UNO."

"You had a tryst with someone every day at school and I didn't know about it?"

"He was the exception to my pattern. Black curly hair, mono brow and sideburns, really dark skin, a thin, long-waisted body? Looked like he never ate and spoke with a sibilant *s*? Come on, Stan, you must remember. He always wore a black leather jacket and the same bleached jeans and scuffed saddle oxfords. We used to smoke pot behind the levee then walk over to the music building. Lenny would slap the leather satchel he carried his music in on top of the upright piano and play the first ten or so bars of 'Für Elise.' I'd sit next to him with my hand on his leg and when he caught a boner I'd suck his long *schlong*. We had the same theory professor.

"Lenny took me home with him for the winter break that year; my mother gave me hell for abandoning her during the holidays. His father was an oil company executive. The Steins had a huge Chanukah party every year at their ranch. I tricked with one of the workmen who came to disassemble the enormous cherrywood table and roll up the Oriental rug and clear them from the dining room. That night while a ten-piece ensemble played fox-trots as couples danced on the parquet floors I fucked Lenny for the first time in his childhood trundle bed, with plastic models of *Star Wars* vessels hanging over us from the ceiling—when he was a kid Lenny wanted to be an astronaut. We were both drunk. He moved to San Francisco and started his own record label called Palindrome. He died in the late Eighties."

"And what does this have to do with the boy on NPR?"

"I'm not sure," Bernard said. "Except that . . . Lenny was gone from the moment he left Oklahoma for UNO—long before he moved to San Francisco. Talking to you about my past I can't help thinking I'm an itinerant. When I lived in New York, I dreamt of New Orleans, when all I'd ever wanted to do before was escape it. It's like some weird stasis. My father was that way. He wanted a place where no one knew him, where he didn't have to worry about satisfying or disappointing anyone.

"Michael would have understood. He always said New York would pulverize me—the noise, the garbage, the inferno subway, the bitter winters, the panhandling. He half-flirted with moving back himself; we lived in the Chelsea Hotel because he didn't want to be trapped in New York. But I loved it there. My friends thought I was crazy for leaving Mecca for Bumfuckegypt. They would never dream of doing it themselves.

"I can hear Michael saying, 'You cannot really return, surely you know that,' and it's true that I had to grow into this life again. Sometimes I forget he died three years ago. It's like I'm having a running conversation with him, a colloquy. I turn to look for Michael, to say something to him. When my father died, the conversation died with him. I didn't have one word left to say to the old man. Not that I'll ever forget the humiliating things he said or did to me. I wish I could forget them."

"Why did you come back, Bernard?"

"I still marvel at the life I had in New York. I played with some interesting performers. I heard all the great ones live. But I couldn't have a career there.

"Right before Michael died, a chair opened up in the Philharmonic, the first one in seven or eight years. A forty-nine-year-old violinist dropped dead of an aneurysm in the Lincoln Center Barnes and Noble, bending over to reach for a book on the bottom shelf. There were twelve-hundred-fifty applicants for the audition to replace him, including me. You could have played brilliantly, been the right person to fill that slot, and if the jury didn't like your interpretation you were screwed. But if you sucked for the seven or eight minutes you had to craft an interpretation of the piece, as I did . . .

"They don't tell you in conservatory that you can spend your life practicing your instrument and not support yourself as a musician, much less maintain your artistic integrity. Orchestras are luxuries and opportunities to play in them have gone from limited to near-nonexistent and dwindling. People would rather throw their money at the next Madonna. I'd have been better off taking typing in high school, like you did. I didn't want to just eke out a living fiddling on the wedding and bar mitzvah circuit, so I came home."

"And then you met Maynard. Do you expect him soon?"

"I'm not sure he'll come today. We had a tiff. Yesterday it rained before dawn, one of those deluges that sends the mind reeling. The thunder woke me. I lay in bed and listened to the rain drumming the roofs of parked cars and pelting my window like retribution. The *staccato* began to let up with the first streaks of light. The crows started in with their racket, like fireworks in my head. I thought I heard strains of Shostakovich's fifteenth quartet on the radio in the nurses' station but I might have imagined it, the morning was so dreary. I had a sense of foreboding.

"Then Maynard showed up and I managed to slip out of bed and go down to the cafeteria with him—not that I dared to eat anything. I stood by the window with a glass of orange juice, staring at the streetlight through the tree limbs and the shadows on the pavement and listening to the cacophony of the cafeteria—the pacing of people down the center aisle, footsteps like water running from a distant faucet, the hushed snickering of a woman reading something maddening in the newspaper, the sounds of chairs scraping the tile floor, tubercular coughs, voices pitched a notch higher than I would have preferred—working it over in my mind, searching for sense in each sound, the gradations of timbre, the pulse, the sighing, breathing, swallowing, snorting, coughing, wondering how I might find harmony, mesh it all together as music. I even gave it a name: 'Touro Infirmary, Sunday Morning, July 9th.' I closed my eyes and gave in to the riot, as if they were playing in my imaginary orchestra pit, allowing myself to drift away, out the window into Uptown as the downpour drenched the city again, drumming the windowpane and sweeping across Prytania Street.

"Then Maynard put his hand on my forehead and grunted. 'Are you all right?' he asked me. He said I looked 'chicken-skinned.' I didn't mind that—it's true—but then he said, 'Why are you sick all of a sudden? Perry Charbonnet has been HIV positive for seventeen years and he's never been sick.'

"For the life of me I couldn't speak. My mouth wouldn't open. I stood at the window and felt dizzy. I couldn't believe he'd actually asked me that."

"I can," Stan said. "He's a foulmouthed brat. You ought to dump him."

"I'm not about to dump him. I miss Maynard when he's not around." Sirens screamed down Prytania. Bernard paused, taking in Stan's expression. "Why do you look shocked? Maynard didn't mean it the way it sounds. You've never liked any of my boyfriends."

"I liked Michael."

"Because he was white."

"I don't like Maynard because he's the spoiled son of a rich Republican judge, Bernard. You're the one who sees only black and white."

"That's not true."

"I don't understand how you don't get it, Bernard. We grew up encouraged to think there are only racial divisions in the South, if we thought about it at all. But it's about class. We were poor, Bernard."

"You weren't that poor."

"My family may have been in 'high cotton,' as my father called it, compared to people like Robin Stark and his sister, but we were poor, Bernard. Moving to New York, you should have discovered that. We both went to Catholic school on scholarship and the bastard stepchild of the state university system. You worked in a bar and I worked in a grocery store."

"It was your father's corner market, Stan. Don't romanticize. My family was always borderline broke and there's nothing romantic about it. I worked for two years in high school to save enough tip money to buy my violin because my mother couldn't afford a new one and I hated making due with a crappy rental. Do you know what she said when I left home instead of pursuing Juilliard? 'If you can afford to live on your own in New Orleans then you can afford to pay for college.'"

"It doesn't change the fact that Maynard hasn't had to work for one goddamn thing he ever wanted," Stan said. "Not even for you, except now when you're lying in the hospital. But if you want it, I'll never say anything about your lover again. Not a goddamn thing."

Bernard had to admit that if Stan questioned why he had come down with hepatitis, he'd have the grace not to ask him. But Bernard was sure that Maynard meant only to suggest that he take better care of himself—no booze, no weed, no poppers, no meat or fatty foods. And Maynard was right. Most of the long-term survivors they knew had had one or two terrible infections before taking more responsibility for their health, deciding to eat well, rest, become centered, deal with issues, join support groups, stop boozing and drugging and whoring around, go on disability, and generally make survival their full-time occupation. But Bernard was not interested in behaving like a good little boy. The mere thought of it exhausted him.

"Please don't be angry, Stan," he said. "I know it's my fault I got hepatitis. My doctor told me to get vaccinated eons ago. I just put off doing it. And I shouldn't have eaten those oysters at Port of Call."

"Oysters. Right."

"What do you mean, 'right'? I went there after a gig a couple of weeks ago. You automatically assumed someone sat on my face?"

"Don't pretend to be offended, Bernard. You've never made a secret of your proclivity for rooting in boys' anuses like a hog after truffles."

"You think I deserve this!" Bernard bellowed.

"I think no such thing, Bernard. Haven't you been telling me lately that you wish you could come to the point in your life where if you stick your tongue up somebody's ass, you at least know the guy's name? *You* said it, not me."

Bernard felt his stomach rising to his throat. "Can you help me into the bathroom, Stan? I think I'm going to throw up."

Stan gave Bernard privacy to do his business. He felt so weak, as though he'd been carrying something heavy for too long. He leaned over the toilet and prepared to retch, his mouth open with labored breathing. But nothing came up. He stood at the sink and looked at himself in the mirror. He needed to shave and brush his teeth, but it would have to wait; he was too tired now. Who was going to look at him, anyway? He thought of the boy in the emergency room—even in this agitated state it prompted stirrings. He'd seemed so familiar. A trick of light made Bernard focus on his eyelashes in the mirror, jolted him. Then memory punished him.

Bernard shuddered. He closed his eyes and saw the other boy, recalled the contours and textures of his body, the resigned expression on his face. What had he done? The details flooded back. He knocked his head painfully against the mirror, trying to make them stop.

Alarmed at the sound, Stan pushed the door open. Bernard collapsed into his arms. Stan eased him back to the bed.

"He had the face of an angel," Bernard whispered.

"What are you talking about?" Stan asked, settling Bernard against the pillows.

"A freshman I picked up in front of Audubon Park."

Stan's tension eased. "Another frat boy," he said. "Your specialty."

"He wasn't a frat boy," Bernard said. "He was in the ROTC program at Tulane, taking summer classes. I've never told anyone about him."

"When was this?"

"Nineteen eighty-one. July third, to be precise."

Ancient history.

That was the day the report of a rare cancer "seen in homosexuals" appeared in the *New York Times*, but Bernard and his buddies hadn't heard about it yet and even if they had it wouldn't have applied to them. They had no way of knowing that half of them eventually would get it themselves or that four of them would end up dead, one from a stroke at twenty-nine, one a suicide, and the other two from AIDS complications. They'd just seen *Harold and Maude* and were partying in the parking lot of the suburban cinema at the Sena Mall, torqued up on rotgut Taaka vodka and orange juice they drank from a plastic jug, smoking cigarettes and listening to The Cure in a pool of tangerine light from the street lamps. The rain had let up as they exited the theater. Bernard drove off alone.

Even after graduating Bernard tended to hunt guys a little too free-range for Stan's taste, usually students and frats from Tulane and Loyola Universities. Stan had said it always amazed him how smooth Bernard was about sussing them out of his old feeding grounds—Audubon Park, the Tilton Library, the Student Union, and Fat Harry's tavern on St. Charles Avenue, where he had been quite the fixture in the old days. Bernard didn't pick them on demeanor alone. His scowl may have masked his hunger, may have undermined their self-confidence, but they went with Bernard willingly. He assumed the boys knew what was going on. He'd walk up to them and talk, learn bits and pieces of their lives, a condensed version of secrets, stories collected, partners disclosed, cryptic messages discerned; Bernard listened in earnest and it confused them. They liked his bravery. He let them off the hook from rejection. Now and then someone escaped him, smelling entrapment or walking away embarrassed, but whether they were naïve or jaded, Bernard usually got what he wanted.

He tore down rain-slick St. Charles Avenue along Audubon Park beneath the canopy of oak boughs, the ink-black street mottled with streetlight, past dim mansion facades. He spotted a boy in a blue U.S. Navy tank top jogging downtown, away from the campus, his shoulder blades peeking from the cut of his shirt like the rapidly beating wings of a hummingbird, all a blur, then glimpsed the boy receding in the rearview mirror.

He swung the MG convertible into the intersection, across the streetcar tracks in the neutral ground of the median, and doubled back a few blocks, cruising with one hand on the wheel, his elbow hanging out of the car, and his other hand jammed into the top of his half-buttoned khakis on his hardening cock. He circled the boy twice, maybe three times. The boy's awkward gait, the glance over his shoulder when the MG was about to pass, told Bernard the boy knew he was being tailed, but he kept a good pace and in the convoluted logic of the hunt Bernard read the absence of hostility as a signal for him to home in.

The boy stopped running, walked hunched over with his arms rocking back and forth, trying to catch his breath. Bernard pulled the car across the neutral ground again and drove past him up the avenue. Turning onto Eleonore Street (Professor Bateman lived farther down, toward the river), he parked a few yards from the dark corner under an oak tree and idled the engine.

He lit a cigarette and watched in the rearview mirror as the boy approached the intersection, stopped in the neutral ground, and turned to face the car. He did a skittish dance of indecision and curiosity, crossing to the other side of the street and back again, his flaccid dick flopping inside his nylon running shorts that stuck to him from sweat; the seam rode up the crack of his ass. Bernard waited, his arm draped across the back of the seat, until finally the boy looked both ways and crossed the eastbound lane, the median, the westbound lane, and walked down the other side of Eleonore Street, past dark mansions behind stone fences and wrought-iron gates, crossed the street, and approached the car.

He appeared to be Asian, and was smooth and thin with sinewy legs, a small chest, and long arms. He wore a crew cut and sweet black-framed glasses with an elastic headband around the back of his head. He wouldn't look at Bernard. He didn't know what to do with his hands; one went defensively to his stomach, slipped up under his shirt, stroked the taut muscles and black down at his navel. He was definitely curious but stood far enough away to make a mad dash if necessary.

"What's up?" Bernard asked.

The boy folded his arms and kept scanning the avenue for cars.

Bernard asked if he was ROTC, and he nodded. When asked if he was a freshman the boy said no. Bernard felt sure he was lying. "Want to come to my place?" he said, as though it were the natural next question.

"I guess so," the boy answered, caught off guard.

Bernard told him to get in the car and reached to unlock the passenger door. The boy opened the door and slid in with a languidness painful to watch, then slouched in his seat. He asked Bernard if they were going far. Bernard ignored him, imagining the boy lathering his cock with spit, what it would be like to bury his face in the boy's ass. Soon, he thought, gripping the wheel.

The MG careened along St. Charles Avenue amid the leaden thunder of streetcars, fifty or so blocks to Canal and into the French Quarter to Chartres Street, across from the Hotel Provincial. Bernard parked on the street then led the boy by the hand to the wrought-iron gated alley between two Creole townhouses, down the dark alley that seemed to sway beneath his feet, and across the courtyard to the *garçonnière*. After fumbling with the keys he unlocked the door and they went inside. Bernard nodded for the boy to sit on the sofa. The boy obeyed.

Bernard went to the bathroom and took a long piss, then stood in the hall transfixed, watching the boy pick at the black hair on his legs, studying it. The boy looked up. Bernard retreated to the kitchen, unable to stand the gaze, and poured himself a bourbon.

He returned to the living room, sat beside the boy on the sofa, put his hand on the boy's leg. The boy stared at the hand, his leg trembling. Bernard gently asked him his name—he mumbled something Bernard didn't remember—then took him to the bedroom.

He pulled the boy's tank top over his head, slid the gym shorts and jock down his legs, and held the boy's elbow as he stepped out of them. He groped the boy.

"What's this?" the boy asked.

"Poppers," Bernard said. "Amyl nitrate. Inhale slowly."

"What's it do?"

"*Ssh!* You'll see."

"Oh!" the boy exclaimed.

Bernard kicked off his bucks, climbed out of his khakis, fumbled with the buttons on his shirt. He pushed the boy down by his shoulders, grabbed his skull, and, holding the boy's jaw in his other hand, fed him his cock, easing the boy's head back and forth, making him swallow all of it.

He pulled the boy up and shoved him onto the bed, examined the boy's erection then rolled him over onto his stomach so that he was stretched out beneath him. He kneaded the boy's neck and shoulder muscles. His lips traced the ridge of the boy's spine down to the crack of his ass, his hands kneading the cheeks as he buried his face between them, lathering the pucker with his tongue. The boy moaned. Bernard spat and the boy spasmed, then shuddered as Bernard slid one, two, three fingers inside him, trilling in and out. The kid was all nerve endings.

It drove Bernard crazy. He greased his cock with Crisco from the can under his bed and, snarling, sank himself into the boy, his muscles knotted, the smack of his groin against the boy's buttocks like wind thudding glass. He heard the boy's lungs deflate, watched red flush from his face downward to the cleft of his shoulder blades. The boy coughed and whimpered, gripping the sheets with both hands and writhing as Bernard worked his cock deep inside, pumping slowly.

Bernard felt nothing but relief radiating from the rhythm of their fucking, saw nothing as he ground the boy into the bed, his muscles contracting as he drew out the supple line like a bow across strings, slow, measured, controlled, suspended in sensation, hovering in beauty, oblivious to the boy.

He came perfectly, like rain, then pulled out and stood, reflexively flicking on the desk lamp. The boy didn't respond when Bernard asked him if he came.

Bernard turned around and saw blood. It was everywhere: on the blue sheets, on Bernard's dick, smeared on his abdomen, on the cheeks of the boy's ass, in the small of his back. Bernard ran to the bathroom and returned with towels. He flipped the boy over, holding a towel under his ass. The boy raised his forearm against the light and bit his bottom lip.

"Why didn't you tell me I was hurting you?"

"I couldn't," the boy whispered.

"I'm taking you to the hospital," Bernard said, not believing he'd suggested it.

"No!" the boy cried. His eyelashes flashed.

A line of seraphs blinked in Bernard's mind. "You're hemorrhaging," he said.

"I can't," the boy insisted, shaking violently. "My parents, the Navy." He began to sob.

Bernard crawled into bed and held him, told him everything would be all right. After a time the boy fell silent and Bernard propped him up in the bed with the towel between his legs.

Bernard felt bile rising to his throat. He couldn't stand the blood. He leapt from the bed and ran to the john, stooped over the commode, vomited. He ran his hands under the tap. He gargled water and spat into the sink, imagining different scenarios and outcomes, all grim.

He couldn't show the boy his fear. He didn't want him to panic. He took the edge off with two short, neat bourbons. He remembered smoking a few cigarettes one after another.

Eventually the bleeding stopped, Bernard could not recall how long it took, and something of his cold, rational self emerged. He carried the boy to the bathroom, suddenly aware that the radio was playing a Mozart piano sonata. He sat the boy on the toilet and undid his laces, realizing he had screwed him with his tennis shoes on. He pulled the shoes and socks off the boy's big, flat feet and led him to the tub, washed him, and toweled him dry. They didn't speak. This was an intimacy Bernard did not want and he refused the boy's glances, knowing it must hurt him.

The kid climbed into his shorts and sat on the edge of the bed. Bernard asked if he was okay. The boy said his glasses were missing. Bernard hunted around the apartment until he found them under the bed.

While Bernard searched, the boy studied framed photographs on the nightstand beside the bed. There was one of Bernard taken on the platform at the Charing Cross Road underground station in London, the walls behind him layered like a de Kooning painting, with ripped and torn handbills and a Campari poster of a well-dressed woman in a Givenchy coat standing on the ledge of a building (like a still from a Pedro Almodóvar film), with the wickedly clever caption to the effect that she would jump if offered another *pinot grigio*. There was one of a kid standing with an Indian chief in a headdress at the Grand Canyon, and a sepia-tinted vintage photo of a teenage girl in a sailor's uniform in front of the McCrory's five-and-dime store on Canal Street.

"That's my maternal grandmother at Mardi Gras in 1924," Bernard told him. The boy picked up a photograph of a nearly bald kid in a plaid shirt and Buster Brown shorts at the entrance to the Zephyr ride at Pontchartrain Beach Amusement Park. "And that's me." Bernard took the picture and handed over the glasses. "My father liked to terrorize me with roller coasters."

Bernard drove the boy back to Tulane, swinging the car into the parking lot at Sharp Hall, the boy's dormitory. The two sat in the front seat with their heads bowed. Bernard checked the rearview mirror. Getting his nerve up, the boy asked Bernard if he could write to him, his tongue cleaving to the roof of his mouth as he asked for Bernard's address, his voice catching. Bernard couldn't tell him no. He scribbled it down on the back of a gas credit card receipt with a pen he kept in the glove compartment. The boy's shoes made a grating sound as he crossed the gravel parking lot to the dormitory.

Bernard drove back to his apartment with the top up, the stereo blaring. Inside he stripped the sheets from the bed and stuffed them with the bloodied towels into a black plastic garbage bag then jammed the bag into the dumpster in the backyard behind the carriage house. He scoured the tub and sink, blotted the mattress ticking with cold water until most of the blood was gone. Then he opened the bedroom windows to air out the mattress.

He put bedding on the couch and lay with the television on, thinking how lucky he felt to have gotten out of the situation unscathed. If he had taken the boy to the hospital, what would have happened? Had he given any real thought to the consequences, he might have owned up to what he had done. But he wanted to be rid of the boy. He lit a joint to kill the smell of sex in the room. The next morning he ate a bowl of cornflakes like nothing had happened.

"Geez," Stan said.

"I wasn't prepared for the aftermath," Bernard told him. "Over the summer break the boy sent me long letters—quiet, lonely letters written in a crabbed hand. I read only a few of them. He told me he was from Guam. His father was an American officer stationed in San Diego, an engineer. His mother was a schoolteacher from Seoul. He was an only child. His family moved a lot. They vacationed most of August in the West. The letters were travelogues, descriptions of what he had done, the places he went, the books he read on the road in the family car, how long it took to get where they were going. He wrote me from Yellowstone, sent me postcards from as far away as Mount Rushmore. His last letter was from the Grand Canyon. He wrote about coming to a ledge at the North Rim and watching the canyon deepen as the sun set, an enigma of light and shadow like his feelings for me, he said. He never wrote about what happened, what I did to him, never asked why I didn't respond to his letters. I remember thinking he wrote them at night, that they were like nocturnes.

"Now that I think of it, I must have read quite a few of them. I got a steady stream. I tried to write and tell him to stop but thought it might encourage him to continue and I didn't want that. I knew eventually the letters would stop coming. But I couldn't take getting them, their very existence upset me. I don't know why I wasn't content to simply throw them away. I had to shred them. I cut them into strips with scissors and stuffed the scraps in the trash. Are you surprised?"

"Nothing you do surprises me anymore, Bernard. Did you ever see him again?"

"I assume he returned to Tulane in the fall but I didn't see him. The first few months of autumn I avoided my old haunts. Gradually I pushed him from my mind. He would have graduated as an ensign, gone off to Officer Candidate School, maybe served in the Gulf War."

Bernard remembered the *solfège* of cicadas in the dark park eighteen years ago, the smell of freshly mown golf courses, the old oak trees, all those boys he'd fucked on those humid summer nights like a sauna. He flashed to his dream, the horror on the boy's face, his overwhelming beauty. The boy was gone and Bernard had not thought of him for years—or so he'd believed. Somehow he'd become the locus of regret. He wondered what the boy looked like after all this time.

"I lost my virginity in the sleazy Crescent Motel on Airline Highway," he told Stan, "to a mortician with a bushy mustache and the smoothest palms who worked at the Bultman Funeral Home. He pummeled me face down on a twin bed then ran into the bathroom to get the shit off his dick after he came. I saw him hunch over the toilet bowl, retching, watched him rinse his mouth out with the shot of whiskey he had ready in a tumbler. I lay on my stomach *filled* with him, watching the blue neon sign pulse VACANCY through a ripped curtain while he got dressed, feeling nothing but shame."

Bernard wiped his eyes with the back of his hand. He heard Stan's slow, measured breathing. Look at the repugnance on his face, Bernard thought. Stan could darken a room with his sulking.

"If the boy is alive"—somehow Bernard couldn't bear to think of him dead—"and he remembers me, I don't want it to be as the gargoyle who first fucked him."

Bernard sensed that Stan understood none of this, that it fell upon deaf ears. His mood soured.

"You relish it, don't you, Stan?"

"What are you talking about?"

"My regret."

"Don't be silly," Stan said.

"I scarred him for life, Stan."

"You're being melodramatic. Not that you were blameless, but boys are resilient. Look at you."

"How in hell do you know?" he muttered. "*Were you there?*"

"Thankfully I wasn't," Stan said. "Maybe that was the wrong thing to say."

"When Michael died, I lost interest in life. I never said anything because I didn't want to be a nuisance."

"Don't try to guilt-trip me, Bernard."

"I'm not. I hung on, didn't I?

A rap on the door startled them.

A young man in a white lab coat and blue surgical scrubs entered the room. He had long dreadlocks, a gold ring in his nose, and wore a Queer Nation pin in his lapel and a stethoscope around his neck. "Hey, there, I'm Terry," he announced cheerfully, accustomed to interrupting *tête-à-têtes*. "I'm here to check your bilirubin count. Bilirubins make you itch. But first I have to take your temperature."

Terry popped the digital thermometer in Bernard's mouth. When it beeped he regarded the tiny monitor.

"Normal," he said.

"That's probably the only thing normal about me," Bernard said, adding as he held out his arm, "Do you think you could hide the syringe? I'm a little squeamish about needles. If I see it, I'll pass out."

"Should I leave?" Stan asked.

"Actually, may I leave too?" Bernard said.

"You stay put," Terry told Bernard, putting a hand on his shoulder. "That won't be necessary," he said to Stan. "Unless you want to leave. This will only take a minute."

He rolled Bernard's left arm toward him and rested the elbow on the bed. Wrapping a rubber cord as a tourniquet below the POSITIVE tattoo on the biceps, he thumped the crook of the arm, searching for a vein, swabbed it, and proffered a syringe.

Bernard winced. He averted his gaze to the window as his blood filled the tube. His mouth was dry but he wouldn't ask Stan to get him a glass of water. He didn't want to be alone. He glanced at the marks on his arm from scratching. Tears streamed from the corners of his eyes.

"I heard from Bartly Dunn," Stan said, to fill the lull in talk. "He asked after you. I told him I was seeing you today."

"Is that supposed to cheer me up, Stan?"

"Sorry. Bartly is the Bearer of Bad News, isn't he? He can be grimmer than Grimm, sometimes."

The nurse withdrew the needle, swabbed Bernard's arm with a cotton ball, and stretched a bandage over it. He slipped the filled vial into the pocket of his lab coat. "All done," he said.

"There goes the umpteenth tube of blood," Bernard blurted. "Is the needle gone yet?" he asked.

"It's gone, Mr. Percy. You take care now, you hear?"

The young man eased the door closed behind him. As the latch clicked, Bernard grabbed Stan's hand.

Stan smiled, elated. "I'm sorry," he said. "I should leave, and let you rest."

"Don't go yet. I'll just drift into a fog again."

Bernard closed his eyes and, in spite of himself, dozed off. Stan sat frozen, afraid that if he moved he'd wake him. The television murmured over the next bed for the man in the coma. Day had drained completely from the room; outside it was growing darker by degrees. Window lights began checkerboarding the skyline with pinspots.

Stan looked down at Bernard's hand in his own, noticed the gold ring on Bernard's left thumb. Was that new? A gift from Maynard? What was that relationship about? Stan had never understood Bernard's attraction to Maynard. He assumed that Bernard had been easy prey to Maynard's blandishments. Bernard loved the *tremolo* of first love but got bored by its more *legato* passages. Perhaps Maynard was that way too, because they both tricked around. But if Bernard loved him, it must mean Maynard had pleasure to give. And being Bernard's boyfriend couldn't be easy. He preferred his sex clandestine and anonymous. Undoubtedly, Bernard kept Maynard at arm's length. Much as he hated to admit it, Stan had to respect Maynard for hanging in there.

Still, there must be little pleasure in the calculus of Bernard's love. Bernard seemed to equate missing someone with loving him. He had learned this from his father, who from what Stan had heard kept Bernard on tenterhooks, drifting in and out of his life with unpredictable arrivals and abrupt departures, promising to be somewhere then disappearing. Love meant absence to Bernard. He'd been conditioned to accept pain as the price of love—a cruel means of control.

Then again, how many times had Stan poured himself into whatever personality attracted him at the moment, those late afternoons when he had a reprieve from the demands of work and school and family, when he felt most alone? In spite of all this, he felt vindicated in his judgment of Maynard.

Sometimes Bernard frightened him, the way he brooded. What was that about? What did he really feel? He wished he could see through Bernard's eyes. Stan thought of the long letter Bernard had written to him from New York during his first winter there. One phrase in particular stood out: *Winter itself coils in response to some internal mechanism.* Bernard said he heard colors in music, green apples and swirling yellow leaves, or a bite in the air. Stan sometimes had the sinking feeling it was Bernard who should have been the writer. It wasn't hard for Stan to tell stories about himself because it wasn't really him, he was really pretty empty and the stories only served to gloss over it. He feared that emptiness more than anything. So he made believe, invented little dramas because that was what New Orleanians did.

"How long was I conked out?" Bernard asked suddenly.

"Ten minutes, maybe."

"That's a start," Bernard said. "I'm so tired, Stan. Are you going to jot all this down when you get home? It wouldn't be the first time. I know everything I told you is on the record—that's always the case with you writers. You take copious notes on everything. Michael ransacked my life for his little *roman à clef*, remember? Don't worry, you have my permission. But do me a favor: if you write about this, fictionalize it more. I don't want to feel poached the way I did when I finally read the manuscript of *The Hotel Enola*. It was too creepy."

Stan tried not to react visibly, though the remark stung him and inwardly he was cringing. Had he ever betrayed Bernard's confidences in fiction? It was true he took inspiration from Bernard. How could he resist the impulse to write about him? And this was raw stuff. Stan remembered details from Michael's novel, about having sex with Bernard, how the clavicle of Bernard's chest always blushed when he came, how he made little grunts of pleasure, how Bernard called his foreskin a "turtleneck." For the Bernard character, fucking was artifice and lust hurt him. He had a visceral sensation from beauty. During sex he might give what he thought his partner wanted but

felt only detachment himself, numbness, which prevented him from coming despite the relentless rocking of his body. He might as well be fucking
the wall, it was so rudimentary. What business did Stan have knowing such
things about Bernard?

Where had that come from? He thought about what embarrassed him. He
had always imagined Bernard making love without exertion, his lips parted
in ecstasy, his smile rich with irony and repose. And after all, who knew how
much of it Michael had invented? Even so, Stan knew that he would likely
write down the scene in the hospital, because it was his life too and it was
the only thing he knew how to do. Hadn't Bernard always said he wanted
Michael to write a novel about him, so that long after they were gone there
would be that book? For Bernard, books were immortal, or so he said. But
that wasn't true, Stan thought. Books languish and die unread. If people
don't burn them first.

"I'm exhausted," Bernard said. "I need to close my eyes again for a minute."

"Do you want me to leave now?"

"Stay until I fall asleep."

"Fine. I'll come back tomorrow."

"Do you know what Maynard said to me last night? He said we were a lot
alike—you and me. Does that surprise you?"

"Not really."

"You know, Stan, when I look at you I see myself as we were about ten
years ago. It's like you're a mirror."

Bernard's hand slipped from Stan's palm.

2.

Stan tiptoed across the room, slid soundlessly through the doorway, crept
past the nurse's station, and took the elevator down to the lobby then stood
in the ambulance well at the emergency room entrance and lit a cigarette. A
young intern in green surgical scrubs and a navy down vest huddled nearby,
also smoking. Every time Stan had a cigarette he cursed Bernard for getting
him hooked as a freshman at UNO. Stan nursed his cigarette, feeling like a
deserter. He inhaled deeply; smoke seared his lungs, grew inside his head,
fanned out through his mouth and nostrils, whirled in the windy ambulance

well. The world seemed tentative; he felt disjointed. He dropped the cigarette to the pavement and crushed it with his foot. He looked at his watch; he'd been with Bernard almost two hours.

Bernard's story had scalded him. It encapsulated Bernard; everything Stan knew about him seemed compressed into it like snapshots in an album. It contained motivation, psychology, Bernard's recollection of history projected into mirrors of an infinite regress, past, present, future. But he wondered if Bernard had told him all of it. Why did this kid haunt Bernard so? Had the boy's letters declared his love for Bernard? Did he despair at never hearing from Bernard again? What about the boy's complicity in his undoing?

And why had Bernard allowed this glimpse into himself now? Rilke wrote that our deaths bloom from within us. Was it some failure of imagination on Stan's part not to have heard panic underneath Bernard's bravado, existential terror that his days were truly numbered? The thought chilled Stan. He could no longer pretend to himself that time wasn't running out.

What was it like to be this man, Stan wondered. Bernard had once told him that Tchaikovsky said music was not the expression of emotion but of the memory of emotion. Did Bernard feel anything as a child, until he felt loss? Did he ever feel joy, ever feel real intimacy? Was he able to say, "I felt this"? He might have remembered moments lived but did he understand them? Emotion was retrospective, it required self-awareness, recognition, epiphany. At least that's what Stan believed. Michael had written that for Bernard desire was motion—he wanted sex to take him somewhere—and sex was the tincture that infused everything.

What if he'd told Bernard he used to watch him cruising the third floor men's room in Earl K. Long Library? That walking home from the student newspaper office one night, he'd seen Bernard parking his car on the grass under a live oak tree near the Popp Fountain in City Park and followed him into the woods, and another time followed him at a discreet distance throughout the Quarter. He'd expected to be caught, but Bernard went about his business oblivious. What had Stan learned about Bernard that he hadn't already suspected? Nothing really, except what an ordinary life he led in New Orleans, although surely he scored more than Stan did.

Do I resent him? Stan wondered. Probably. Bernard had an essential optimism—or arrogance, depending on one's outlook—that all of his life experiences were part and parcel of his growth as an artist. He savored experience rather than endured it. How else was he to survive, if he didn't think that way? He had faith that he had something to say in his music, that people would get something out of it. Stan couldn't say that about his writing, at least not yet. He'd written that piece for an anthology that won a gay literary prize and found his face in the Vivant section of the newspaper one Friday last spring but sometimes he wondered if he had ever written one true thing besides that. As his twenty-fifth high school reunion approached he had no novel and it bothered him. If he had been made of heartier stuff, he might have locked himself in his apartment for a lost weekend, took some speed, and cranked out crap, just to say he had finished one. He had come up in the world from his life as a clerk stocking and blocking the dog food aisle in his father's suburban market—he'd been a paralegal in a larger Southern firm, well paid with three weeks vacation and domestic partnership benefits. But he'd left that to pursue a dream he wasn't sure existed, or if it did that he could achieve it.

His love life wasn't much better. Stan found himself arguing with himself against doing what his heart told him to. All of the loves of his life had been different and in different degrees, including his new boyfriend, Taylor. This morning Taylor had wanted to have sex and Stan had wanted to work on his writing. They had sex. Afterward Stan couldn't decide if he'd wanted to work to avoid the sex or vice versa. Everything seemed false to him, like the sentiments in pop song lyrics or canned sitcom laughter. The question was, was it better to have even this experience? We love them and they abandon us; we yield to them, acquiesce as if sex might allow us a privileged glimpse into the psyches of others, and still they leave us.

He'd thought he loved Bernard for the qualities he now realized he envied, believed himself indifferent to Bernard's penchant for throwing caution to the wind, what Stan saw as his capriciousness. The fact was that Bernard had been a boundary. He made Stan recognize how sheltered his own life was.

Night had deliquesced into mist; watercolor silhouettes of distant city spires agitated behind the scrim at their point of evanescence, tawdry auguries of death. The dip in air pressure impending another storm made Stan breathless. He felt empty, sucked into vertigo, outside of time. He crossed the street, worrying the keys in his pocket. A green-and-white NOPSI electrical service truck nearly struck him. Wind whipped the trees, scattering leaves and plastic bags across his path. The weather had changed so quickly. He scurried down the cracked, buckling sidewalk, rounded the corner of Washington Avenue and Prytania Street where the old skating rink had been turned into a little mall of shops.

He crossed at the corner and stopped in front of the Garden District Book Shop, took a long look at the phantom self reflected in the window, superimposed across the display of books. His image blurred as he stepped closer to the glass for shelter and copies of the anthology with his coming-out piece emerged into focus before him.

Stan had chosen to write about what he and Robin Stark had done together for the anthology. He remembered the cicadas at the marshy riverbank pulsing through the willows, the lapping of the water, the buzz of mosquitoes, the smell of mosquito spray. It felt like Southern Gothic but it had been real. Stan thought he had never written anything so honest. He wondered if anyone saw the anger shimmering off the page in graphic, clinical detail. The indictment.

In middle school, Stan and Robin were the kids no one else spoke to, except each other. During recess Stan shared his lunch with Robin. They would sit together and read the sappy love poetry they'd written. Robin's legs were always bruised with welts from his father's belt. The same was true of his sister, Lily. How parents who'd named their children after a flower and a bird could beat them, Stan could not fathom. Robin was the first person he talked into standing up for himself. He'd convinced Robin to call the police about his parents' abuse; Robin and Lily were subsequently placed in a foster home. Stan had adored Robin. He thought Robin looked like Leonard Whiting, whom he'd gone to see thirteen times in *Romeo and Juliet* two years before, he had such a crush.

By the time they were in high school Robin had turned into a jock but they'd remained friends. Stan remembered how he sat in the Volkswagen at the Time Saver convenience store while Robin got beer. "Get some Off spray, will you?" he'd called from the Beetle.

They'd walked along River Road, between the meandering west bank levee and ominous oak trees lining the Mississippi. Twenty minutes from suburban New Orleans orange groves and fruit and vegetable stands appeared, road signs, mile markers, an occasional water tower cropping up on odd vistas of flat delta landscape. The sky glowed like Tang, from the oil refinery on the east bank; the lights of the refinery shimmered on the inky river water as darkness rolled in. The crisp air smelled of sulfur and milkweed and burning leaves. About a hundred-fifty yards past the Chalmette-Algiers ferry landing, between the heave of the levee and the muddy lip of bank in the river's *batture* (Robin pronounced it *batcher*), they reached a small grove of cypress and oak trees and scrub magnolia. Stan wondered how Robin had discovered it.

One six pack of Moosehead was all it took. Robin let Stan slide his jeans down his hairy blond legs and take him in his mouth. Spent brass bullet casings, a few beer cans gnarled by target practice, littered the spot where Stan knelt in the soft river silt and wet grass, his eyes tearing as he parted Robin's legs and traced with his nose an invisible line in Robin's bush, the tangle of blond pubic curls. He cupped Robin's balls, reveling in the smell of talc and sweat, the buttery taste of Robin's thick cock. After he swallowed Robin's brine, Robin pulled him up by the shoulders and kissed him, tasting his own seed as his mouth inhaled Stan's tongue. Stan came without touching himself.

They'd drifted apart after that night, their friendship unable to survive the awesome power of the forbidden territory they'd traversed. In their senior year at Archbishop Shaw, Robin was accepted into the diocesan seminary college north of Covington, Louisiana, exposing him to the ridicule of his jock friends. But one foggy Sunday morning just before he was to begin classes, a train ran over his rickety Volkswagen Beetle in the Westwego pinewoods. The foster family insisted Robin's death had been an accident—his car had stalled on the railroad tracks—but at his tenth-year class reunion Lily told Stan that the car keys had been in the breast pocket of Robin's white button-down shirt, not the ignition. He'd also left a note which their foster mother destroyed. Lily told Stan she believed Robin had been in love with him. Stan told Lily it was heavy crap to lay on him at the reunion.

The rain wouldn't hold off much longer; Stan knew he should go inside the bookstore or be on his way. He turned up his collar against the wind.

Stan felt weighted down with circumstance. The ideal of an ardor so unfathomable it led one to sacrifice everything for one hour of love no longer existed for him. But it had once. Would he go back to that hour, to that sense of triumph he carried with him to this very day, when he'd done his best for the gay community, kneeling in the mud for love? Unquestionably, he told himself. But was he willing to accept that he might never again write anything as real, live without regret no matter how impossible it might seem? He'd always believed that his experiences would lead to something larger. What if that was a lie?

Stories reminded people of who they were, where they came from. And the importance of stories came not with telling the incident but from the context. Memory changed experience, Stan knew that. None of the men he ever took up with reminded him of Robin. Those years had been far away. He had not planned to forget them. But the fact of them begged a rain of questions. He had felt this way once. It was like him to recognize this too late. It crossed his mind that he might not be able to forget everything he had remembered today. His inability to foresee outcomes hampered him at every turn. The thought struck him: that's what his novel should be about.

Stan closed his eyes and a picture from years before surfaced. Bernard was standing in candlelight in Rutherford Minyard's home in the French Quarter, flirting with the nerdy violist from the music school. "Don't fret it," he said, twiddling with the fob of his pocket watch. The pun flew completely over the young man's head. Bernard glanced his way as he ambled into the dining room humming "Under a Blanket of Blue," his silhouette framed in the entrance. Stan recalled Bernard's vintage three-button worsted wool tuxedo, the shimmer of fabric as he passed, the English calfskin pumps beneath frayed trouser cuffs, the threadbare elegance. Bernard had been tall and thin before starting at the gym a few years later. Now he was rail-thin again. But the contours of his jawbone, cheeks, and forehead beneath the buzz cut and goatee still suggested beauty.

Rutherford's salon followed a concert at the music school. Who else had been there? Michael Stroud, Violet Watkins, Roscoe Claiborne, Patricia McCall. They'd listened to Rutherford and Bernard perform the *menuetto* movement from Mozart's violin and piano sonata in E minor. As Rutherford sat at the piano, Bernard positioned his violin on the chin rest under his cheek—his cheek seemed to clench the instrument—and with a flick of the wrist tapped the cambering page of sheet music on the stand with the tip of his bow.

When Bernard rehearsed, he'd touch his middle finger to his tongue before turning a page, tug at his earlobe when he read, his imperious eyes scanning the score as his bowing cajoled the instrument to plow through an *allegro*, wending his way through the exposition, the violin singeing the air. He'd stop, draw a pencil from behind his ear, announce, "More *legato*, top of bar thirty," and mark the score with scratches on the page. But in performance he rarely consulted the score, referring instead to the picture of it in his head as he sat on the edge of his chair, eyes closed, torso pivoting gently, tapping time with his foot, thrashing the strings incisively with what he called his "impasto" when the composer called for *brio*.

Bernard was so present in the music, delighting in surprises big and small, scowling during a passage as if beauty had assaulted his senses. He had superb technique. Stan envied his immersion—the delicious angle formed by fore-arm, elbow, and arm, the comma of Bernard's wrist as he pulled the bow across the strings, the fluid trilling of his fingertips over the fingerboard, the incredible lightness of his stance lending the impression of defying gravity. He was incapable of ugliness. His playing could stir even the coldest listener. Standing near the piano, arms folded, Stan had listened with the yearning of one who'd always wished to play himself.

The sight had inspired Stan. The need to give voice to it overwhelmed him. He'd drafted a sketch for a story that would contain what he felt that evening. But how do you describe experience without dissecting it into paltry explanations? He tried to write the scene, describing Bernard's mannerisms, his composure. The words wilted feeling, evaporated emotion. He'd sit with pen in hand and brood, searching for a portal. If he was having a good day, words trickled out. Sometimes the launchpad would be a dream Stan had written down, half awake, the night before; in the morning he'd leaf through the scrawled pages over a cup of coffee and discover bits and pieces of the week dropped into the Cuisinart of his subconscious and served lukewarm and a little thick, like the gazpacho at his friend Roscoe's restaurant. Stan would sit at his desk waiting for a vista to open in his imagination; occasion-ally the fog lifted and at least he could see the path.

He'd wanted to write a novel about an intimation, a novel that would express what he felt about certain figurations as Bernard played them, what snippets of Bernard's music meant to him—had always meant to him. Since the first time he'd heard it, walking across the commons in front of the UNO library on his way to meet Bernard at the music building, Bernard's playing had carved a place in Stan where quiet and solitude could exist, accompanied the events of Stan's life. Bernard's music provided a soundtrack to Stan's personal movie, added counterpoise. In an art that abstracted time, Bernard had created timelessness. Stan felt incidental to Bernard's music. And more than his music—his temperament, his very breath.

Stan tried to write it, to make it real as the *ping* of thunder on a window-pane, but the words *clanged*. Yet words were all he had. Frustrated, he'd finally locked the work in his desk drawer and walked away from it.

Stan felt suspicious of such exaggerations now, standing before the Garden District Book Shop, although he could not say he regretted thinking any of it. He wondered what Bernard would make of all this. He felt guilty for what Bernard didn't know: Stan, too, harbored secrets. He had a double life with

Bernard. One Stan inhabited the city, the other leapt along a tangential path in his imagination where the impulse to smash through life, to tear body from soul, glowed with possibilities. For all his cynicism, Stan believed in the phantom self, the core of him a radiating, animating physicality that wanted to move separately. In a parallel world, Bernard and he would have been lovers. He still lusted after his old friend.

The sky opened. Stan went into the bookstore to wait out the downpour.

FIN DE SIÈCLE

Your note found me suffering from the residual doldrums of the end of summer and a little bit of nausea from the food poisoning from the Italian restaurant on North Rampart Street. But it did raise my spirits immensely. I'm glad that things seem to be going well for you. I've been working hard lately, but somehow not writing nearly enough. Life goes on in the Crescent City.

I miss you and think about you always, especially now when the leaves are gone from the trees and my mind's eye seems to make an easy leap from my window, flies out and around the city to that corner near your old apartment on Governor Nicholls. I remember the totally improper passion I found there. I'll never forget the way we held each other, fucking with wordless anguish, our hearts in our mouths. I don't regret anything we ever did. There's very little I regret. Something Kyle said to me a while ago sticks in mind—that every choice involves some sort of loss, and that if you spent all your time worrying about the losses you wouldn't make any choices. Life has its hidden jeopardies, it's fraught with them at every turn. One just has to go on. You understand this. We both understand this.

I had read your last letter, Michael. When I got here Wednesday afternoon, I took a cab straight to Odd Fellows Rest and wandered the rows of tombs for two hours, looking for your headstone. On Friday night I went to a Bogart double feature at the Saenger, then walked over to Decatur Street in the rain afterward and went into Sidney's News Stand to buy Saturday's paper. Drifting down Decatur, I skimmed the front page. Under the balcony of The

Mint, I heard her voice wafting from the bar like a presentiment. I looked up and saw the gilded marquee on the sidewalk: *Fortunate Champagne: Two Shows Nightly.*

I didn't know she was in town. I couldn't know. How I wish I could have told you, Michael. How I wish I could have made you understand what hearing her meant to me. . . .

I bribe the maitre d' to let me in without a jacket and tie. He spirits me down to a good table as Fortunate drifts across the room leading a beam of light and ripples of applause. I haven't ever seen her so beautiful, not when she played the dives along North Rampart Street. She shimmers darkly, sheathed in beaded black organza that throws light like crushed onyx. She sees me. She eases into a rendition of "Cry Me a River," singing only to me, casting me adrift on its blue swell, plunging me into a shoal of bass, piano, tenor sax. She clutches the moment, holds it in a clenched fist to her breast, in closed eyes, in lips quivering words, making the familiar into something completely foreign and unexpected, and I am drawn into the stream of her lament. It's distilled through me. Every gesture beckons me to escape.

After her last set, I wait for her in the shadows of the tiny bar by the courtyard.

"Tom Cahill? My goodness, it is you," Fortunate whispers. "Mother has missed you."

I turn to her and smile. She's wearing a black picture hat with peacock feathers cascading behind her. She throws her long arms around me and kisses my cheek.

"It's good to see you, Fortunate. It's been a while," I say. "You look like you've seen a ghost."

"I have," she says. "You dropped off the face of the earth. What happened to you? Where's your hair? One of the bar boys you used to run with told me you had disappeared, and then he saw your old apartment for rent and figured you had died. *No one* voluntarily gives up an apartment in the Quarter. Remember that one-armed attorney, Leon? He told me that your sojourn in New York was a dismal failure, that you were practically penniless and then you got sick and died. I tried to find you. My word. When I saw you tonight . . ." She holds my face in her hands, staring at me in disbelief. "Forgive my bad manners. Come, darling, let's get out of here."

"Let me buy you a cocktail." I step out to the street and flag a taxi. A black-and-white Checker skids to the curb. "The Monteleone," I tell the driver.

"Don't do that again," Fortunate says. "Don't you dare leave Mother again without telling us."

I can't see her face in the dark cab. "I promise," I say. "Someday soon, I'm going to tell you why I left, even though it doesn't matter. He could take care of himself. He didn't need me. He never did."

"But what brings you back, dear? I know—this whole damn city exists to remind us of him."

She extracts a cigarette from a little silver case I recognize as one of the gifts you gave her. I slouch in the seat, dig in my trouser pocket for my Zippo, ceremoniously light her up. She touches my hand, inhales, nods, rustling the feathers in her hat.

"How did you happen to catch my show?" she asks. "I'm glad you did. What did you think?"

"It was wonderful. But you didn't sing my song."

"Maybe later," she says, laughing. "I've been getting some gigs in New York lately, at this great little club on Bleecker Street. I've got one in St. Louis next week. Sunday night I'm leaving on the *City of New Orleans*."

"Why are you taking the train?"

"You know how I hate to fly," she says.

I had forgotten. The driver takes us into the Rue St. Anne, then into the Rue Royale to the Montelcone Hotel. We stroll through the grand lobby into the gaudy Carousel Bar and sit at the rotating mahogany bar where we can see the passersby on Royale through the windows, at least for a while.

"Who are you cruising?" Fortunate asks.

"Guess," I say.

She pivots on her stool.

"You missed him."

"What are we drinking?" Fortunate whispers. "Mother is so *parched*."

"Order anything you want."

"What's your pleasure?" asks the bartender.

"Two dirty martinis," I say, taking off my glasses.

"Just a child's portion of vermouth for me—with a twist," Fortunate adds.

The bartender grins and turns away.

I light two cigarettes and pass one to Fortunate, thinking of Jake's remark at the end of *The Sun Also Rises*. "No matter how vulgar a hotel is, the bar is always nice," I say to her. She coos and nods. The bartender presents us with our martinis. We sit drinking and smoking. Smoke wafts to the ceiling and dissipates above us.

"What's your name?" Fortunate calls to the bartender.

"Turk."

"I get it," she says. "The fez. I'm pleased to make your acquaintance, Turk. Every time you see this glass nearly empty, you may take the liberty of concocting another."

"What happened to Casper, the other bartender?" I ask Turk.

"Gone for a few months now," he says.

"I'm sorry to hear that. It will be six years ago, the day after tomorrow," I tell Fortunate in the mirror.

"What? That you met Michael?"

"In this very bar."

"So that's what brings you back."

I ask if anyone was with him at the end, if he said anything to her about me.

"I can't say it got any easier after Kyle and Gary," she says. "You don't become immune to loss even though you know what to expect. Michael got worse quickly right after you left. He kept pleading with me to take him out of the hospital, and who could blame him? Not that he didn't have good care. There was a nurse on his floor, she was so butch you just *knew* she pissed through a funnel. But, Tom, the way she picked him up was something to behold. You'd think he was made of spun glass—so brittle and frail, like my momma when she had *the cancer*. That woman would hold Michael in her arms while the orderlies changed his sheets, and there wasn't a peep out of him. You should've seen the love on that nurse's face. It was the only peaceful moment he had during his day. It broke my heart. I'm the one who checked him out of Touro Infirmary and drove him to his parents' fishing camp."

"On the Irish Bayou? He took me there sometimes."

"'Hang in there sweetie,' I told him, 'while your ugly stepsister goes out a minute to the Kay-Bee and gets her some fortification.' And I'm thinking about those first few months before his mind started to slip, that brief moment of mirth he had—two months, maybe—when he would start in the morning and plunge himself into the city, his city. I drove up a ways and bought a little pint bottle of bourbon and carried it back to the camp. I always forget to sit on the left side when the train crosses that rickety trestle over the Rigolets. I hate looking out the window and seeing the camps on their stilts. Every time

I take the *Crescent* to New York, I recollect how it felt to leave him. We may have said two words to each other on the drive out there that cold Monday morning late in October. The sun rising over the marsh. The house closed for the season. The pipes belching rusty water when I opened the faucet. I don't think I could've done it if I hadn't known in my heart how bad off he was, if he hadn't been the third man I'd seen go this way. I don't think I'd have had the courage."

Suddenly I'm coasting along the deserted strip of Chef Menteur Highway in your red two-seater, the wind like a thousand flags flapping at our heads, remembering the detour we took to Little Woods five summers ago, on a return trip to New Orleans from Pensacola Beach. Fire burned in the marsh, its looming black funnel cloud carrying the smell and taste of creosote far inland. I snapped your profile with the new camera you gave me: dark sunglasses, wind whipping your hair—the only photograph of you I claimed in my escape. I had never beheld such a vision, me the Moon-landing kid, the welder's son. You said something to me I couldn't hear in the open convertible. I smiled, thinking how much I wanted to fuck you. We couldn't get to the camp soon enough. A semi barreled past us at twice our speed and sucked us into the vacuum of its wake, making us swoon. The car lurched forward. You gripped the wheel, slipped your foot off the gas, and glanced into the rearview mirror to see where the trailer had left a hole in space. Then you eased the car onto the gravel shoulder and lit a cigarette to catch your breath. Smoke fanned above your head. You grabbed a Dixie longneck from the six-pack behind your seat. I jumped out to take pictures of the long line of shacks that squatted on high pylons along the highway that seemed so woebegone and desolate to me, like a Hopper painting. Ahead of us I could see the city limits, the procession of sleazy motor inns, used car lots, junkyards, bait shops, filling stations.

We parked at a boat launch and strolled along the bottle cap and oyster shell path to your parents' camp. We climbed steps to the crest of the levee, then followed the boardwalk about fifty feet out over the water to the clapboard bungalow on its stilts. The camp looked neglected, the white paint peeling, the pylons stripped and split. We went through a gate with its overhead sign "The Strouds" burned into the weathered wood. You told me the climax of *King Creole* had been filmed here, with Elvis Presley and Carolyn Jones, and when I noticed the chicken-wire boxes hanging in the rafters, you told me they were crab traps.

On the porch at the back of the house facing the water, weathered wicker chairs leaned against the wall. We went down the long pier that jutted into Lake Pontchartrain.

"The lake always smells like sex to me," you said, removing your T-shirt and stuffing it into the back pocket of your khakis. "Like semen. Primordial."

The pier smelled like mildewed canvas. You kicked off your deck shoes and stood at the edge, looking down into the water like you were about to dive. I watched you through the camera viewfinder, seeing a strikingly mature man, barrel-chested, barefoot, self-conscious, and realized how perfectly alone we were. You waited for me to take your picture and I didn't. I let that picture go.

"Hear that sound?" you asked. A boat engine snarled in the distance, gulls screeched riotously above us. "Ever since I was a child I've been taken with it. The sound of the waves lapping against the pylons." You dropped the cigarette to the dock and crushed it with your bare foot.

I listened again. Blankness gave way to scudding waves underneath the camp. Spray hissed against the pylons. The lake whispered to me a rhapsodic refrain: *It shall be you.*

Later, there was music too—Mozart's B-flat piano sonata, I read on the album cover in the light of the big amber hurricane lamp. The plaintive first movement slipped by as you rotated in my lap on the hideaway bed. Then silence. We must have realized it as we stopped fucking. You asked me, "Do you want to put something else on?"

Now fragments of that music well up, the C-minor episode from the *adagio*, the way those chords sang out during our sex. You feel music long before you understand it. It had never crossed my mind that I might not be able to forget you. You once said that writing was an act of forgetting, memory drained into prose, kept at bay, kept better that way. It was there in the story. You would write the life we fervently wished we'd had.

"His heart stopped in his sleep," Fortunate says. "It petered out, the doctor said." She crushes her cigarette in an alabaster ashtray. "This isn't how I wanted to remember him to you."

"I need to know," I say. "Tell me everything."

"There *was* something Michael wanted me to tell you, Tom."

"What is it?"

"No. Let's not talk about it now."

We have another round, smoke cigarettes, and stare out the window in silence. Great swaths of rain fall on the Rue Royale. I can't stand to look at it any longer. Fortunate takes my hand.

And it's early morning three summers ago. We're cruising up Canal Street past the Cemeteries, on our way to Pensacola Beach again. We happened upon a film crew with its trucks, vans, lights, and slowed to watch the tuxedoed musicians, the blooming black umbrellas, the mourning Negro women waving and fluttering handkerchiefs limp like calla lilies, sultry and erotic, to the scintillation of coronets, the wail of trombones. It reminded me of my first Carnival, lurid and festive. As the languorous procession trickled through the gates of Odd Fellows Rest, you blurted out that you had caught it, probably from Kyle. Then we saw Fortunate and you parked the car.

I remember how she held a small bunch of white tea roses, the way her ivory silk dress clung to her dark, dark skin in the humidity, how she sang with such bitter exuberance, "Yes, we will gather at the river—the beautiful, the beautiful river." Later she said the director had wanted to shoot the funeral of some local blues legend but ended up staging his own. When the procession flowed down Canal Street, you followed them in the second line, leaving me at the cemetery gate, and it occurred to me how much life had turned into a bad medieval morality play—we fuck and then we die. That night, when I asked how you could leave me standing alone after such a revelation, you said it was to see Fortunate dressed in white. It was all you could think of at the time.

"Are you okay?" asks Fortunate, squeezing my hand. "Want another drink?"

"Anyplace but here," I say.

At Victor's, where Fortunate plays the Wurlitzer, we dance until the bartender pulls the plug, choking the jukebox on a Dorsey tune, "I'm Getting Sentimental Over You," then wind up in the Rue St. Philippe as the rain slacks off. Now we wander in the Rue Royale under balconies, dodging the puddles and accumulated rainwater plummeting from the overhangs of slate roofs and awnings and eaves, saying nothing. I smell Fortunate's perfume, burning incense. The street is empty and cool. We barely see the street lamps through the fog. As we cross into the Rue Bourbon, we hear revelers heckling like ghouls on the balconies of bars, and I realize we've been looking for you in the old haunts.

We go into Lafitte's Blacksmith Shop, where a fire crackles in the fireplace. Candles flicker white in indigo glasses on the bar and magnolia blooms float in a great bowl on the piano in the back room. Miss Lilly sits at the keyboard, playing and singing "The Nearness of You," off-key. A couple of elderly gentlemen sip cognac in the shadows. They know Fortunate. One of them calls her "our greedy songbird." Fortunate laughs. She goes over to them and they speak together in the patois. They offer to buy us drinks. I tell the waiter we'll have what they're having. Fortunate and I sit at the piano, raise our glasses to the gentlemen, and light Lucky Strikes.

"You're remembering the first time we met?" Fortunate asks me, smoke curling exquisitely out of her mouth. She's French-inhaling the darkness.

"Nonsense," I say.

She shrugs. "Michael brought you here, his new discovery. We all sat singing—Kyle, Tommy, Michael, you, and me. You and Michael kept dredging up ballads one after the other, and I asked you where you learned to play the piano like that. Michael said, 'He's just drunk.'"

"Funny how you make it feel like yesterday, Fortunate."

"It feels like now to me. The rain does it."

"Hadn't been a month since I came down to New Orleans. I knew I was a hick, but knew I belonged here too. He asked me three questions, questions I've been rolling around in my mind ever since: Who am I? What do I want? What the hell am I doing here?"

"Don't you mistake for one minute that Michael had all the answers, dear."

"He knew more than I did. Or he made it seem like it."

"He was twenty years older than us," Fortunate says.

"There's a *noir*-ish story in Michael's last collection called 'Sanitized For Your Protection.' When I read it I heard his voice in my head, telling me our lives. There was one detail—that I had somehow missed getting my senior class yearbook picture taken—that I fixated on, and I had to think, did that really happen to me or did he make it up? Had I already left home? It made sense that I might have skipped the hoopla, but I couldn't remember if it had actually happened. My memory is like a sieve these days."

"Mine, too."

"Michael always said it was inevitable that he'd write about us. I kept a journal when I was a kid. Never told Michael this, but I burned it. Father found it under my mattress and read it, asked me how I could write such trash, made me burn it behind the garage. I was fifteen. I cried when I lit the pages. The ashes curled up from the flame and flew everywhere on the smoke. He knew what it was doing to me. I hated him for that. None of what I wrote ever came back to me. It was then I understood that Natchez was a hellhole. I'm sorry, Fortunate. Reckon I'm a little cocktailed."

She touches my face in a way that suddenly makes me fear her. "It's all that booze you've been drinking," she whispers. "Let's go."

"I do know what it means, to miss New Orleans."

Fortunate sings my song under her breath against the staccato of rain, her voice smoky, brandied, as we stagger back to the Fairmont Hotel. We'd gone to the Café du Monde for steaming cups of *café au lait*, but it did no good. We'd talked about Sarah, Ella, Billie—how you worshipped them. Now she wants to walk in the rain. I ask her about her dress, her hat.

"I'll get new ones," she says.

Then we're huddled together in the Rue Bourbon. The porters are sweeping out the strip joints. We drift past hustlers heading home from their johns. The streets are deserted. These last hours before dawn make me hold my breath. Solitude confronts me everywhere, seeps from every alley and alcove of this reliquary place. I hear it in the rain. It's like being made of shadow: everything that passes me, passes through me, leaving me still, far behind, afraid.

We dash up Baronne Street from Canal, run sopping wet into the cavernous lobby of the Fairmont, past the silent Blue Room, past the bank of phone booths like confessionals, past the front desk, through the lobby to the elevator cages, breathless and cold as the attendant pulls open the bronze accordion doors, Fortunate whispering in my ear with the sad ebullience of a war bride.

I don't remember being ushered into my suite, though I know everything had already been decided. Then she appears, a silhouette against the window blinds, disrobed, cupping her small breasts, and stillness settles everywhere like manna.

"I haven't ever with . . . ," I try to tell her as she removes my glasses and undresses me.

"*Improvise*," she says.

We fall across the bed. She mounts me slowly, immersing me. And now I see plainly where the labyrinth of night has led.

"I don't think I can," I tell her.

She clutches the back of my head and drowns my face in her breasts. "That's it. Take me. See," she whispers. "Yes, do this for me."

But I'm remembering you, imagining how much her darkness feels like you, how I want to change her into you. She seems to know this, and still we do it.

I wake to find her in the window, wrapped in my paisley silk robe, smoking. I climb into boxers and join her on the fire escape. Rain chimes on the cold steel steps. A siren screams somewhere in the firmament below us. Through a sliver of space between zigzagging, rusted fire escapes, we watch the motionless river of ink, its billowing mists, the first streaks of light shivering in the east. I kiss the nape of her neck. Her skin tastes like warm milk and rain.

"It's a little disconcerting to stay in a hotel room in your hometown," I say. Of course, I've spent time before in hotel rooms in New Orleans, with this out-of-town trick or that conventioneer, the senior prom after-party (who remembered anything after the first plastic cup of Jungle Juice?), but I've never spent the night, watching cable TV or ordering breakfast from room service.

"Do you love my breasts?" she asks.

I touch her skin, examine the freckles. Feel her hair, stare into her eyes. Hold her fingers in the palm of my hand. Inhale her.

"Totally. Tragically. Fatally," I say.

"Fatally?" She laughs. "We're probably both fatal, because of who we are."

I say nothing.

"Do you remember when you were with Michael in the Port of Call?" she asks.

"There were so many times, Fortunate."

"After the two of you had been together for a month or so."

"I remember. But how do you know about it?"

"He told me he wanted to tell you the secret then."

I think of the time you and I were sitting in the Port of Call and you said dryly, "I created this city." And I believed you. Alphonse was shucking oysters on the zinc bar, filling the ice bed in our beer tray. It was a Friday afternoon when the oysters were a dollar a dozen. The place smelled a little raw, which was the reason, I always thought, you liked going there.

"Is that why you stay?" I asked you.

"It's not the only reason," you said, taking a gulp from your longneck.

I remember the peeling Winesap wallpaper and the ceiling fans that hung from the rafters. One swooped above us, churning the smoke and brine from the oysters, the other wobbled sonorously. I picture that big Dixie Beer neon sign that I know was blue but feels black-and-white like an old movie, when I remember it now. You didn't say anything else, but I still have the vaguest reminiscence that I knew then you were keeping something from me, I could almost see it on your face.

I turn to Fortunate. She looks at me gravely.

"Michael was my father," she says. She shields the flame of a match and lights another cigarette. I watch as she draws on it, tilts her head back to blow a plume of smoke into the flurrying rain. She's waiting.

"But how?" I ask.

"It might have happened like this, like what happened between us. I don't know. He was young then. Momma never would talk about it. I always wanted to know what my daddy was like, but she wouldn't say. I knew he had to be white—you know when you're different. We lived on Thalia Street then, and I'd imagine my daddy was a movie star, like Burt Lancaster. Momma wrote to all the movie stars. She didn't like going to the show, even after she didn't have to sit in the Colored balcony, so we'd stay up late on weekends watching movies on the TV, fall asleep on the sofa, and wake up in the morning to the snow."

She takes a final pull on her cigarette, drops it in a puddle on the fire escape step, and it blinks out. I know she feels the stillness. It's embalmed in her smoke, steeped in the rain's peppery smell.

I wonder how true her story is, but I can't bring myself to question whatever past she feels the need to steal from you. We both know you invented lives for us. Maybe she just wants to believe in something. I look at her in the reflected light from the room. Her eyes have a sacred intensity, like a Bach fugue. It makes me want to accept her myth. If I look at her again, I might see that her eyes are definitely yours, the color of honey.

She looks at me. "Say something. Anything. *Please.*"

"What's there to say?" I tell her.

"Is it really so strange?" she asks.

"No. I don't reckon so."

The sound of a riverboat calliope wakes me. It's evening. I'm still with Fortunate.

I find her sunk into the big white porcelain tub, my robe at its claw feet. She sucks on a Lucky Strike and soaks in the froth of her bath, humming something that only seems familiar. I come in and stand by the door of the dressing room. I dress in a rumpled shirt and linen pants.

"I watched you sleep all afternoon," she says, sponging her shoulders. "You looked so tired, so beautiful."

"*You* made me that way."

"I guess I did, didn't I?" She's been looking at herself in the mirror she holds. She drops the mirror in the tub and waves smoke away from her face. Water beads in her ebony hair.

"Any regrets?"

I tell her I have a few.

"What's to become of us, Tom? Will you stay? Will you go?"

"Three questions, Fortunate?"

"I'm the greedy songbird, remember?"

"I remember." I stare at the arabesque in the tiled floor and the slatted, vibrating bars of light and shadow from the blinds and the transom, trying to think of what I can possibly say to her. "I'll leave again one day, when I don't know. I'm not on a timetable now."

"You could follow me. We could wake up at night together, not knowing where in God's name we are, all exhausted, still motion sick from the rolling of the train, wondering what hotel we're in. You would search for me in the ashtray. On the matchbook, that's where to find the name of the hotel, on the matchbook."

"I don't know, Fortunate. I think I'm going to stay here a while. I've been looking for something for a long time."

"What makes you think you'll find it here?"

"I've looked everywhere else."

"I think you'll end up losing it, if you stay. I mean really losing it."

"I'm tired of traipsing around trying to outrun his memory, Fortunate. I need to find peace."

"You think you want that now, but remember, you and I are itinerants." She lifts her leg to sponge it, then does her shoulders as the light fades from the window. "Memory is so vengeful. It'll eat you alive, if you let it." She looks meaningfully at me, dropping her cigarette to the floor. "And we both know you're going to let it, Tom."

"Why tell me your secret now, Fortunate?" She doesn't answer me, just lights another cigarette. I persist. "Why?"

"No reason." She turns away. "I wondered if you really loved him," she says under her breath. I can almost see the words form in the blue smoke.

"Michael sent me away," I say. "Told me he didn't want me around when his time came. I didn't want to leave him."

I'm lying and she knows it. I had to go. I couldn't stand to watch what you and I both knew was coming. I want to explain to her.

"It doesn't matter now," she says.

"The hell it doesn't."

I wish it didn't matter. I wish I could be more like Fortunate, wish I could follow her and we could bore our way through a pitch-black Delta night on the train playing Hearts with a couple of old men from Memphis, laughing and drinking and smoking as the hours flip past our window with each turn of the cards and the *thud-thwack, thud-thwack, thud-thwack* rhythm of the train on the rails.

But I can't. To do that I'd have to pretend I never knew you, Michael, and that I could never manage, any more than I can lie to Fortunate.

Evening comes. Fortunate steps into the elevator cage and the attendant pulls the accordion door closed. She asks if we'll see each other again. I tell her I'll look for her wherever I happen to be. She says that suits her. Fortunate has been as I remember you. Everything and nothing. Holding her finally made it so. The elevator winds downward, sundering us.

Now it's Sunday evening and I'm perched on a stool at the bar in the Monteleone, recollecting. One May you and I stood in Jackson Square watching the firefighters prop damaged paintings along the Cabildo's wrought-iron fence as the museum burned. I knew then I would leave you, Michael. Leave your city. I didn't know it would never leave me. I can't forget the last thing you said as you stood under the tarpaulin of the Clover Grill a couple of weeks later, barefoot, coughing, a cigarette dangling from your lips, watching me throw my luggage in the trunk of a Checker taxi. It was another hot Memorial Day. Thunder rolled in from the north over Lake Ponchartrain.

"Take care of yourself," I told you.

"I always do," you said. Your next words stay in my head like an incantation. "No matter what's happened, we've ruined each other for ever belonging to anyone else." I wish I could forget them. But here I sit, drinking and smoking, and talking to the dead. Or to myself, which I reckon is what a good many people in hotel bars do. It's the dead who hold on to us. The living let us go.

RISK FACTORS

"ARE WE HAVING ORAL SAKS FOR LUNCH?" Calvert asked John. I gathered "Oral Saks" was code for shopping. The conversations of Calvert and John had wormed their way into my daydream. For weeks I could not help but overhear them. They blithely ignored everyone within earshot, blurting out whatever was on their minds, no matter how unspeakable or inappropriate, not so much to shock or amuse but because it was innate to them, like an eye twitch or a bad case of Tourette's syndrome. I found their conversations titillating. My racquetball buddies weren't nearly so scintillating and informative.

"We have that mandatory video conference at twelve-thirty," John said.

"Do we have any idea what it's about?" Calvert asked.

"Not a word," John replied.

John and Calvert shared the cubicle outside my office. Calvert was my secretary. My previous secretary, an actress with an eating disorder, left candy and cookies on the counter of her cubicle, which we had dubbed the "Grazing Wall." Though she seemed never to touch the stuff herself, she took great pleasure in feeding the staff on our floor.

"By the way," John said. "Just so you know, I have first dibs on the two delicious new associates securities poached from Butterfield & Peabody."

"I saw the blond one on Eighth Avenue this weekend," Calvert said. "The Doogie Howser look-alike. Remember him from television?"

"Vaguely. Where did you see him?"

"At the Big Cup."

"He's gay?" John asked.

"Buff body, bleached hair, lives in Chelsea. You do the math, Ms. Street."

"I never see anyone famous."

"Not the real Doogie Howser—the look-alike associate."

"The brunette is a major *slurp*—empirically divine, like a Kennedy," John said.

"I don't know," Calvert said. "He's too moody."

"I'm sure you wouldn't kick him out of bed, Della. You always wanted to be a full-service secretary."

"He did say hello to me in the bathroom this morning."

"Lucky you. Did you blow him?"

"Excuse me, Ms. Street?"

"I'd have had my way with him right there, thrown him down and gone to town. They'd have had to block the door with police tape and get a HAZMAT crew to clean up after us."

"I suppose a handjob is the natural extension of a handshake," said Calvert. "But he's such an oddball. Have you checked his backstory?"

"I've done a little investigating," John admitted. "He obviously got hitched to the first girl who ever kissed him back. Married her the year after Columbia Law School, fresh from a clerkship with an Eastern District judge. A strawberry blonde with freckles. Cute, but very Peppermint Patty. I bet she calls the shots in that marriage. He can hardly get a word in edgewise. I feel sorry for him."

I glanced at the wedding picture on my desk.

"She has good taste though," John continued.

"The dress?"

"That too. Definitely Vera Wang."

"How do you know?"

"That she calls the shots? From the one-sided conversations," John said.

"Be careful," said Calvert. "My ugly stepsister always warned me, 'Don't shit where you eat.' It's a slippery slope to hell, once you start eroticizing your bosses."

"I don't care," John said.

It was the stunningly clear and cold November Monday morning before Thanksgiving, during the limbo between Election Day and the judicial selection of President Bush, when I overheard Calvert and his diabolical cubicle mate. The video they referred to was on sexual harassment, and Corcoran, Fuchs, Broyard, Harris & Baum had sent a firm-wide e-mail memorandum to all personnel requiring them to view it. One of the more realistic vignettes portrayed two "insensitive" male colleagues hovering over a computer terminal, laughing about an unseen pornographic image on the monitor. A seated third colleague asked the two men, "What was the best sex you ever had?" A young female colleague in the adjacent cubicle overheard the question and ensuing banter and reported it to the human resources administrator. The scene had gotten under my skin. Together with John and Calvert's conversation, it had the unintended effect of underscoring my burgeoning identity crisis.

Physically, Calvert and John reminded me of the bold wrestlers in high school who had gotten all the sex. They were both tanned, strapping young sophisticates, bald with goatees, always dressed in fetching pastel cashmere sweaters and black wool stretch pants. They strutted the halls of our floor as if a soundtrack of boleros looped permanently through their addled brains, brazenly calling each other "Della" or "Ms. Street," purring about their Saturday romps in Chelsea sex clubs. Never mind that Barbara Leyland, the head of the securities practice and John's boss, was no Perry Mason. From these *tête-à-têtes* I had deduced that Calvert and John pursued the enterprise of hooking up with mind-boggling seriousness, collecting conquests like I collected books. Part of my morning amusement consisted of trying to decipher how much of their talk was hubris. I refused to believe in their singleness of purpose. Not that I found what passed for conversation among my fellow associates any more elevating. I despised having to read the sports pages to keep up with the batting averages. I hated my buddies' dick-wagging about who had the biggest client or the smallest cell phone.

I'd left my hometown to go to a New York law school, to procrastinate my adolescence. I'm a recovering school addict. You need to know this because no one in New York is just a secretary or a lawyer. No one is just a seducer, any more than one is just a legal secretary. When I was a summer associate at Braeburn & Rome, the secretarial pools were filled with would-be thespians, prima donnas, and soubrettes—all high-maintenance personalities.

Calvert had never hit on me, and wouldn't have given me the time of day if I weren't his boss. It didn't dawn on me until the firm hired John that I was completely out of Calvert's league. I don't know why their inattention mattered to me. I had a decent body. I was fit. I had been on the golf team in high school and college, even earned a letter. I wore good clothes. I had been told I was a dead ringer for Tucker Carlson.

Nor could I completely fathom why I was so fascinated with them, except that I felt snubbed. I began to wonder if I was a closet case. Spotting at the gym or glances in the sauna never led to any serious quandaries. I didn't know if I could actually go through with one of my hazily imagined trysts, but I knew it couldn't be healthy to feel so frustrated. Laura and I had been married for ten years, right out of college. She had teased me about how all of my close friends in New Orleans were gay and in the closet. But she said she would give me the benefit of the doubt, although I don't think she really suspected anything of the sort about me. We had a daughter and a son, twins, both of whom had started at the Friends School two years earlier, where Laura was a teacher. I was past president of the block association and we belonged to the local grocery cooperative, the last bastion of ecological vegetarian liberalism in a largely gentrified neighborhood in the middle of Brooklyn where most of the men were like me, rather soft, quasi-effete, denatured, and ostensibly straight. Or testosterone-rich and gay.

In the waning "irrational exuberance" of the High Tech Boom, I had noticed that I'd gravitated into the orbit of gay men. This event seemed to coincide with the arrival of my new administrative assistant, who let it be known that he preferred the title "secretary."

Calvert and John stalked the forty-sixth-floor Corcoran offices like pumas in Prada. The data processing department also teemed with high-maintenance men each more polished than the next, and I could not be certain they had always been there and I had only begun to notice them. How had they become the new epitome of masculinity? My golfing buddies, though they would have been loath to admit they even contemplated the question, were mystified—they would never have used that word—as to why the media culture was so infatuated with gay men.

But gay men were inevitably, I noticed, the best-looking guys on the street, the most sinewy at the gym. I couldn't go into Bloomingdale's to buy a tie without confronting one of them. And they all made me feel like an inadequate fop in comparison. But while I was embarrassed by how this *commedia dell'arte* pantomime of masculinity by certain gays had become the ideal, I must admit that I found it hard not to be jealous of, or at least intoxicated by, the pheromones pouring off their buff bodies like a Viagra cloud.

It probably didn't help my psychological state that I had been restless and disgruntled at work after nearly six years of billing twenty-four-hundred hours annually. I wanted off the partnership track. I was tired of trying to wrest time for myself away from my desk and its piles of files but always finding a reason I needed to be there. Rumors had circulated that I actually lived in my office. Soon I would have to order in and eat at my desk like the other associates, but for now I was probably the only senior associate in Corcoran's Business & Technology Group who actually took a full hour for lunch every day outside the office.

Sometimes I would drift over to the Museum of Modern Art and sit reading in the room with Monet's mammoth Water Lilies panel of the Japanese footbridge at Giverny, just to escape the pressure, the rancid whiff of regularity and conformity. Sometimes I wandered to the Equitable Galleries or strolled to the Waldorf-Astoria Hotel to visit Golden Argosy, the rare-books dealer there. I collected modern first editions, though lately I had been trying to curb my habit. Who had time to read them or the space to keep them?

Most days I sat in the coffee bar across the street from my midtown office, though the chain's slick, shiny espresso machines, cookie-cutter décor, and "lite jazz" piped in over the sound of steaming milk aspired to a warmth and fuzziness I found irritating. I usually carried a book and ended up watching people. Lately I had been focusing on the manic middle-aged porter who mumbled as he cleared away the lunch debris of tourists—cellophane, paper towels, dirty dishes, sandwich fragments—cleaning tables with frantic energy for what I imagined was little more than minimum wage. In contrast to the faceless hordes streaming down Broadway, his specificity was oddly engaging. When I began to notice someone—someone I might see every day, it didn't matter where, in the subway, in the deli where I bought my morning bagel—the next time I ran into him I would realize that I had been waiting to see him again. It was comforting to acknowledge that fact, to admit to myself that I was looking forward to seeing him. I could connect with him on some level.

The day after the video presentation, I went to the coffee bar and saw the handsome guy I'd been trading glances with for about a week. He could have been an actor on the cover of *Details* magazine: dusky blond, pouty lips, chiseled bone structure, and hazel eyes. He wore a new twist on Buddy Holly eyeglasses, navy stretch twills, expensive black penny loafers without socks—the tops of his ankles showed—and a periwinkle sweater. His hair was cropped close around the sides and back but moppy on top. I felt like a dork in my cords and button-down denim shirt, sitting upright and prim on a stool at the counter that ran across the storefront.

"What are you doing?" he asked.

I turned, startled. He was talking on his cell phone.

"Is this a bad time?" he said. "For heaven's sake, girlfriend, why are you listening to that? I'm watching the Letterman lemmings."

My eyes followed his gaze outside, to the bundled French tourists leaking out of the Novotel hotel across the street, who trudged up bustling Broadway in the snow to join the throngs queued at the door and snaking around the corner of the Ed Sullivan Theater, whose blue-and-yellow marquee promoted the residency of *The Late Show with David Letterman.*

"You don't need to keep reminding me," Mr. Buddy Holly Glasses said. "And just for the record, I did not seduce that married agent in your office. We seduced each other. There is a difference. Wayward married men are such a hot commodity. A hedge against a privacy-leaching boyfriend, right? Why can't you be happy for me? Did you see *Will and Grace* last night? All right. I admit I'm addicted. I can't help myself." Mr. Buddy Holly Glasses had sidled up to the condiment bar and was pouring more half-and-half into his cup. I listened to him tell his friend how one of the characters mentioned something about a joke flying below his "gaydar"—whatever that was. Mr. Buddy Holly Glasses could not believe that mainstream viewers actually understood the punch line.

"And why is it you never see gay men portrayed on television as anything but the witty Cloris Leachman-like neighbor or the glamorous, frivolous life of the party? We're never dowdy and never, never angry. What's that about? That doesn't represent my experience. Of course, it's a comedy. I know that. What about *Bewitched*? I don't think witchcraft, black or white, is an appropriate metaphor of homosexuality."

The cadence of his voice fascinated me. I detected a faint nasal timbre, a trace of the Tidewater in the way he said the diphthong in *about*. One of those Southern boys who thought he could reinvent himself in the city.

"I'm not being heretical," Mr. Buddy Holly Glasses insisted. "I'm just saying that sometimes queens get angry. We're not all pretty and witty. Sometimes we're vicious and rapacious. Sometimes we'll sue our mother to evict her from a rent-controlled apartment. Don't go there, Harlan. I know it's only television, not real life. Enough of this. Let's talk high finance. I need to know—Amalgamated or not?"

I twisted around in my seat, knocking over my cup. Coffee spilled across the counter. I bounced up, scrambling to get out of the way. Mr. Buddy Holly Glasses looked at me curiously. I shrugged and went to the condiment bar.

When I returned with napkins, the manic porter had already begun sopping up the spill with a rag.

Mr. Buddy Holly Glasses had asked his friend about a so-called "New Economy" stock, Amalgamated Diagnostics—"Agnostics," as we called it around the office—the preeminent manufacturer of fiber-optic networking, data encryption, and transmission systems. A company Corcoran happened to represent. The firm had made a killing ten years ago when we took Agnostics public. In lieu of legal fees, Corcoran accepted five hundred thousand shares of Series A and B Preferred Stock, an uncommon practice then among Silicon Valley law firms, and when Agnostics landed on the NASDAQ, Corcoran's equity stake converted to the equivalent of three shares of common stock at a staggering initial public offering price. The stock value proceeded to quadruple in the first six weeks on the market. It was currently hovering just pennies below its all-time, split-adjusted high.

"I do listen to you," Mr. Buddy Holly Glasses said. "Real estate and the stock market are the only things I do listen to you about. I need some friendly advice, or maybe some market-friendly advice, Harlan. You really think I should sell my shares?"

I wanted to shout, "You must sell," attorney-client privilege and insider-trading laws be damned. But I couldn't actually do anything as rash and stupid as insinuate myself into his conversation. I rolled my eyes in mock horror at the mumbling, manic porter. It's only securities fraud if you act on the knowledge, I told myself with a twinge of guilt.

"I was hoping to hold out a couple of months more. Okay, I get the picture."

The friend of Mr. Buddy Holly Glasses apparently had insisted the last hurrah for the Internet bull market had already started. Eighty percent since the beginning of the year, I thought, with the technology-laden NASDAQ sinking to a two-year low last week. What Mr. Buddy Holly Glasses did not seem to realize was that Agnostics had already joined, according to those in the know, the ranks of the New Economy downtrodden as the *cognoscenti* dumped shares on the hungry wider market.

While Agnostics had continued to book unit orders for their servers through the summer, the kind of orders upon which those high-risk, advertiser-supported sites depended—the NuevoKiosk.coms and Gurgle.coms of the Web—these same sites put the brakes on capital expenditures after Labor Day. Agnostics responded by slashing margins in an effort to stimulate sales, offering deferments and financing incentives on its infrastructure upgrades. Longer sales cycles spelled hemorrhaging cash flow and the greater likelihood of even more write-downs on the uncollected revenue. Fast approaching the end of the fiscal year, Agnostics still had difficulty collecting cash. Only income from the company's enormous and well-diversified investment portfolio in the third quarter propped up the bottom line, helping avoid a downward revision in earnings estimates.

But how long could Agnostics count on its investments to sustain this illusion of growth? Mr. Buddy Holly Glasses might have known about some of their problems if he'd dug for information behind the company's hype. I calculated that he was probably twenty-something, two, three years tops beyond college, nine years younger than me, and I pictured him living in a studio apartment on the Upper West Side, paying exorbitant rent.

He flicked his cell phone shut and turned to me. "Sorry I was so loud," he said. "I hate people who talk on cell phones in public places."

I cleared my throat. "I've been trying to place your accent," I blurted. "Virginia?"

"Very good! New Orleans," he said, smiling. "By way of Virginia. Navy brat. How'd you guess?"

"I'm from New Orleans."

"Oh my God. Where did you go to high school?"

Whenever a New Orleanian met another for the first time, this was always the first question.

"Ben Franklin," I answered.

"Jesuit."

I had gone to the public magnet school. He had gone to the upper-crust parochial school.

I heard the whole story in torrential detail. His father, a nuclear engineer, was a Delta Jew from a Greenwood mercantile family who'd managed to hold their own against the Wal-Mart juggernaut in North Mississippi. His mother was New Orleans *crème de la crème*, an Episcopalian. His father had converted when the two married.

"My father retired a couple of months into my senior year of high school, then had a stroke and died. I miss him," Mr. Buddy Holly Glasses said. "My mother died this year. She had been a New Orleans debutante—Queen of the Mystik Krewe of Comus, a Newcomb girl. A real witch. She married the best-looking guy at Tulane and never let him forget he was a notch below her station.

"Spent the better part of my childhood in Norfolk and two years at a military academy before moving to New Orleans, where my mother stuck me in Jesuit because the Jesuits are known for their pedagogy. They dismember their students' beliefs and rebuild their faith tenet by tenet, the 'Jesuit Way.' I slid through the gauntlet relatively unscathed, came out to my parents at sixteen. Hated most of my classmates, who were all either repressed or stuck on themselves. Went to Tulane like my father and unlike him graduated with degrees in English and music theory. Came to New York, snagged an internship writing content for MediaCafe.com, then moved elsewhere to a job as a technical editor. I'm waiting for the rest of my options to vest in January before I bolt for Paris to find a French boyfriend."

Mr. Buddy Holly Glasses had moved to a stool next to me during his monologue. The breezy way he rattled off his *curriculum vitae* stunned me. If I had clammed up, unable to speak, it wouldn't have mattered. I couldn't get a word in edgewise. When he came up for air, I interjected, "I'm a Tulane alumnus. MBA, before law school up here. Who was your friend on the phone?"

"Harlan? He's my best friend, a real estate broker to the rich and famous." He snickered. "We're sisters in 'Bouvier conspiracy.'"

I offered him my name.

"My name's Ernest," he said. "Ernest Zwick. Come here often?"

"I'm out to lunch."

"Do you mean that figuratively? It's four o'clock," he said. "So are you, like, a practicing lawyer? I don't know anyone who actually practices law. Harlan's a lawyer."

"Securities." I told him how I had come to work for Corcoran, and groused about my work without mentioning Laura or the kids. I talked about what it was like to shovel venture capital into the Internet stoker and what was going to happen when the New Economy imploded. "There's no creativity in it," I said, sipping my *latte*. "At least you get to write for a living. I draft interminable SEC registration statements and NASDAQ forms."

"I hardly call writing server manuals creative," he retorted. He asked if my firm handled mass toxic torts, product liability defense work. When I answered yes he wrinkled his nose and said he busied himself at work writing a post-postmodern sci-fi thriller screenplay on the sly, something about carcinogens leaching into the groundwater and the side effects of dioxin and PCB accumulation in the systems of adolescent boys. It sounded like a cross between Philip K. Dick and *Lord of the Flies*. He'd had himself tested and traces of seventy-two of the one-hundred-fifty-or-so known carcinogens had been discovered in his body.

"Speaking of shilling," he said. "I want to write a dystopian novel about the plan for the reinstitution of slavery in America. The GOP gets a Colin Powell-like character to sell the country on the plan as social security for the poor, with a guaranteed minimum wage for life. That would be some spin, wouldn't it? After all, we already have welfare reform, which is sort of like indentured servitude anyway. Right? I saw this cardboard sign the other day in front of a kid slumped on the sidewalk: 'Will code HTML for food.'"

An hour whizzed by. I let slip about my wife and family, hoping alarm bells would ring in both our heads, that Ernest would bristle and I would draw back from the precipice, then eyed him to assess the impact. He checked out the wedding ring on my hand. I noticed that he wore a thin gold band on his right hand, and for a confused moment wondered if he too was married. He gave me a complicit smile. I sidled closer and, knowing I shouldn't, told Ernest about Laura wanting a third child. Adrenaline rushed to my head. Having divulged a secret elated me. I felt as if I'd given Ernest my ATM password, a key to a room of my life. I should guard what I say, I thought, then spilled more beans, admiring my impetuosity while part of me eavesdropped with incredulity.

Snow swirled outside on Broadway. Every time the street door opened, a blast of cold air sideswiped us and we shuddered in the warm, suddenly cozy coffee bar. I kept glancing at Ernest as if I had a tic, and he kept catching me—we were disconcertingly in sync. "Jazz Month," the placard at the counter announced, and the store obliged with a real jazz CD instead of its usual watered-down fare—*Blue Train* by John Coltrane. As I was thinking how much I liked that album, a retinue of people burst into the store, at the center of whom was a gorgeous, gargantuan Jamaican woman in a sable coat and black leather boots.

"Oh my God, it's Immaculata!" Ernest shrieked.

"I recognize her. Who is she?" I asked.

"The supermodel—L'Oréal's new girl. She's so gorgeous and rich."

"So that's who she is. I must see her every other month, riding the elevator. I work on the floor above the offices for a French fashion magazine."

"You're so fortunate," he said.

We stared silently, basking in the woman's fame. It felt weirdly intimate, like I had known this guy for years.

"Back to the legal sweatshop," I said, glancing at my watch.

"I've got to go too," Ernest said. "Off to the gym. Despite my grandfather's saying that 'Episcopalians don't do calisthenics in public.'"

The wind swept down Broadway and at irregular intervals an updraft in the canyon of buildings sent snow skyward, creating an illusion that we were falling through space. A homeless man pursed his lips and stuck his tongue out at me then scurried along the sidewalk. I stood shocked, feeling somehow that I deserved the gesture.

Ernest chortled. "Don't take it personally—the poor, hapless dude," he said. "Saint Augustine wrote that we are all homeless, meant for another city, and our desperation is evidence of our immortal souls. He reminds us we live in dual cities simultaneously—the eternal and the temporal. Have you read *City of God*?"

Evidently he had had more than a smattering of theology under the Jesuits. "Excerpts in an undergraduate philosophy course," I answered. "I hardly read literature in college. I'm devoting my thirties to catching up. You have a strange look on your face."

"I didn't say I believed Augustine."

"Well, got to go," I said, then hazarded, "Hope to see you again."

"Ditto," he called as I fled into the snow.

"Remember last year when Barbara Leyland burned her bra in the kitchen sink?" Laura asked, eyeing me across the table.

Our dining room was oppressive with its Scandinavian furniture and spare, cold linen wallpaper. I couldn't figure out why we ate here instead of in the kitchen. Laura invariably finished dinner after the kids and I did. I had helped her cobble together a quick stir-fry from leftover steak and vegetables. Before dinner she had bathed the twins, and I'd promised to read them a story if they got ready for bed. Now I sat at the table with her, staring into space, thinking how unalike we were.

Laura was tall—six feet in heels—a giant when she stood next to me. She was self-assured and had no problem asserting her independence. She was physically active, pulling weeds in the garden in summer, commiserating in the bleachers with mothers of other eight-year-olds during Saturday play-dates with the twins or rushing out with them to the Brooklyn Museum for the kids' art program, after dabbing on ChapStick and a little blush. She was wearing my "GO WAVE" sweatshirt, her skin translucent white like bisque porcelain (although she tanned easily when the weather turned hot). And I was hoping I would synchronize with Ernest again.

"Is something wrong, Elliott?" Laura said. "You seem far away."

My stomach spasmed. "What are you talking about?" I snapped.

"Sorry, Mr. Grump. I was reminding you about the Stern-Leylands' holiday cocktail party," she said. "The one where your boss burned her bra. Are you down in the dumps again?"

"Barbara is stressing me out with this registration statement she has me working on," I lied, wondering what Laura would say if I told her I had flirted with a man today, if I dared to speak it aloud. Would she be shocked? Would she sulk or go ballistic? Or would she take it as a joke and shrug it off like she had the jokes I'd made in college, half-mocking, half-ironic, half-true?

Suddenly I longed for those days before the pressures of graduate school and law school and having to support a family, my little undergraduate dorm life at LSU when I shared quarters with an asexual computer geek I had known from Franklin. I was fond of David despite his irritating fastidiousness and endless prattle. Laura referred to him flippantly in private as my border collie roommate (she had been reared on her family's thoroughbred horse farm outside Lexington, Kentucky), a bright specimen for his breed, intensely loyal to the point of neediness, as perpetually present as a shadow. We'd heard David finally married during Spring Break festivities last year in Pensacola Beach, Florida—a buxom blonde rock station disc jockey named Dallas. We had no idea he had even been dating.

After dinner, Laura and I tried to make love but nothing worked right. We kissed, then disengaged and lay in bed waiting for lightning to strike. Exhausted, I rolled over and thought of Ernest. Laura headed for the bathroom, then to the hall and upstairs to the third floor to check on the twins, close the curtains in their rooms, pick up a stack of papers from her office next to their bedrooms. Her nightly routine. Back in bed, she flipped on the television and worked on her eighth-grade lesson plan, which I noticed was about *Canterbury Tales* and the idea of pilgrimage. Then she marked papers.

I read in bed and watched her, glancing at the television from time to time. She tired easily, and would leave Letterman on loud to help her get through the stack. But at twelve-fifteen her eyelids dropped to half-mast and the pen grew slack in her hand.

"Why don't you call it a night, honey?" I suggested.

"Can't. Two or three more essays to grade."

"You're a goner," I said, grabbing the remote control and switching to another channel. "Go to sleep."

She pecked me on the forehead and rolled over, covering her head with a pillow. I channel surfed for a few minutes, then settled on a rerun of *Bewitched*, turning down the volume. Some of these episodes I knew by heart; here was yet another where Darrin and Samantha were worried that their snooping neighbor Mrs. Kravitz had spied Samantha using witchcraft.

I thought about the incongruity and irony between the actor and the character: wife with an innate talent forced to repress its expression—to live in a closet, as it were—while the threat of exposure and the wrath of the wife's mother drives the narrative of each episode. I had read somewhere that Dick Sargent, the actor who played Darrin—the staid, repressed model Sixties sitcom husband—had been gay "in real life."

I switched channels. *How to Succeed in Business Without Really Trying*: "A secretary is not a toy . . ." I recognized the scene instantly. I turned off the television.

Now I couldn't sleep. I padded downstairs to the kitchen and made some chamomile tea with valerian, staring at the tincture as it imbued the tea. I took a shower and tried to masturbate. I couldn't stop thinking of Corcoran's sexual harassment video.

When David Hecht and I were sophomores, his younger brother spent the weekend of the LSU *vs.* Tulane football game with us in our dorm room, having taken the Greyhound bus from New Orleans up to Baton Rouge. A senior in high school, Barry had always been the bad boy of the block, but with the intellectual wattage of his older brother. He admitted having had sex with the chaperone on his senior class trip to the Bahamas. Barry thrived on his adversarial relationship with David. "You are such a goober," he would complain. David would counter with how reckless and unkempt Barry was by his standards. I considered Barry fairly well-groomed for a teenager.

David studied piano and on weekends worked as a disc jockey for WLSU. On Saturday night, I was studying my history textbook when Barry came into our room from the shower wearing nothing but a towel around his waist. I thought he was beautiful but I didn't trust the vocabulary I had for equating beauty and masculinity or even boyishness. I watched his reflection in the window as he combed his hair in the mirror hanging on the interior side of David's closet door. He sprayed his armpits with his brother's deodorant he found among the boxes of macaroni and cheese and ramen noodles there, the cans of Vienna sausages and tuna and the threadbare, mismatched bath towels. David was already at work. On the radio he was playing Steely Dan; I had just heard the phrase "no static at all" when heat exploded through my body.

Barry had touched my back. Had he seen me staring at his reflection? Had I wanted him to? His touch took me by surprise, yet I did not flinch and I did not turn to face him. There was no point in telling him to stop. Curiosity might have been my only genuine emotion in those days, my resistance to mystery practically nil. I was like the Southern Baptists in my mother's family with whom I spent summers, shunted off to aunts in dry counties after my parents' divorce: if they saw a snake by the cistern they had to hunker down and touch it, to test their faith.

Those first minutes held the most electricity, the most ferocious hunger in my life. Everything burned itself into my memory: the stale air of the room, the Right Guard's scent (still so erotic to me), the cinder block dorm room walls coated in thick, cake icing swirls of sky blue paint, the coffee stain like the rings of Saturn spiraling over the silver glitter galaxy design in my Formica desk, the hardness of the chair, the thrumming of my pulse in my ears. The lightness of Barry's fingertips as he caressed the nape of my neck, the crown of my close-cropped head, almost too painful to bear as he followed some maze I never knew existed. I would never forget that first contact, the inexplicable connection with Barry.

I turned and looked up, trying to search his eyes, but he would not look at me. This impulse to touch me had taken him by surprise as well. I stood from my chair, took the tip of his chin in my hand, and gravely kissed him on the mouth. The magnitude of this act amazed me. How long had I fought to put doing something like this out of my mind? The thought flashed through me that this was Columbus Day weekend and I had discovered the New World.

We threw ourselves onto my bunk. He wanted me inside him. He fidgeted and squirmed in my lap until he'd worked my cock deep in his ass. I asked if I was hurting him—did I want an excuse to stop?—and he shook his head no as I cradled him with my arms, feeling sweat in the runnel of his back. We rocked back and forth, panting, for desperate minutes or hours until we came.

The room smelled like sex and shit. We jumped out of the bunk. I grabbed the towel from the floor where he had flung it and thrust it to my mouth, fighting the urge to vomit; but the vertigo and nausea passed. Gulping to regain my composure, my heart heaved then galloped in my chest cavity. I couldn't believe we had actually done it, that I had crossed this boundary with another guy. I tried not to relish what had occurred between us, the sensation of falling, the aloneness, the heaviness of my body, tried to imagine what would have happened if I had stopped him, if I had flown off the handle and sneered, "What the fuck are you doing, Barry?" Not because I regretted what had happened—had I not somehow seen this coming? At the same time I couldn't help thinking that the kid who'd fucked his best friend's lanky brother was not me. That kid acted braver and more foolish. That kid didn't exist. This was not really the way I was. I heard David's voice announcing a set, and realized the radio had been playing the whole time.

We showered separately. Barry sniffed the underarm of his T-shirt before pulling it over his head, then curled up next to me in the bottom bunk. I told him he could not stay with me all night, he had to go back to his sleeping bag on the floor, David would return soon from the campus radio station. Barry put his head on my chest, licking my nipples, tracing the line of blond hair down to my navel. He knelt beside the bed and I let him suck me off. Then we fell asleep.

How did he know I would acquiesce? David was on his way to the dormitory; we'd heard him sign off the air, exchanging banter with the overnight announcer as we lay in bed together. I might have tried to calculate how long it would take him to make the lonely trek across the campus, but I dozed off. Sunday morning, David left a note (which he rarely did), saying he was going to the practice rooms to work on the Scriabin piece. How could he not have seen his brother in bed with me? But the three of us never said a word about it. The silence was itself obscene.

When Barry did not come up to LSU the following weekend, I was at once bereft and relieved. I did not know that he had decided to apply to Iowa until David told me after Christmas break. Barry had received a scholarship and would go away to school after graduation.

However briefly, Barry had wrenched me out of my complacent life and I responded by making a devout effort to forget what we had done that night. I pledged a fraternity and moved into the fraternity house, entering what I later called my "decadent" phase. I got a tattoo of my new Greek letters on my right ankle and went to see *The Rocky Horror Picture Show*. I once watched a fraternity brother blow a Deke in the steam room at the gymnasium, but I never dabbled myself.

The next semester, a month or so after the holiday break, I met Laura. She was sitting with a group of sorority sisters on the lawn balustrade in front of the library. I recognized her from a photograph in the campus newspaper the features editor had taken in the courtyard of the liberal arts building. I went up to her and said, "I saw your picture in the *Reveille.*" Surprised, flattered, she talked to me. By Easter we were dating steadily and by the time we left for summer break we had decided to get married after graduation.

And now Corcoran's sexual harassment video had prodded me to answer the Internet vignette's question, "What was the best sex you ever had?" Though I had never thought to ask myself before, I now had to admit the unequivocal answer.

Tuesday morning I sat at my computer wondering what had become of Barry. I had heard intermittent news through his brother over the years. I remembered he'd been a contestant on *Jeopardy*, but lost, and had a small role as a photographer in a movie about a law student cum novelist, called *Making Rain*, that was shot in New Orleans and led to some notoriety at the Toronto Film Festival. I typed "Barry Reynolds Hecht" into the search engine (another Corcoran client) and instantly found ten or twelve entries for his name, detailing aspects of his writing career, his Calhoun Dodd Fiction Prize for a novel called *Life*, his teaching at Washington University in St. Louis. I clicked on what appeared to be the most recent entry and was immediately directed to the Web site of the nonprofit publishing house that released his new book, a short, experimental coming-of-age novel called *Eye* in which the vowel "i" never appears. On my way back to Brooklyn that evening, I took a detour to Three Lives & Company bookstore in Greenwich Village and picked up an autographed copy. I read the first paragraph:

> *Eye seduced Amos Jot. Eye wanted that understood before he began the story. For Eye was about to come clean to someone who mattered rather a lot, at least for more than just a moment, and Amos would not have deserved the ugly treatment. Eye would tell all for the money. Eye trusted Amos would comprehend the reason because Amos was an attorney. Amos would understand how a loathsome deed could be done for the money. And Amos could afford the embarrassment.*

My hands shook as I carried the book to the clerk.

I read it that week, on the train in the mornings and on my lunch breaks at MoMA, where no one I knew was likely to see me. The dust jacket had a photograph of Barry smiling sweetly on the back. He hadn't changed much— was perhaps a little more fleshed out—and the photograph captured his impishness, the twinkle in his eyes. The novel was well written, told in that coy, earnest, funny voice I remembered. Barry had a knack for encapsulating an adolescent mentality, drawing out the tale, filling in the narrative. But the passages about the obnoxious older brother's friend who debauched the seventeen-year-old *soigné* schoolboy as the brother's voice boomed over the airwaves were ludicrous. What was Barry talking about? Hadn't he seduced me? Still, I found the book touching in its artifice, and wondered briefly if I should send him a note.

On Saturday I took the twins to a silly animated matinee then checked out the Rare Book Show at the Park Avenue Armory. But on Sunday I had to go in to the office. Corcoran's "eat-what-you-kill" compensation and bonus structure packages kept its partners and associates racking up billable hours seven days a week. We did not call Corcoran the "Velvet Gutter" for nothing.

And now "Dot-Com" was Corcoran's middle name. Corcoran had ushered into the bullpen more IPOs than any other international law firm. When the apocalypse came and all those Dot-Coms became Dot-Bombs, Corcoran's four hundred partners proclaimed they had no worries about the firm's ledgers; their mergers and acquisitions practice would certainly pick up the slack—and whatever M&A could not contribute to the coffers, securities litigation and bankruptcy practices would mop up the mess, as it had done after the Bush *père* savings-and-loan debacle. Corcoran would welcome the class-action shareholder lawsuits and bankruptcy filings as manna from heaven.

I worked on the prospectus for a new biotechnology initial public offering Barbara Leyland had ordered me to draft at the last minute, after leaving a message on my office voice mail: "I'm calling from the delivery room. I gave birth to Elijah at 3:33 a.m. Send out an e-mail, Elliott, that I will not be in the office. Clients can reach me on my cell phone if they need me."

I wrote the Risk Factors section for the corporation's lead product in clinical trials, JJ180 (tentatively named Zervan), a new selective serotonin reuptake inhibitor. Then I left a message for the corporation's general counsel and called Laura to say I would be home around seven o'clock. I decided to take a break at the coffee bar on the off-chance Ernest might appear, my great aunt Ally-Mae's voice sniggering in my head, "You will be turning over a bad bed of worms, if you do."

The weather had turned bone-chillingly cold and a razzle-dazzle of snow swarmed under streetlights down Broadway. At the risk of catching pneumonia, I took up a position near the door so I could keep track of the comings and goings. I sat there for an hour; by five o'clock it was getting dark outside. I wished for clement weather again. Shades of Friday night's discussion had hardly dampened my guilt. When I realized the coffee bar must not be on Ernest's weekend schedule, I finished my skinny *latte* and began to stuff the straw and napkins in my dirty paper cup.

Then Ernest strolled in, wearing a sleek blue cashmere turtleneck sweater, black stretch pants, black boots, and an elegant leather car coat, still talking on his cell phone. He raked back his hair and pulled on his earlobe. I watched him giggle and chat as he placed his order. The coffee bar was nearly empty. Occasional tourists straggled in but never lingered. The counter boy, in dreadlocks, took an instant shine to Ernest; I could tell by the way he was annoyed at his speaking on the cell phone and not giving him the time of day besides a coffee order. Ernest waited at the counter for his *latte*, interjected into his conversation a "Thanks" to the counter boy, and turned to walk out.

Then he noticed me. "I've got to run, Harlan. See you in a while," he said to the phone and walked over, beaming.

"Elliott! Remember me from the other day? I just got out of the gym across the street and I need my pick-me-up." He displayed his cup. "Then I'm off to a party. My friend Harlan is launching a new search engine for his real estate brokerage. Say, would you like to come? You could network." He glanced down at my yellow legal pad. "It'll be more fun than Risk Factors and there's sure to be great food." He raked through his hair again and gave me a smile. "Come with me, Elliott," he urged. "Harlan is my oldest friend from New Orleans—well, he's originally from St. Bernard Parish, but we don't hold it against him—and he's a scream. You must see his apartment. Oh my God, what a steal. This old woman died and her husband wanted to dump the place cheap because of the estate taxes and Harlan just scooped it up."

"Are you looking to buy an apartment?" I asked, following Ernest outside into the snow.

"Isn't everyone?" he said. He pulled a pack of cigarettes from his pocket. "Now I understand why New Yorkers are constantly prospecting for real estate. It's impossible to find a decent apartment in this city without blowing a broker." He snorted smoke from his nostrils, arched an eyebrow at me. "Seriously. I was looking. But I gave up on finding something I could afford and decided to move to Paris."

"It's obscene," I offered. "What people are willing to spend on a Manhattan apartment these days."

"I wouldn't pay an arm and a leg for just anything."

"I guess not," I said. "I'm wary of those who are still irrationally exuberant about the economy's prospects."

Ernest stepped from the curb in the swirling snow to flag a cab, pivoting on his foot like a dancer, his arm outstretched, his thumb, index, and middle fingers open as if he were changing a lightbulb. As I admired his stance a cab skidded to within an inch of him. He didn't flinch. He flicked his cigarette to the street, swung the car door open, and jumped in. I climbed in after him. The cab pulled onto Fiftieth Street.

"So you think the economy is a train wreck waiting to happen?" he asked, a placid, contented expression on his face. He didn't have a clue.

"Your words. But one day soon the bubble will burst." I pictured the Agnostics draft financial report on my desk. "The venture capital spigot will close and all but a few of the heartier Internet companies will have to furlough employees and file for bankruptcy protection."

Ernest caught me checking him out in his peripheral vision, and grimaced. On paper, Ernest was probably worth a nice chunk of change at the moment. But soon the story would be different.

"Why don't you look for a co-op in my neighborhood?" I asked, wondering what possessed me to say it.

"Where's that?"

"Prospect Heights, Brooklyn."

He shot me a look as if I had just suggested he have a colonoscopy. "Wuthering Heights?" he said tonelessly, staring at the driver's rearview mirror. "Are you whacked?" He turned to face me. "Get out of this car. *Get out* of the car."

I couldn't tell if he was serious.

"*Gotcha!*" he howled. Then he clutched my leg and I jumped out of my skin. "Darling, I was only yanking your chain. Oh my God, that was a good one. Speaking of which, yesterday I went with Harlan to an open house and he said if I pretended I wanted the apartment, he'd find me a great deal on one in Chelsea, in the London Terrace building."

"You were his shill?"

"Not exactly. I didn't do anything fraudulent. I didn't say I wanted the apartment. I only acted intrigued."

"I'm not persuaded," I said, shaking my head. "Talk about the odiousness of attorneys—brokers are the worst, strictly bottom-feeders. Does your friend Harlan scour obituaries and the probate petition filings in surrogate's court for hot prospects?"

A quizzical expression came over Ernest's face. "Brokers do that?"

"Unethical ones."

"Harlan's ethical. I think."

He craned his head to look around us. We were snarled in traffic. "I think we should get out and walk," he suggested.

"Fine," I said.

The cab pulled to the corner and Ernest flipped the driver a five. We walked east along Fiftieth Street.

"Don't slip!" I said.

"I have to watch my knee," Ernest said. "I tore my ACL last year when I fell from a ladder at the Strand reaching for a book."

"What was the title?"

"I believe it was *A Breathtaking Work of Withering Chutzpah.*"

"That'll teach you to go to bookstores," I said. "You'll wind up like Leonard Bast in *Howards End* with a bookcase on top of you. Are you suing?"

"I'm not that litigious."

We arrived a little winded at Sutton Place South as the last light drained from the sky. Snow had accumulated in the streets, blanketing traffic; I wondered how I would ever get back to Brooklyn. A taciturn doorman in black overcoat and gold epaulets ushered us into a private elevator. On the fourteenth floor a short stout man in a black silk kimono greeted us in the foyer.

"Darling Ernest."

"I take back all the rotten things I've ever said about you, Harlan."

"Is that any way to greet the hostess? And who is this wonder?" he asked about me. "Come in and have some saki. Let me take your coats."

He handed them to a very tall, gaunt Asian man in a white dinner jacket who appeared from a room off the foyer that had been made into a makeshift coat-check, with racks of furs and leather coats. He must be a model, I thought as Harlan whisked us out of the foyer into the hall on a cloud of patchouli incense to the strains of "Moonlight Serenade."

"For the *feng shui*," Ernest whispered as I stared incredulously at the enormous floor-to-ceiling aquarium before us filled with orange and red iridescent *koi*.

The vast apartment was decorated with a homogeneous if strident taste. Painted and inlaid screens, mahogany and teak furniture, terra-cotta statuary, enormous blue Chinese porcelain tea jars, ceramics like fetish objects on seemingly every lacquered surface, the odd smattering of white banquet chairs adding an incongruous element such as one might see at a gallery lecture. About a hundred-fifty people thronged the sunken living room. We descended a spiral staircase of rose travertine, the *popping* of champagne corks punctuating the din.

"Does anyone know how to barbecue?" someone in the crowd shouted.

"I do!" someone else responded, to laughter and scattered applause.

"There's a sucker born every minute," yet another retorted.

I wondered what they were talking about. "How long have you known Harlan?" I asked Ernest.

"Since Jesuit," he said. "Isn't he a scream? And what a salesman."

I could hardly hear him. I felt decidedly out of place among the models of both genders and every ethnicity. Surveying the crowd I noticed a woman nodding toward us. An Hermès scarf was drawn taut around her chin; her expertly barbered, bowl-cut straight black hair had a marcel wave in it. She'd been eyeing us since the moment we descended into the living room.

I slipped away from Ernest as he was chattering on about a friend of a friend of a friend from New Orleans, out to the terrace where white-hatted yakitori chefs in wool overcoats flipped kabobs on two long, freestanding gas hibachis under a candy-striped awning, pouring Tsingtao over the searing kabobs. At least a hundred bottles of Veuve Clicquot stood in formation, marooned in a snowbank on the wraparound terrace. I moved through the crowd to the edge, where people huddled under the awning smoking, pretending not to notice the cold. The snow had tapered off; the street below looked like a pool of milk while tips of city spires peeked from above clouds. I spied Ernest inside in animated conversation (lots of hand gestures) with two buzz-cut boys also wearing Buddy Holly glasses—Ernest multiplied. Counterparts of him peppered the crowd. I felt a twinge of envy and disgust.

"Will you open this for me?" asked a voice below my eye level. I looked down.

"Sure," I said, taking the champagne bottle from a little person in tight leather jeans and a bomber jacket.

The bottle was so cold and wet from snow it clung to my skin, burning, but I enjoyed peeling the foil off the cork and twisting the wire, the slow tension of the cork in my hand as I gripped the bottle and twisted it from the bottom. The cork thudded into my palm with a muffled *pop* and the whole bottle shuddered in spumeless release. It was the first time I had ever actually opened a bottle employing this method without making a mess and I was secretly thrilled. I handed the bottle to the little person. He took a swig, leapt up, and pecked me on the cheek then slipped through the sliding glass door into the crowd on the mezzanine.

Dumbfounded, I floated around the corner of the terrace to the west side of the building. Except for taxi horns below like muted oboes and bassoons, I was alone, shivering with cold. But the view was too entrancing to leave. I surrendered to unearthly stillness.

Then Ernest emerged through French doors, a highball pressed to his forehead, scowling. "What are you doing out here?" he asked.

"Freezing my ass off. What are you doing?"

"Hiding."

"From?"

Before he could answer, the little person with the champagne bottle joined us.

"Ernes-*tina!*" he shouted. "I wondered where you had gone to. Want to do a line?"

Ernest groaned. "No thanks," he said, then shrugged and followed the little person inside.

I glanced at my watch. It was seven-thirty; Laura must be wondering what happened to me. I stole through another set of French doors to check my office voice mail on my cell phone. No messages.

This room appeared to be the library. Fire roared in a Frank Lloyd Wright-inspired fireplace, and above the koa wood mantel, set off by votive candles in indigo glass squares, hung a suite of four Japanese woodcut prints such as Wright himself had avidly collected, depicting a flock of cranes amid boughs of spring foliage, tendrils of cherry blossoms. The library was paneled with deep-grained mahogany. Two lapidary kimonos (obviously created to flout imperial sumptuary laws) encased in glass-paned frames hung opposite the fireplace. Four red leather thrones guarded the entrance from the hall.

Ernest returned, without his little friend.

"I like the desk," I said, nodding at the small writing desk made of faux bamboo in the Victorian-Japanese style in front of the fireplace.

"*Escritoire*," he sniffled.

On the desk lay a book with a title I recognized, *The Picture of Dorian Gray*. I picked it up to admire the leather-and-gold binding. "It's a first edition," I told Ernest.

"I'm a bit bewildered by Wilde," he said. "Why he's so important. I know it may be politically incorrect to say so, but why is he considered a gay martyr? He got what he deserved after the Alfred Douglas trial—he took advantage of lower-class boys."

I shrugged. I had no comment to offer, one way or the other. Ernest excused himself, saying he was going to "the loo" and then wanted to reconnoiter the bar. Alone again, I peered into the cabinet that served as a bookcase. I didn't recognize any of the titles—Michael Stroud's novel *The Hotel Enola*; Cornell Winesberry's *History of Jazz* (with improbable blue irises on the cover); a Kenneth Roy Kors monograph on Henry Chadwick, the sculptor. But I had read a recent review of Rayburn Birdseye's collection of alternating villanelles and sestinas, *The Despondent Correspondent*.

I pulled out the book, checked to see if it was a first edition, then cracked it open at the middle and read the first line of a poem, trying to parse it. A voice startled me.

"That book is definitely minor Birdseye."

I turned and recognized the beautiful African-American woman with the Hermès scarf and marcel wave in her hair who earlier had been eyeing Ernest and me.

"I've found it's best to read him when you're half asleep," she said. "He makes perfect sense if you're not trying to understand him. Some critics don't appreciate his obscurantism and his diction often grates. But don't tell that to the lover—he's the man who owns this apartment. Poor Dr. Birdseye leapt from that very terrace two months ago. Trouble in paradise, as they say. Your boyfriend's fucking cute."

"Excuse me?" It sounded as if she had said "boy-*fiend*."

"Isn't he yours? The boy you're with? You two make a great couple."

"He's just an acquaintance, really."

"How long have you known him?

"Since Monday?"

"*Hmm.*" She pursed her lips. "Are you in the Industry? You look like you might not be."

I wasn't sure which industry she meant. "I'm an attorney," I said, reflexively fishing in my shirt pocket for a business card.

"We're in *need* of a new attorney in this crowd," she said, accepting my card. "Say, my girlfriend and I really are looking for someone—to donate to our cause." She mimed a pregnant belly with her hand.

"I beg your pardon?"

"You know, sperm? Jizz?"

"I'm quite happily married," I said, mortified.

"Oh, well, buzzkill."

Thankfully, Ernest returned bearing two cosmopolitans in giant martini glasses. Rather than explain why I shouldn't be drinking these days, I accepted the glass and held it.

"Don't I know you from New Orleans?" Ernest asked the semen-seeker.

"Possibly. Where did you go to high school?"

"Jesuit."

"Archbishop Chapelle," she said. "Didn't you date Frank Deloussye?"

"Oh my God, yes," Ernest answered. "Frank was my first boyfriend in high school. I haven't heard his name in years."

"That fuckwad is my cousin."

"Frank was an asshole, but I met some of my best friends through him. Elliott's from New Orleans too."

"I had a feeling you might be," she said to me.

I excused myself and returned to the terrace. Ernest followed a moment later.

"What's up, dude?" he asked.

"That woman just asked me to donate sperm to her and her girlfriend," I said.

"You've got to be joking."

"She thought we were together. I guess they've been checking out all the male couples."

"That's so *hilare*," Ernest said. "Do you know who her girlfriend is? She's on *New York Voyeur*, that late-night cable program. I never watch it. Her cousin Frank had a punk band in New Orleans in the late Eighties called the Wet Puppies. They were pretty popular. Imagine Thaïs Gautreau Parker wanting a turkey-baster baby."

"I thought that was just a lesbian old wives' tale."

"I don't think so. What I want to know is, how can she walk in those heels?"

I needed to extricate myself from this slipstream. I worried that an acquaintance would see me pinned to the wall in a questionable conversation.

"I have to go to the john," I said abruptly.

I fled into the hall. In the bathroom I downed the martini then made my way through the crowd to the foyer, where I used my cell phone to order a car to take me back to the office.

"Ernest left," the valet said, passing me my overcoat. "He asked me to give you this."

He handed me a business card. I pocketed it reflexively and took the elevator to the lobby and waited for the car to pick me up. Guests streamed out of the elevator at odd intervals while the young doorman, who looked like Bruce Willis circa *Moonlighting*, sulked and scowled behind his podium. After about twenty minutes, he motioned to me that my car had pulled to the curb, and opened the door for me.

I asked the driver to wait while I ran up to my office. I'd barely missed the ten o'clock curfew and had to sign in for a building pass. The elevator in my office's bank stopped at every floor. "I guess we're on the local," the janitor in the car murmured.

I used my office phone to call Laura and tell her I was on my way home.

"What are you doing still at the office?" she asked.

"The People's Work," I said. "The Corcoran Bloc doesn't know the Cold War is over."

"You're a laugh riot, Elliott," she said in a tone of voice I was not accustomed to. "I'm sure that's what being a lawyer must feel like sometimes. I called you around five o'clock. Where were you?"

Having a circle jerk with my secretaries, I thought. "I must have gone for coffee," I said.

"Try to get home at a decent hour. Your children miss you and so do I."

The line went dead. I swiveled around to look out at Broadway and hung up the phone.

The Corcoran offices occupied the forty-sixth through fifty-third floors of a black megalithic building three blocks north of Times Square on Broadway. On days when the clouds were low we seemed airborne. My window overlooked a Calvin Klein underwear billboard on the building across from us in the Mall of America Times Square had become; I often felt like the eyes of Scott Fitzgerald's Dr. T. J. Eckleburg were upon me.

As the car crawled downtown along Broadway, I kept mulling over the party, the fact that I had gone to it, the kiss by the little person, the request for my genetic material, the terrace in the snow. Everyone looked so young, so hip. I argued briefly with the driver about not taking the Brooklyn Bridge then settled into the leather seat of the sedan, like a big sofa, and closed my eyes. The car carried me along in a haze where the snow floated past me and Ernest's voice chided me for running away. I must have nodded off; the next I realized I was on Park Place. Our brownstone, quaintly pewtered in the half-light of the street lamp and the reflected snow, felt miraculous to see. Laura had shoveled the steps. Lights burned in the living room but the rest of the house was dark. My family were all snuggled in bed, sound asleep.

I ran up the steps and fumbled with my keys before I got inside. In the warm, lamplit foyer I glanced at the mail, gently set my keys in the gold ceramic bowl where Laura kept the garden gate key, the spare front door key, and the keys to the Gellers' house next door. The twins had made me a "We-miss-you-Daddy" collage card from magazine cutouts and construction paper. It occurred to me that Christmas was around the corner and my days would get longer as the clients and their underwriters tightened the noose around my neck. My stomach gripped me—the time-crunch spasm, I thought, and automatically headed to the kitchen for a glass of milk.

I sat in darkness looking at the rectangle of tangerine light that was our backyard. Why did I go running off with some strange man to an even stranger party, I asked myself. This was my home, warm and real. Somehow I still didn't believe it, staring out the kitchen window with my glass of milk in hand. I went outside to where I had hidden a pack of cigarettes under the lid of the gas grill, and had a quick smoke.

I climbed across the bed to kiss Laura on the forehead like Prince Charming. "You couldn't get home sooner?" she moaned. "You smell like barbecue."

I might have told her I had gone to a party, told her about the apartment, the Asian cooks and their tremendous hibachi, the snowbank of champagne bottles. I might have described the lesbian couple who wanted my sperm, though on second thought I did not want to stimulate the ongoing discussion about Laura wanting another child. I've kidded her, threatening to have a secret vasectomy. But something in me held back despite the drink I'd downed in the bathroom at the party. The giddy possibility of exposing myself frightened me. I shuddered imagining her reaction to my saying, "This lesbian couple wanted my sperm."

Laura wanted to hear all the latest office gossip. We went downstairs to the kitchen and she fixed me a plate of the leftover *penne alla grappa* she had made for dinner. She ate from my plate as we sat at the kitchen bar with two forks. Then we climbed the stairs to the kids' room on the third floor. We stood in the doorway of their room as we've done nearly every night since we first moved into this house, and imagined it painted yellow and blue instead of white. The children, towheaded like Laura's side of the family with matching short haircuts, still appeared identical at eight, and sometimes our extended family was hard-pressed to correctly identify Emily from Olin. Laura joked that I would soon have the same trouble telling them apart. I knew she worried I didn't see them enough and she was right. She hardly ever gave me a hard time about it but I knew she would not be distraught if I were to accept a position as in-house counsel at some conservative company and left the stress of the Velvet Gutter behind me.

I fell asleep as soon as my head hit the pillow. When the alarm rang on Monday morning, I smacked the snooze button without looking at the time. After several repeats of this process I glanced at the glaring red digits. I was an hour late. Laura and the kids had already left for school and the house was completely still. I skipped listening to National Public Radio's *Morning Edition* as I took a shower. I fumbled with myself, conjuring thoughts of Ernest, trying to get aroused, but nothing worked.

The snow had started to melt without it getting sooty and too trampled. Sunday had begun to take on the chimerical quality of a Rothko painting: stark, empty, searing. On the train I thought about how New Yorkers spend three hours a day trying not to talk to people they don't know but see all week commuting to and from work. The size of the city was an abstraction. It didn't take long to realize how small it really was.

At the office Calvert cornered me in the hall, grabbing my arm. I froze.

"Hey, Elliott," he whispered. "I saw you last night at Harlan Wodhouse's party."

"Couldn't have been me. I was in the office," I said. "I hear there are rumors that I actually live here."

"You've got a *doppelgänger* in the city then," Calvert said with a smirk. "He sure did look like you."

I fled into my office and shut the door.

I saw Ernest again about two weeks later, on the Tuesday between Christmas and New Year's Eve. With no time to go out, I had been ordering sushi and eating lunch at my desk again. But I knew that my whole routine was about to be undone. Our clients and their underwriters had pressed us to accelerate the process, in a desperate bid to launch the initial public offerings already in the pipeline before year's end. I sensed that this mad rush was too late—the market had already crested. My initial skepticism over stock valuations seemed justified and I felt relieved that I hadn't bought into the hype. When brokers cold-called, I told them I was into municipal bonds. Thankfully it was the partners' job to manage the clients' expectations.

Waiting in line for the automatic teller machine at the bank near my office before going to work, watching CNN on the monitors hanging from the lobby ceiling, I stood mesmerized by the NASDAQ ticker crawl across the bottom of the screen. Each red symbol registered the steep decline in nearly every New Economy issue. Agnostics had just announced its intention to lay off five thousand employees nationwide—normally not necessarily bad news to the market but the stock had already tanked five-and-a-half points after the opening bell, dragging down the entire sector. I felt a certain satisfaction from having pulled the bulk of the family's savings out of mutual funds into money market accounts over the past several months. I was notoriously risk-adverse when it came to investing our nest egg. The kids' college fund was spared for now.

Waiting for the ATM to dispense cash, I looked into the security mirror above the terminal and spied Ernest at the table behind me, going through his backpack. I slipped silently toward the door, hoping he had not seen me, and stepped outside. I hadn't gone far when I wished I'd said hello. I returned to the bank lobby to look for him, but he was already gone.

At the office I remembered Ernest's business card. I removed it from my overcoat pocket where it had sat since the valet at Harlan's party gave it to me, and discovered that Ernest worked for Agnostic. I tried to imagine how his day had started. I could not. I didn't have enough due diligence. He would probably lose his job as he had hoped and light out for Paris with a lot less money, but he would finish his book. And I would never see him again. I wanted to do something with the card, something irrevocable like put it in the shredder. Instead I held it for a long while then tossed it in my trash can.

That Friday night Laura and I went to the Leyland-Sterns' annual cocktail party at the San Remo on the Upper West Side. It wouldn't have been the holiday season without the associates in our office groveling before Edgar Stern or currying Barbara Leyland's favor. Everyone except Laura and me seemed to be commiserating about the latest downturn in the economy. I wasn't surprised to find a gaggle of associates standing in a corner of the library, out of earshot of the host and hostess, gossiping about those senior associates rumored to be made partner.

"If it's a lawyer joke, I won't listen," I overheard Edgar say to someone I did not recognize.

"It is, but—wait, don't go. It's really funny," the young man said. "There's a man in a hot air balloon, see. And he discovers he's lost as well as being late for an important date. So he adds ballast and descends, and spots a woman walking down the road. 'Pardon, pardon,' he calls to her. 'Would you please help me? I promised a friend I would meet her an hour ago and I don't know where I am.' The woman says, 'You're in a red-and-blue hot air balloon, approximately twenty feet above the ground at latitude sixty-nine degrees north and longitude sixty-nine degrees west.' The balloonist says, 'You must be an associate.' She replies yes and asks how he knew. He tells her that everything she reported may be technically correct but he has no idea what to make of the information. 'In fact,' he tells her, 'I'm still lost, you haven't been any help, and you've delayed my trip.' The associate retorts, 'You must be a partner.' He answers in the affirmative and wonders aloud how she knew. She replies, 'You don't know where you are or where you are going. You've risen to where you are due to an enormous quantity of hot air. You made a promise you have no idea how to keep but you expect people beneath you to solve your problem. The fact is you are in exactly the same position you were in before you interrupted my stroll, but now, somehow, it's all my fault.'"

Edgar chuckled. We all smiled. "That wasn't very bright of him," I whispered in Laura's ear, thinking that if the joke teller was an associate I'd just witnessed a train wreck. Laura walked across the room to greet Barbara.

Edgar pulled me aside to ask what I'd thought of the sexual harassment video, as the one senior associate member of the hiring committee.

"I thought it was effective," I said. "Too bad the Attorney General didn't have one like it to show the President."

We had been following the latest news of President Clinton's travails. Despite his acquittal by the Senate, a new independent prosecutor had impaneled a grand jury in August to investigate whether Clinton should face criminal charges once he left office. With the Bush inauguration less than a month away, the right wing clamor for an indictment had become a cacophony.

"I doubt if it would have done any good," Edgar said, "regardless of the President's peccadilloes. I don't blame Lewinsky so much as those paleo-Republican hypocrites who want to see Clinton hang. Still, you see people like Gennifer Flowers and Monica Lewinsky in the newspapers or on TV and wonder what insatiable, bottomless pit of need for attention leads them to want celebrity.

"So," Edgar continued, a little drunk, "yesterday I asked old Avery Cabot if he had read the case in the law journal about the bankruptcy partner at Priestly, Cogan & Shin who dropped M&Ms down the blouse of his female associate. You know what he had the nerve to ask me? 'Were the M&Ms *green*?'"

"I've heard him myself," I said, "on more than one occasion, lamenting the lost, halcyon era of 'the full-service secretary.'"

"It's a race against the clock between his retirement and a sexual harassment lawsuit. Let's give him a male summer associate this year."

I nodded agreement, surprised at the new level of intimacy between us.

Two associates asked Edgar for advice about a research project he'd assigned them; I took the opportunity to make my way across the crowded living room. Laura was holding forth to several women gathered around her beneath one of de Kooning's enormous red-and-white Alzheimer's-era paintings. She waved to me as I slipped behind them on my way toward the arch into the dining room, meanwhile telling her audience, "That's why women identify with her characters so much—even her cat has to be a victim."

Barbara laughed as Laura continued. "She doesn't think she needs men, which is a crock, except in an Anita Brookner novel where the heroines are always of independent means. I'd like to send Ms. Brookner an e-mail and ask her, 'Why don't you make one of these characters poor? *Can* you write that?'"

In the dining room I fell into conversation with the young cosmopolite who had told the bad lawyer joke. "I bet you have a whole repertoire," I said as we perused the buffet table.

"A few," he said.

"Are you a lawyer?"

"A violinist."

He said he was a friend of Edgar Stern's youngest daughter from a previous marriage, Sally, also a graduate student at Oberlin. His name was Bertram and he reminded me of Calvert, my secretary, if a little younger: in his early twenties, bald, with a thick black goatee and silver earrings. His penetrating, transparent blue eyes held something I instinctively recognized. He boasted that his deep tan was the result of a recent ecotourist trip to the jungles of Costa Rica, said he had just arrived from the airport and was famished.

We grazed the crudités, nibbled at the crab and herb Gorgonzola canapés, sampled the bacon-wrapped prunes. While we chatted his eyes drifted to the view through the window. Central Park lay like a yawning cavity of darkness punctuated by pale snow and web-like shadows of bare tree branches in intermittent pools of lamplight along invisible paths.

He looked down at my ring hand clutching the cheese knife. "So," he said, "are you ... attached?" His voice was so redolent with subtext I stopped chewing the cracker in my mouth and held my breath an instant before swallowing.

Our eyes met. "Married," I answered, perhaps too timidly, the word like a bell in my head, my pulse quickening. "She's in the living room."

I nodded toward the circle of women gathered around Laura—and out of the corner of my eye saw her jump from her conversation and dash across the living room toward me like a woman possessed. But she couldn't possibly have heard me. She didn't even notice Bertram.

"I'm so bored, Elliott," she moaned in my ear. "Let's leave."

I shrugged, said, "I'll get our coats."

"Oh, dear, I'm sorry," she said, turning to Bertram. "Did I interrupt?"

"Not really," I said. "We were just chatting about Costa Rica. Laura, this is Bertram, a friend of Sally's."

"A pleasure," she said. "Ten minutes, darling. We've got to get home to the twins."

Bertram smiled as Laura excused herself to say good night to Barbara in the foyer, his face betraying not so much amusement as empathy and interest.

Suddenly I felt relieved, as if a burden had been lifted.

ACKNOWLEDGMENTS

I wish to express my deepest gratitude to my spouse, Jeffrey Dreiblatt, and my friend Vance Philip Hedderel, as well as to my teachers, editors, colleagues, and friends, Jonathan Baumbach, Brian Bouldrey, Christopher Bram, Stephen Cipriano, Jameson Currier, Hal Espen, Caroline Fraser, Robert Gianetto, the late Patrick Giles, Bently Graham, Peter Ketchum, Carter King, Garland Richard Kyle, Ramon Pereda, Marisa Schwartz, Draper Shreeve, Peter Spielberg, Nikki Smith, Donald Weise, Garold Whisler, Edmund White, and Nancy Yost; and lastly, to my first editor, mentor, and friend, Patrick Merla, whose imprint upon these pages is as indelible as a watermark. Their encouragement and support meant the world to me during the writing of these stories and I proudly acknowledge how immeasurably they have enriched my writing life.

ABOUT THE AUTHOR

William Sterling Walker's stories have been anthologized in *Best American Gay Fiction 2* and the Lambda Award–winning *Fresh Men: New Voices in Gay Fiction*, after first appearing in *modern words, Harrington Gay Men's Fiction Quarterly*, and *The James White Review*. His nonfiction account of coming out appeared in the Lambda Award–winning anthology *Boys Like Us: Gay Writers Tell Their Coming Out Stories*. He wrote the biographical entries on poet James Merrill and film director Douglas Sirk for *The Scribner Encyclopedia of American Lives*. He has written for many publications, including the *Boston Book Review* and *Publishers Weekly*. He holds a Master of Fine Arts degree in creative writing from Brooklyn College. A native of New Orleans, he now resides in Brooklyn, with his spouse, the artist Jeffrey Dreiblatt.

CPSIA information can be obtained at www.ICGtesting.com
Printed in the USA
LVOW06s1938140813

347904LV00016B/1294/P